THE AMERICAN STRANGLER

PRAISE

"A bleak and unnerving examination of justice in America."

KIRKUS REVIEWS

"This fast-paced study of an expert surgeon's descent into violent vigilantism will be cathartic for readers enraged by malpractice lawsuits and the lawyers who file them. Great for fans of Ted Galdi's An American Cage or L.A. Couriel's *The Milk Moon Assassin: Betrayal and Vengeance in the Killing Hills*."

BOOKLIFE

"It is disturbing, shocking, captivating, gripping, gritty. What a great read, I thoroughly enjoyed it."

SHANNON'S BOOK REVIEWS

"Dark, twisted, compelling, thought-provoking, shocking, gritty, and gripping—*The American Strangler* is all of those and more."

MOMMA SAYS

"Amazing. Absolutely amazing. Fleisher is an absolute literary wizard!"

A QUINTILLION WORDS

THE AMERICAN STRANGLER

ROBERT M. FLEISHER

PRIMARY PRESS

First published by Black Rose Writing 2020
First Primary Press edition 2024

PUBLISHED BY PRIMARY PRESS
a division of Primary Productions LLC
www.primary-productions.com
New York, New York

Library of Congress Control Number: 2024950014
ISBN: 978-0-982-8441-6-8

Second edition, November 2024
Printed in the U.S.A.

Thanks to my dear family and friends for allowing me to be part of their lives. The essence of life is all about relationships. For these connections, I am grateful.

Thank you to Mike Garrett for your editorial guidance.

THE AMERICAN STRANGLER

One useless man is called a disgrace. Two or more are called a law firm.
—John Adams, 1776

The first thing we do, let's kill all the lawyers.
—William Shakespeare, *Henry VI*

The last thing we do, let's kill all the lawyers.
—Ron Rellick, *The American Strangler*

CHAPTER
ONE

THOUGH HE APPEARED to navigate life's passage with ease, recent events kept him from exorcizing the demons tormenting his conscious thoughts. He ran from a relentless circumstance of evil intent. With each stride, he saw the ground beneath him dissolve like loose sand. His soul was the hunted, his mind the hunter.

He placed the pill far back onto his tongue and swallowed hard. Mounting angst contorted every muscle in his neck. He never took a Xanax before. He never engaged in recreational drugs. He never drank.

The emptiness of the room magnified the echo of heavy foot-steps. Four muscular men went about their work much in the manner of mindless robots. Over and over they made the trip from the house to the truck carrying elegant furniture, artwork, and the boxes stacked in each room.

The sedative effect of the Xanax did not affect his mood. His thoughts drifted. He saw many obnoxious, selfish people that day. The stress to perform turned intolerable.

I see the patients. I hear their voices. It's become an endless chatter. Instead of concentrating on their problems, I stare with a blank expression at their irritable faces. I never felt this way before. All I see are the flaws in their complexion; the wrinkles, blemishes, and dark patches that visit their skin like a plague.

"Excuse me, sir," said one man, balancing two large boxes in his arms. "I gotta get through here."

Lifted just above the threshold of deep thought he responded, "Oh, sure."

He moved out of the young man's path and walked to the undressed window. With a fixed gaze, he stared into the distance, looking at nothing in particular.

I used to reason there were more kind people in the world than nasty ones, but for the life of me, they seem reduced in numbers from the past.

A pile of junk mail sat on the sill, left there by the housemaid before being dismissed from service. As mindless therapy, he glanced at the envelopes, determined what he needed to read, and flung the fodder into the empty box next to him for recycling.

One piece caught his attention. The outer envelope stated, "DON'T LOSE EVERYTHING YOU WORKED HARD FOR TO THE PREDATORS OF THE LEGAL PROFESSION!"

He saw this mailing many times in the past. It meant nothing before, but now it was too late. He placed his finger beneath the sealed flap and attacked the messenger. A searing burn preceded the realization that the envelop tore open his flesh. Unlike other paper cuts, this wound traveled deeper.

The hollow high-pitched sound of petite footsteps heard crossing the room intruded upon his solitude.

"What happened to your finger?" she inquired.

He ignored her question and stated, "This fiasco should have never happened to us."

With an expression defining despair, he shook his head from side to side.

"What can we do?" she asked.

"Nothing. Not a damn thing we can do."

"What about Florida?"

"They'll get that too."

"The beach house?"

"That they can't take."

The leader of the men approached. He held the last box between his strong arms. Sweat and grime from his labor darkened a badly worn blue denim shirt. His bulging forearm bore a faded tattoo blurred by time. Still, remnants of a once proud eagle, wings spread and mounted, remained for all to admire.

"You can lock up now," he said without emotion or commentary as he exited.

Two souls now stood naked before a world of their perceived injustice. They had become the residue of a defective system manipulated by design. No more dreams to live for, only emptiness and torment stood ready to visit upon them.

How did I get here? Every problem has solutions, logical solutions. God, I know this! The ruination of my existence is about to unfold. How did I get here?

CHAPTER
TWO

AT EIGHT P.M., Dr. Ron Rellick and his wife Susan walked the corridor of the Philadelphia International Airport heading for a last visit to their Florida retreat. They had to pack their personal effects before foreclosure on the property took place.

Susan, a blonde of perfection and grace, had long straight hair worn in a style that looked best on a face with classic features. Hers was imposing. She had a long nose and plump lips set within most prominent cheekbones. Her eyes, wide set, had a seductive appeal. The wholesomeness enveloping her beauty did not lend itself to the status of glamour, but charm. At forty, she showed no signs of decline, and people often mistook her for a woman ten years younger.

Ron stood tall and lean with broad shoulders. His hair was dark, almost black. In recent years, some gray sculpted his temples, defining the distinguished look of graceful aging. Though always well groomed, the shadow of his ever-present beard expressed masculinity. He wore distinct and prominent facial features. Ron and Susan complimented each other, looking like a couple created for Madison Avenue.

"Oh, shit!" Ron exclaimed as the metal detector came into view.

"What's the problem?" asked Susan with grave concern. Ron never cursed, so when he used profanity, it garnered attention.

"I forgot to leave the Mace home."

"Don't you remember what happened the last time you forgot? You set off the alarm."

"Yeah," he said with a chuckle.

"They thought you were an international terrorist. Police and the Canine Unit showed up to assist the TSA as they searched all of our luggage. Not funny."

"You're right, love. However, my belt buckle set off the alarm, not the Mace. They would never have found it if the buckle didn't set off the metal detector."

"Just throw it away," Susan scolded.

"Screw it. I'm taking it with me. There's violence all over Florida. Christ, tourists can't come to America without fear of turning down the wrong street and getting killed. I know it's not much, but it makes me feel safe."

Ron left the plastic container of Mace in his pocket and placed his briefcase upon the conveyor belt. He stared at the luggage checkers with an air of disdain as he walked through the metal detector without incident. Their flight proved uneventful.

They arrived at the high-rise condo by twelve-thirty A.M. Accustomed to late hours, Ron experienced no burden to his mind or body. He felt sorry for Susan, who couldn't keep her eyes open. She undressed and lay nude beneath silver satin sheets, draping the sensuous curves of her body. In a matter of seconds, she breathed the slow rhythm of deep sleep.

Ron's libido, being the casualty of stress and aggravation, left him blind to her beauty. Instead of physical desire, all the day's thoughts preyed on Ron to the point of obsession. He tried to sleep, but past events chased away all attempts toward slumber.

By one-thirty A.M. the facts of the incident from seven years before filled his mind. He still saw the petulant little man holding his cheek, moaning. Three other lawsuits played out in his memory as well—but different—being fraudulent petty claims. When the attorneys realized the cases had no merit, they never got beyond discovery before being dropped.

Greed motivates these whores. They lie for money, looking to make an easy buck. They orchestrate the scheme, then rehearse the words.

His thoughts, somewhat disjointed, indulged the pace of his beating chest.

Damn it! Slow down. Seems like my heart will jump right out of my body. Can't keep beating like this. Why can't I get this shit off my mind? It's sinful, but who's the sinner? Deterrents don't exist. "Why not take a chance and fake a suit?" they figure. What's perjury anyway? Too many slaps on soiled wrists. They live in the gutter. They pray to the gods of gold and silver. Maybe if I just sit. This infernal throbbing has got to stop.

He sat on the side of his bed and twisted from his waist, left, then right. His hands gripped his temples as disjointed thoughts continued to grow more contentious.

What a sick system! The bigger bucks attract the best talent. It's set up for unlimited gain for the plaintiff's side, while the defense attorneys are the hourly workers. Adversaries, they swear to tell the truth. What bull-shit! Somebody has to be lying. They tell two different stories, so who's the liar? It doesn't matter anymore. There is no truth, no honor, no deterrents. None. It's all about the sacred money.

Ron looked at the clock that now read two-thirty A.M. The second Xanax did not help. After tossing and turning in bed, Ron decided to go for a walk on the beach. He reasoned he would contain his scrambled thoughts by embracing the sound of the ocean, a pleasure that always relaxed him. His heart pounded in unison with the ringing in his ears. Out of control, he let his psyche wreak havoc upon his body.

Ron fumbled for his clothes that lay on the chair next to the bed. To avoid waking Susan, he dressed in the dark and left the apartment. He walked the deserted corridor toward the elevators.

This condo at the ocean in Florida was but another perk Ron

enjoyed because of his diligence and hard work. The building housed the "Who's Who" of the nouveau riche. From Silicon Valley retirees, who in short years amassed hundreds of millions of dollars, to garment industry mavens of New York City, this was home to the elite from various endeavors.

Ron was the only doctor to travel in such circles; not because of the income from his oral surgical practice, but because of his patent on an ingenious bone-restructuring device. Johnson and Johnson paid him five million dollars along with a percentage of sales for the right to market the unique instrument.

For years, Ron had thoughts of packing it in and settling in this land of sunshine. The abuses of the system made working no longer seem worth the risks they forced him to take every day. He amassed enough money to retire in style. The rewards of practice left his graces long ago.

Ron was not the workaholic his friends accused him of being. Instead, he felt he helped people at a level unmatched by anyone, anywhere. He was not just good; he was the best. A moral obligation kept him in practice to help those who needed his services.

Ron pioneered sophisticated surgical techniques to reconstruct facial bones destroyed by injury, disease, or congenital disability. Many cases were performed pro bono, supported by the routine oral surgical procedures. He never wanted to give up the noble part of practice.

Descending from the thirty-fourth-floor penthouse, Ron felt the Mace in his pocket.

I don't need this in a gated community, he thought.

Crime had become an ever-present threat to all but those who could afford to build walls and use guards for relative safety. The wealthy became incarcerated by their fears.

Ron experienced the familiar sensation in his stomach and groin telling him the elevator was about to stop and let another restless soul board on the twenty-fifth floor at two-forty A.M.

The doors opened, and ironic as the day dealt cruelty, there stood the epitome of all things wrong with the legal system,

Nathan Mittenberg, the leading Philadelphia sleaze-advertising attorney. He stepped onto the elevator with his arrogant, nose-in-the-air attitude displayed like a peacock in full glory.

I don't believe it's him, that parasite, Mittenberg. "Have you been injured in an accident or by a doctor? I'll get you the money you deserve!" Those wretched commercials! Look at him with that smug, erudite pretense.

Mittenberg glanced at Ron and offered a gratuitous smile.

You make me sick! Ron thought, and while he did not speak a word, a face contorted by disgust revealed his feelings. Mittenberg turned away.

He can sense my disdain.

Ron felt his neck bulge as the pressure inside his head soared. Primal rage dominated, and it felt foreign to him. He could not control the physical changes overtaking his being, but he understood their origin. Ron's body stiffened as sweat leaked from every pore in his face. His mouth became dry and his tongue stuck to the roof of his mouth. His muscles tensed. Leg spasms caused him to lose balance. He grabbed on to the rail surrounding the elevator to steady himself. Mittenberg inched up against the closed door as he watched with an unsettled expression while Ron's transformation ensued.

I'm having trouble breathing. I feel like I'll jump out of my skin. It's not time to show my weakness. That's what these lawyers want. That's what they do. He's trying to break me. Attack until you don't know what's real. They twist and distort until confusion leads to doubt.

The floors raced by, but for Ron time slowed. His enduring hatred became the spark for foul deed. He tried to fight an uncontrolled jerking motion causing him to pull the Mace from his pocket. In an instant, he emptied the canister into the face of his foe.

Mittenberg's hands leaped to his eyes, and he cried out in pain. Gasping sounds replaced the screams, then an eerie silence ensued. A sudden struggle to re-inflate his lungs produced yet another bout of screams, louder than the original. He tumbled to the floor with a force that jolted the elevator. Ron steadied himself on the rail to keep from falling.

What have I done? This isn't real. It, it can't be. Oh my God! What have I done?

Ron fought for air while clawing the elevator wall to support his failing legs. He watched Mittenberg writhing on the floor screaming. The act, the expected consequences, the approaching lobby floor all spoke to his sensibilities. He had to do something fast. Logic and reason had to take over for the insanity that ruled just moments ago.

He's got to stop screaming. Quiet, quiet!

Disjointed thoughts turned Ron's silent horror into an abhorrence manifest in his now demonic voice.

"You pig, you greedy pig! How does it feel getting put down, you scum?"

Ron had to silence Mittenberg, who rocked while crouched in a fetal position.

With the precision of a martial-arts expert, Ron plunged his hand onto Mittenberg's throat. As a head and neck surgeon, he identified the exact position of the cricothyroid cartilage and knew how fast he could snap it. This fatal act would stop further shrieks coming from Mittenberg. With deft hands, Ron pressed the cartilage back over the larynx and released his grip, knowing the terminal nature of this action. In short order, the victim stopped grabbing at his burning eyes and suffocated.

When Ron looked up to see the floor number on the elevator panel, he realized his hand was on the emergency stop button, halting their car just above the lobby. This reflexive survival response gave him the time needed to commit the act and now time to collect his thoughts. Possessed by some external force, Ron reached into his pocket, pulled out a one-hundred-dollar note, and stuffed it into the mouth of the lifeless form.

Water running down his leg, the result of a failed sphincter, pulled Ron back to real time. The slow-motion stopped, and he understood what he had done. Though the psychotic episode ended, Ron recognized life, as he lived it, had ended, too.

He released the emergency stop, knowing they hovered above the lobby. Certain doom waited for Ron if anyone stood there expecting this lift.

The doors opened. The chime signaling the arrival sounded.

"It's here."

The sound of someone running toward him came on fast. Again, a voice called out, "Come on! It's here!"

With footsteps approaching, Ron hit the twelfth floor and close-door buttons together. He recognized it would surprise the lobby people to find the elevator taking off. They might remember where it would next stop. In an ensuing investigation the last floor Ron wanted anyone to remember was thirty-four, his floor.

At twelve, he stepped out and dragged Mittenberg's limp body halfway through the threshold to act as a prop, keeping the elevator doors open. It wouldn't be long before someone found the body.

In a detached manner, Ron removed Mittenberg's lapel handkerchief and wiped off the rail he used to brace himself, the wall and each button in the elevator. Just before he was about to step over the corpse, he thought about any other precautions to cover his tracks. Having read about latent fingerprints, he wiped the neck of his victim and retrieved the one-hundred-dollar note.

The fewer clues, the better, he thought, ready to return the money to his pocket. With rage dictating a change of mind, he threw the bill to the floor and rubbed it on the carpet with his shoe. He kicked it over and rubbed again to make sure all fingerprints disappeared. Ron lifted the bill with the handkerchief and, exerting a final thrust of passion, he shoved it back into Mittenberg's stiffening lips.

"Go buy yourself some ethics, asshole!" He scoffed.

Ron ran up twenty-two flights of stairs, and he felt his chest bursting. The wretched stench of urine, supplied by the janitors and laborers who used the fire towers as their urinals, filled each gasping breath with the foulest taste. Ron pictured the night concierge fetching the stranded elevator and summoning the police. In actuality, the concierge would unlock one of the other three elevators always removed from service after midnight. This protocol assured Ron time to assess his dilemma in the safety of his quarters. Rushing toward the door of his unit, he collapsed to his knees. His key fell five feet in front of him. With little strength to draw upon, he crawled forward, grasped the key, and pulled himself up to his door. He entered.

Susan remained sound asleep. Ron crept into bed, trembling. Exhaustion extinguished the roiling fury that only moments before drove him to violent actions. He could not fathom what controlling force possessed him. He sweat profusely and felt a deep chill from the soothing breeze of the ceiling fan. The blades appeared to recede as he lay in the darkness of his deed and drifted toward unconsciousness.

CHAPTER
THREE

AT EIGHT A.M., the distinctive eight notes of the door chime broke the morning silence. In lavish high-rise condominiums, a call from the concierge always preceded anyone from reaching the apartment doors. This unexpected intrusion caused concern.

"Ron, Ron, someone's at the door. Who could it be?" Susan whispered as they both lay in bed.

A glance at the clock told Ron the day began without him; a day he would soon prefer to escape.

"You get it," he replied. "It's probably the maintenance people."

Susan put on her lush terry robe and walked to the entrance.

Ron sat up with a disorientated mind and sunken heart. He had the strange sense of awakening from a nightmare but wasn't sure it was a dream. Sleep only afforded him a brief reprieve from the terror of the previous night. As slumber lifted, a clouded recollection gave way to the reality of his actions. A hollow notion of gloom grew stronger as the details of his nocturnal foray came into focus. He ran to the bathroom, stripped, and jumped into the shower. He needed to clear his head.

While safe in her towering fortress, Susan approached the door with an uncomfortable sense of hesitation. She hoped the unannounced visitors would be maintenance men as Ron suggested. When opening the door, leaving the chain lock secured, the sight confirmed her apprehension. She pulled the robe tight to her chest as if to provide protection from the strangers. In the hallway stood a paunchy short man accompanied by a lean six-footer. The unexpected guests did not belong. Nor did they look like they belonged together.

The short man wore a cheap, ill-fitted, and worn sports jacket. It clashed with the plaid of the underlying wrinkled shirt tucked into trousers too short. His eyes set deep into a face weathered by the sun. A vertical line of stress ran between untamed brows and ended mid-forehead. Other telltale wrinkles mapped out difficult roads traveled.

The tall man dressed like a fashion model. He wore an expensive suit. His shirt and tie sat well on a body of perfect form. Piercing eyes and a strong chin gave him the appearance of inquiry and strength. A gel or tonic of some type held every hair in perfect order.

"Mrs. Rellick, I'm Detective Rice from the homicide unit of the Dade County Sheriff's Office," the short man stated, "and this is Special Agent Grey."

Before he said another word, Susan's face turned white, and she gasped. "My children!"

She forever worried about an imagined tragedy befalling her life's treasure, "the children."

"No, no, I'm sorry if I scared you, ma'am. We're here because someone murdered a tenant in the building last night," said the diminutive detective with a tone of genuine apology.

He held a listing for the residents of each unit retrieved from the front desk.

"We gotta ask all the guests some questions. Is Mr. Rellick in?"

"Just one moment," Susan said, leaving the door chained, as she excused herself to summon Ron. She saw that he was in the shower and returned to reschedule their interview.

"Mr. Rellick is showering. Come back in an hour," she said through the limited opening of the chained door.

"No problem, lady."

"Who died?" Susan queried.

"*Murdered*, ma'am, *murdered*," Detective Rice corrected with emphasis.

Susan shuddered and placed her hands to her face as the distinction between death and murder resonated.

"Don't mean to upset you, ma'am, but some hotshot lawyer, Mittenberg was the target. They tell me he's not from around here. I mean, he lives here, but he works in Philadelphia. Did you know him?"

"The name sounds familiar," said Susan, wiping tears from her eyes, realizing the gravity of the situation. She tilted her head right and looked to the ceiling trying to recall the name.

"Sounds familiar. That's what several people told me, all from up north; Philadelphia region. You from up north?"

"We are. Maybe he was a politician," she volunteered.

"I don't know. We'll know soon enough though. Again, I apologize for scaring you, miss."

Susan offered a forced smile, and the men left.

Over five-hundred families lived in the complex of buildings. Few knew their neighbors in the sprawling, impersonal communities of modern times. Susan didn't know Mittenberg. He could have lived on her floor and she'd still not know him. She greeted many name-less faces in the course of her travels through the lavish halls and the lush palm-filled grounds. Maybe Mittenberg was one of them. The name sounded familiar.

Susan sat in the kitchen sipping her morning brew of exotic tea. The herbal aroma filled the air. Though she gazed at the calm, deep blue ocean viewed from the floor to ceiling windows, an uncomfortable misgiving spawned by her conversation with the detective graced her face.

When Ron entered the room, he saw something amiss in her demeanor.

"What's wrong?"

"Do you know a Mittenberg?" Susan inquired without a usual morning greet.

"Mittenberg? On this floor? What did he want?" replied Ron, playing dumb.

"He wanted nothing. He's dead."

Though he expected this news, Ron had to act surprised.

"Dead? I thought you said he was here."

"No, I asked if you were acquainted with him. Some detectives came to the door. That's who rang. They wanted to discuss a murder, and—"

Ron felt his heart skip a beat, and before she continued, he interrupted.

"Did they think you were the murderer?" queried Ron, in jest, but intending to see how accusatory they acted.

"Come on, Ron. They said they had to interview everyone. They'll be back in an hour."

"I'm sorry. This is terrible. It's not a joking matter, but jest keeps me sane in a world gone mad."

When the doorbell rang again, Ron greeted the detectives with Susan by his side.

"Good morning, Mr. Rellick. I'm Detective Rice."

Before he spoke another word, Ron put his wrists out as if waiting for handcuffs, and he said, "I've been expecting you."

After an uncomfortable pause, Ron smiled. He then offered a polite chuckle as Detective Rice laughed. Susan looked confused as the humor traveled right past her.

Ron had the gift. He could ingratiate himself to just about anyone, anywhere. His friendly manner and wittiness opened doors and put people at ease. His humor did not affect Agent Grey, whose reserved countenance remained unyielding.

"I'm sorry to bother you nice folks, but we have to go through certain routines when there's a homicide. Agent Grey, here, is from the Philadelphia office of the FBI."

"I didn't think the FBI took an interest in local homicides," Ron stated.

"It appears the victim engaged in some big interstate car accident scam. I suppose your wife mentioned someone murdered a Mr. Mittenberg last night. He was the head honcho at a big Philadelphia law firm, Mittenberg, Mason, and Gordon."

Detective Rice paused with purpose. He waited to see who would speak next. The awkward silence forced a response.

"We never left the building after we returned from Philadelphia. It was late last night," said Ron, offering nothing more.

"The crime occurred in the building, sir," said Detective Rice. "While you and the Mrs. didn't leave the building, did you perhaps go to the lobby or hear any sounds coming from the hallway?"

"In this building? You couldn't hear a fire alarm through all the insulation. People here want solitude," Ron explained.

"At one point I woke up. I don't know why. I heard a loud noise or something, and you weren't in bed," Susan volunteered, looking straight at Ron.

Ron's heart sunk.

Agent Grey's eyes darted from Susan to Ron several times, searching for some hidden signs of body language that might reveal a lead.

"I remember wondering where you were." She deliberated for a moment. "Then I heard the toilet flush."

"For a second there I thought you would give me away, dear." Ron paused. "But it looks like my enlarged prostate saved me."

They all laughed, except for Agent Grey.

Grey's cold manner and lack of response to social graces troubled Ron. Agent Grey did not speak a word. He just stared into the eyes of each person as they spoke.

Why would a federal agent based in Philadelphia be on the case of a Florida homicide? How did he get here so fast? Could Mittenberg have been under surveillance? Do they know I killed him?

"Well, there isn't more to discuss," said Rice. "I would appreciate your input if you remember anything. It seems not too many people liked this Mittenberg. I suspect he got involved with some organized crime types based on the way he died."

"Is there any reason for us to fear for our safety? Like a thug getting past security to rob an apartment. Like those home invasions I see on the news. What about the security cameras?"

Ron hoped his questions would throw off any suspicion since he did not take money from Mittenberg's body.

"Cameras were out of service for an upgrade. Figures. On the one night they may have helped. No, sir. This looks like a revenge crime, a hate crime, or a professional hit," explained Rice.

"How can you be sure?" Ron added..

"The killer didn't take any money, and Mittenberg had a couple thousand on him. No street crook would miss the cash."

"What kind of car insurance fraud was he involved in?" asked Susan.

"At the moment, it appears he and his team hired drivers to go around the country and crash into each other after loading up on auto insurance. They sued and made off with some big bucks claiming serious injuries. At least that's the way Agent Grey here explained it to me."

Agent Grey looked angry that Detective Rice provided so much information in such an unprofessional and sloppy investigative process.

"Well, you know, until convicted in a court of law they're innocent," Susan offered.

"I can assure you they're guilty, and we'll get the rest of them soon enough," countered Agent Grey in a manner bordering on aggravated hostility.

It was the routine murder interrogation for Rice. Ron, having the mind of a lawyer, passed it with honors because of his brilliant manner of thinking ahead, never forgetting logical sequencing, and never afraid of making contradictory statements.

Ron's composure surprised him after having committed murder; the ultimate sin in the Ten Commandments he so cherished. He did not show signs of sorrow. His heart remained steady, and he did not feel in the least bit nervous during the interrogation, other than the one moment Susan may have given away his alibi. The calm confounded him.

Ron's survival defenses jumped in on a primal level, allowing him to perform during his interview with Rice, but he fell apart the moment the detectives left. He gave Susan a hug and exited to the bathroom, wanting to be alone. Tremendous guilt overwhelmed him, his heart pounded, perspiration leaked from every pore, and his breathing felt labored. He splashed cold water onto his face and took several deep breaths. In a matter of a few seconds, a spirit of accomplishment replaced the guilt with an uneasy sense of pride for his actions. He looked into the bathroom mirror. In this solitude, his frown and worry melted away. He felt good.

"RON, WHEN YOU SAY, 'LOSING CONTROL,' do you feel as though you want to harm yourself or anyone?"

An awkward pause hung heavy in the air.

"Ron, are you listening to me? When you say, 'losing control,' do you feel as though you want to harm yourself or anyone else?"

"That's it! That's my precise point!"

"What do you mean, Ron?"

"Twenty years ago that wouldn't have been your first question every time we meet. Today, you begin with that obligatory question to see if the patients are planning on doing any harm to themselves or others. And why? Because if your patients hurt themselves, or someone else, the system will hold you responsible. Their family will sue your ass, so you'd better cover that ass with those detailed notations you write in the patient chart showing you asked all the right questions. Even then, they'll second guess you until they have a jury of laymen convinced you screwed up."

It hurt Steve Lagerfeld to see his long-time friend reduced to a shell of himself as he confessed his weaknesses.

They went through their undergraduate years together at Temple University. Coming from humble means, neither could afford any of the prestigious schools. In college, they got serious about education, and Steve gained entrance into Ivy League professional schools through scholarships.

Approaching their mid-forties, it was apparent Ron had aged much better than Steve. His gray hair grew rather sparse, giving the appearance of a thin veil letting most of his scalp show. A prominent nose balanced the mid-life, telltale bifocals at its tip. His posture exaggerated his rounded shoulders, midriff bulge, and frail arms, all more noticeable while sitting in his chair. Steve's mind, however, was sharp. Many powerbrokers and society dames shared their innermost secrets with him during the never-ending therapy sessions of the well to do.

Steve practiced psychiatry for years and saw many sad cases. He had a simple rule. He did not treat family or friends. To avoid the risks associated with personal involvement, he referred familiar people to a colleague. Ron seeking help was an exception. Steve knew Ron's ego kept him from getting help. When the request came, he would not turn him away.

Steve continued taking notes.

"Well, am I right?" asked Ron.

"This diatribe is about the lawsuit, isn't it?"

"You answer my question, and I'll answer yours."

Steve put his pen down and stared into Ron's eyes as he responded.

"You're right. What can I say? Every week I read about cases blaming a doctor or a drug company for the misfortunes of the mentally disturbed. For Christ's sake, they tried to blame Prozac, and the doctors who prescribe it, for the suicides some unstable people commit every day. If they succeeded, we would have lost a good group of drugs to treat depression."

"And who are they?" asked Ron.

"What do you mean?" said Steve.

"You said, 'they.' They're the fuckin' lawyers."

"Ron, it's the lawsuit, isn't it?"

"Yes, it is, damn it." Ron slammed his hand onto the oversized leather chair.

"That's over, for God's sake. Let it go."

"Steve, I can't let it go. We lost everything."

"Let me tell you something, Ron. You're not the first doctor to see me over the trauma of these experiences. Lawsuits are a normal reason to become stressed. You will get through it. You can build it back up again," said Steve, in a soft reassuring voice. "A lot of the doctors are getting out of town. They're moving down south where the people still have morals. I heard patients even say, 'thank you, Doctor' for helping them down there."

"Move? You can't be serious. I lost my spirit. Do you understand me? They stole my will, my mind. I've changed."

Steve looked down at his notepad as though he understood, but he didn't have an answer.

"You know that repugnant lawyer who's on television?" asked Ron.

"Sure, who doesn't? He was murdered, wasn't he?"

"He was. I laughed at that joker. I thought people were too moral to support such an unprofessional whore. Well, the humor faded as the years went by, and I saw more and more of these ambulance-chasing clowns reminding everyone they can get big money by blaming anyone with deep pockets for misfortunes. Look at our neighbors. They feed on the system. God, they embody it."

Steve understood what preyed on Ron. He, too, attended the parties, Little League games, and assorted events that let the true colors show. He wanted to help Ron from obsessing over all the tumult that is part of the universal human condition.

"What can I tell you, Ron? You present a good case for the fall of the Empire."

They laughed.

"We have to stop focusing on the negativity. I want you to get this prescription filled. It's an antidepressant, and I don't want your crap about how you're not depressed. I'm giving it to you for obsessive-compulsive disorder. It'll take three weeks to see an effect. Then you'll notice every thing won't be an issue."

"I hope you're right."

"Trust me. I'm right! Now you have a lecture in about ten minutes. You don't want to leave your students holding the bag, so get on over there and take out your frustrations on them."

They chuckled, and Ron stood to shake hands with his friend.

"I think we should meet again, Ron. How about next week?"

"Yeah, that would be great. I have this recurring dream. Maybe you can tell me what it means."

"I'm a Behaviorist, not a Freudian. You know we put little credence in dreams, but I'll want to hear about it next time."

CHAPTER
FIVE

PERHAPS THE MEDICATION would erase the bad memory, or at least the guilt, driving Ron mad. He would do anything to reverse the Florida insanity. For now, he kept reliving the events that took him to this evil place.

Ron understood, only too well, the games played to enrich the unscrupulous lawyers, unethical doctors, and greedy people playing the national litigation lottery. That's what he called it. His neighbors were a testament to the ills of the perverted system. The million-dollar homes of his Philadelphia suburb sheltered the nouveau riche. Nothing like the old-money Main Line homes, these dwellings were modern structures with the architectural extravagance of a most pretentious nature.

At least three "accident doctors" lived on the same street as Ron and Steve, so they were well acquainted with them. At various social functions, the professionals bragged about their multimillion-dollar billings. It repulsed Ron to hear about these fraudulent claims. Neighbors related their stories of being referred to medical colleagues of his by the many personal injury attorneys living in this same plush landfill of a community.

While Ron walked to his class to present his seminar, he relived an incident from not too long ago. It felt dream-like to recall the banter at the cocktail party with his neighbors. Janis took great pride in telling her tale.

"I felt so bad for the young kid. He was busing our table, and as he poured the coffee, he dropped the cup in my lap. I jumped up, thinking my thighs were on fire. The poor boy was helpless. He went to blot my wet spot. Get it? My wet spot! Then he backed off, approached, and backed off. It was like he was afraid of pussy."

This kind of language in mixed company, let alone from a woman, made Ron sick. He perceived it as yet another degradation of society. Perhaps he was just not "with it," since the crowd laughed in obvious approval.

"If it didn't hurt so much, I would have been laughing. The manager came over, apologized a hundred times, and wanted to see if I was okay."

Janis carried on and on about how she got home and noticed the equivalence of sunburnt thighs. Her husband, Terry, the owner of an aggressive auto body shop, had "special arrangements" with the neighborhood attorneys for years. He would jack up the repair bills to make the claims high, then do the repairs with cheap parts. The profits helped pay the kickbacks to his lawyer friends. He told Janis to wait until morning, and then call "the best personal injury attorney around," Jerry Rothenberg.

"Do you believe they paid me two-hundred-thousand dollars for a case of sunburnt thighs?" Janis boasted. "I guess I should have done better, because the twit who burnt her pussy at McDonald's got four million dollars. What happened, Jerry?"

She looked to Rothenberg, whose expression of pride for winning her case turned to that of embarrassment.

Again, the chorus showed their approval with hyena-like laughter.

Not to place second, Brad Greenspun played out his story of

how a "fender-bender" resulted in seven stitches below his lip. Many considered the resultant scar to look somewhat sexy. His lawyer, at the deposition, had him feign a lisp as if the accident caused a permanent speech impediment.

"They never wanted a jury to hear me say a word. A hundred-thousand just like that. I shoulda got the Academy Award. I was so fuckin' convincing."

Right! You shoulda got . . . ten years in jail, asshole, thought Ron.

The revelation of lost integrity and defiled character gathered before him at these cocktail parties provided the evidence for the ever-growing acceptance of wealth over moral conviction. Ron could not comprehend how they showed pride in such disgraceful actions.

On the outside, Ron acted civil. These were the parents of his children's friends. They had grown up together. Years of socializing revealed the corruption, making it more and more difficult for Ron to connect with this type.

Ron would often lecture his children on how the dollar had so perverted the values of society that they put people on a pedestal because of what they had, rather than for their character or the quality of their actions.

"Years ago, the neighbors would have ostracized Dr. Laken He would have had to move to a new town where no one knew him. He'd have to start again."

Ron explained to his children the case of Alfred Laken, who lived across the street. Alfred was the first doctor of their acquaintances to get convicted of welfare fraud. His lucrative accident practice did not satisfy his greed. He padded the medical bills of the poor to help finance his gambling habit and lavish lifestyle.

"Dr. Laken only served thirty days in state prison and paid back one hundred thousand dollars to Medicaid. Not bad considering he made at least two million in his fraudulent billings till he got caught," Ron said with a hint of cynicism. While Ron did not like to tell tales, these stories contained good lessons from which the children learned morality.

Ron's children loved the dinnertime banter. The stories were interesting and great gossip. He told them these accounts were not to leave the house.

CHAPTER
SIX

RON STROLLED ONWARD to the lecture hall for his weekly meeting with the surgery residents. The University of Pennsylvania campus bustled with activity. Students moved about in a manner showing drive and determination. Penn was not a party school. These were the future elite leaders, and it showed.

The room was too large for the small class of seven oral surgery residents, but his lectures, popular by word of mouth, attracted many walk-ins. They represented the new generation getting ready to take the reins from a previous lot of burnt out doctors; societal kings no more.

Modern times changed the opinion of the healthcare provider. While once held in high esteem, almost god-like, the portrait of the doctor turned into a common idol, easy to discard. At his lectures, Ron often spoke of the factors contributing to the fall of the reputation doctors once wore with honor.

"You see all too many cases of medical malpractice making the headlines. While we can justify some, only the egregious ones make the front page, and most others have no merit. We never hear about them.

"The public never sees the other side. They don't tell them

about the fraud and the malicious, frivolous claims made by the patients. They keep seeing how the doctors make mistake after mistake. Couple this narrative with the Hollywood movies depicting doctors, hospitals, clergy, and just about every institution as corrupt. What's the result?"

"Great movies, Dr. Rellick," said Bilal, the exchange student from India, who, like many foreigners, was a big fan of the Hollywood productions.

Ron and the other residents laughed.

"You're right. These movies are so wonderful that everyone goes to see them. Then they lose their trust in the institutions that make a society great. It doesn't happen overnight, nor is it one movie, not one article about a bad doctor or a predator priest. It's the multitude of attacks on good things that have a devastating effect on society. The result is an untrusting, paranoid public doubting and questioning everything.

"The sacred relationship between healer and patient becomes undermined. While common sense tells us this failing is bad for society, the first amendment to our Constitution tells us we can't do anything about it. Who are the biggest defenders of our first amendment?"

As he waited for an answer, the sight of what looked like a familiar figure sitting in the shadows toward the back of the lecture hall distracted Ron. He did not recognize the face, but then it became clear. It was Agent Grey.

"That's easy, Dr. Rellick. The lawyers, the ACLU," answered Kim, a petite third-year resident who devoured Ron's every word.

"Keep in mind what they have to gain under the guise of free speech," said Ron as he maintained a fixed gaze upon the man sitting at the back of the hall.

Ron turned and walked to the blackboard. He felt Grey's piercing eyes attempting to penetrate his dark secret as he drew a large dollar sign in response to his own words.

"It's almost impossible to sue someone held in high esteem. When doctors were gods you wouldn't, you couldn't sue them.

Now we live in a world where it's easy to find a jury seeking to punish the doctor, the cop, the church. They revere nothing. Irreverence is what the lawyers want."

With uncanny timing, the bell rang as he delivered his last word. The students gathered their belongings and began their exodus from the lecture hall.

Ron walked up the aisle toward the exit hoping to confront the unwelcome stranger, but he already left. Ron followed on to the campus in pursuit. A glimpse of Grey turning a corner offered a fleeting chance to follow, but the bustling crowds made the task futile.

Great! Now I'm under surveillance, and Grey knows from my lecture I have a motive for killing Mittenberg. No. He can't know what happened. If he knew, he'd take me in for questioning.

He has no clue. It's just a hunch on his part. We're from the same city, so he has to investigate everyone from the Florida condo who lives here. Yeah, that's it. He has nothing on me. It's just routine. I've got to play it cool. And what the hell would I say if I caught up with him? Got to let it go.

CHAPTER
SEVEN

IT WAS seven years since the "Phillip's" debacle began. Seven years ago, Ron's decline started, but all during that time he remained an unsuspecting pawn in the story that would play out in a courtroom and end up in his ruination.

Ron explained it over and over to Sharon Carver, his insurance company appointed defense attorney. She defended doctors from the predatory plaintiffs' bar, and the legal community considered her a specialist.

"It's every doc's nightmare. The day you treat the patient from Hell," Ron explained. "In medical residencies, they have a name for it, PPP, piss-poor plasma. While the American credo states that, 'all men are created equal,' it just ain't so."

"What do you mean?" Sharon asked.

"Everyone recognizes physical differences in appearance, but with healing, laymen think everyone responds the same and always gets better. If complications happen, it's the doctor's fault. That's the way the lawyers see it. From their view, there's no such thing as a plasma or immune system defect. I'm talking about the patient who doesn't respond to anything we do."

Sharon listened to Ron's tale. Every so often she would make a note on her legal pad.

"People understood how certain infections are so virulent, or some people's resistance so weak, that they don't get better."

Sharon looked up, making innocent eye contact with Ron, knowing it would prompt more detail.

"That's right, patients sometimes die," he went on, as if he was responding to Sharon's unspoken lack of understanding. "The legal profession has yet to figure out how to attach blame and sue for a poor resistance. Bacteria and viruses don't have deep pockets, so they have to go after the doctors." Ron's mockery was rather clear.

"Hey, everybody's got to eat," Sharon said, and with a devilish laugh to let Ron know she was on his side.

"Yeah, right. Well, this is how I got involved. He showed up at my office as an emergency."

Ron described his initial contact with Jason Philips, the patient who would lead to his ruination. Sharon took notes. The events played out in his mind over the years, and it affected his psyche in ways he never understood.

"How can I help you, Jason?"

"God, Doc! I'm in terrible pain. Everything hurts. I've been awake for two days now. You gotta help me. I can't go another night like this."

Examination revealed a frail white male with a history of allergy to all antibiotics except clindamycin, a potent, effective drug for more serious infections with the attendant risk of causing a serious form of colitis. A complicating factor involved Jason's long-term history of ulcerative colitis, made the absorption of any drugs a difficulty.

His effeminate manner and feeble constitution made Ron wonder if Jason might have AIDS but chuckled to himself as he pictured the "thought police" arresting him for such an assumption. While he needed to know if Jason had a disease that could alter therapy and keep him from healing, Ron could not order an AIDS test without Jason's consent. During the early days of the AIDS epidemic, doctors could not question patients about HIV status. Ron did not care. The health and healing of his patient was his foremost concern. He inquired despite the new laws.

"Doc, there's no way I'd get AIDS, and I wouldn't want to know, anyway."

Enough, said. Ron knew rather well how politicians turned medical practice on edge once they classified AIDS as a disability, protecting these patients under the Americans with a Disability Act. He would have to follow the universal precautions doctrine and assume the worst, that all patients have serious contagious infections, including AIDS.

After careful examination, imaging, and testing, Ron presented his findings.

"Jason, you have an infection in your jaw, but I suspect you also have an infection in your sinus. We can get treatment started on the dental infection, but you must see an ENT doctor who specializes in treating sinus infections."

"Just pull the tooth that's killing me. If it still hurts, then I'll see the other doctor."

"Whenever we remove a tooth, you might develop numbness in your lip, jaw, cheek, or face because of the surgery."

Ron despised frightening the hell out of every patient to get an informed consent. It was bad enough that surgery scares everyone to death before they get started. Now doctors had to add the finishing touch; fear of the treatment, fear of the caregiver.

Jason did not get well numbed, and he jumped with the slightest pressure every time Ron attempted to remove the infected tooth. Jason's history of complications with general anesthesia prevented its use, making the procedure another of those rough management problems Ron dealt with daily.

To make matters worse, Jason had the classic PPP profile. His friable tissues tore upon reflecting a surgical flap, delayed healing, and a messy surgical site made suturing and post-operative care difficult, even with Ron's deft touch.

Jason bled all over the place, putting Ron under tremendous pressure to protect himself and Bonnie, his nurse. He completed the procedure after an hour of struggling. Jason tried to rise from the operating chair in a most melodramatic fashion, holding his face and appearing he might faint. Ron tilted the chair back to allay any chance of passing out.

"I'd like you to see an ear, nose, and throat specialist. The infection you have seems to be in the sinus more than in your teeth. They can better determine the course of treatment from this point. Get there today."

Spent from his ordeal, Jason labored a response.

"I need to see my family doctor before I go to anyone else."

"If you prefer, but get there today."

"I don't think I can. I want to go home."

At 2:00 am the phone rang. The sound awakened Ron from a deep sleep. Available at anytime for most of his life since his residency meant the call wasn't unexpected, but it never failed to cause worry and start his heart beating rather fast. His service relayed the message that his patient needed a callback.

"Hello, this is Dr. Rellick. How can I help you, Jason?"

"I'm dying here, Doc. I feel worse than I did before you pulled that damn tooth. I think you messed up somehow."

All along Ron recognized Jason needed the ENT service. Not wanting to get into a scientific explanation with an agitated patient, he spoke with command.

"I want you to go right over to Brandon Hospital. I'll call ahead and make sure they have the right team to see you."

Records would show Jason went to the emergency room, but after twenty-four hours, getting a little better, he left against medical advice.

The E.N.T. service felt, as did Ron, the sinus infection was the primary source of infection and not responding to the clindamycin, they put him on an I.V. drip of vancomycin. They wanted to monitor Jason until he stabilized, but he "felt closed in" at hospitals. He removed the I.V. and demanded to leave. They couldn't make him stay. The best they could offer was an increased dose of the oral clindamycin.

Two days later Jason returned to Ron's office with a fever of 102 degrees and looking toxic. Again, Ron suggested hospitalization, but Jason said he would check with his medical doctor first. Ron did not hear from Jason again. Later, he learned Jason put off treatment for another day, then landed in a different hospital where Ron did not have admitting privileges. Now, he would lose track of Jason's progress and care.

When the new doctors worked up Jason for his unyielding infection, he told them since the tooth extraction he'd been getting worse. He never mentioned the sinus infection diagnosed by Ron and the other doctors during his first hospitalization. Based on the flawed history, the new team of doctors told Jason his problem was a tooth infection that spread to his sinus. This flawed statement was all the evidence necessary for Jason and his wife to blame Ron for the poor outcome and injuries.

The infection turned worse, and the new attendings at the local hospital referred Jason to the E.N.T. service of a major teaching hospital. They performed a Caldwell-Luc surgery to drain the sinus through his oral cavity with no improvement. The pressure continued to build, and Jason's orbit came under such stress it destroyed his optic nerve. Jason became blind in one eye, developed a brain abscess, and it looked like he would die. He came through the critical period after two weeks of difficult recovery, and his doctors dismissed him from the hospital.

Five days later Jason's pain returned, along with a spiking fever. This time the confounded doctors transferred Jason to the biggest facility specializing in the care of advanced neurological cases. Dr. Fesik Hitselberger, the world-renowned neurosurgeon, took the case.

Concerned about Jason, Ron called treating physicians daily throughout the ordeal to check on his condition. With the first call to Dr. Hitselberger, his attitude turned most indignant upon learning that Ron removed the original infected tooth.

"So, you're the doctor, or shall I say oral surgeon—that's a dentist if I'm not mistaken, who nearly killed Jason."

"What? What are you saying?" asked Ron in utter amazement.

"I've seen this kind of thing often. Don't deny you had a problem that got out of control. Just admit it. That's why you have insurance."

Ron did not believe what he heard. To place blame on the blameless and relegate a serious medical issue to an expected lawsuit angered Ron, but maintaining decorum, he attempted to detail the case to Hitselberger, who found it easier to create his history rather than to listen to Ron's explanation.

Each time Jason saw a new doctor, the history he told implicated Ron as the "surgeon who pulled my tooth, and the next thing you know I wound up in the hospital."

Hitselberger's reaction wasn't uncommon. Many medical practitioners badmouth other doctors without ever having a full and accurate history. If Hitselberger understood the events, he would never have treated Ron in this manner. His report added to case histories from the ten other doctors who saw Jason all stating, "a sinus infection developed secondary to dental extraction." Over and over, in chart after chart of some of the finest doctors, the jury saw "sinus infection secondary to dental extraction" while ignoring the stated presence of a sinus infection noted in Ron's chart.

After two months and three hospitalizations, Jason recovered. He was blind in one eye and stated he could hardly see out of the other. He walked with a cane to each deposition. Several doctors treated Jason for chronic pain, and addiction following the many Demerol and Percodan prescriptions provided in attempts to manage the agony. He registered with a Methadone clinic to break his prescription opioid dependence.

CHAPTER
EIGHT

SHARON CARVER WAS NO SLOUCH. The insurance company recognized the seriousness of the allegations in this lawsuit, so they assigned their best. They needed their best against Jason's attorney, Edgar Hill. They did not want to settle his case. Ron did nothing wrong, but they had to be realistic knowing the claimed damages were big. Unlike most life insurance companies that can factor in their losses through actuarial tables, liability carriers can never factor in emotion or the unexpected consequences of a courtroom trial.

In pretrial hearings, Ron's insurance company offered one-hundred-thousand dollars to settle.

"Your honor, the insurance carrier will offer $100,000 to close this case. Let's make everyone happy and move on," reasoned Carver on behalf of getting this nightmare over with for Ron. She recognized the offer represented poor bait but had to play the negotiating game to stay in the judge's good graces.

Hill laughed, looked at the judge, and held up six fingers.

"Six," he said.

Judge Sean Donovan, having most of the larger personal injury cases assigned to his docket, responded, "So, you want $600,000 to make this go away?" He raised his bushy brows as a signal for Hill to confirm.

"Not at all your honor," responded Hill with a haughty air of superiority. "I'm talking six million dollars to end this case now."

"That's absurd," Carver countered as she looked to the judge for affirmation.

"Take it or leave it," Hill demanded.

"Edgar, let's find a number that works for everybody," Judge Donovan insisted.

"Sean, this is a solid case. I'm not playing around here. This matter is worth double if we go before a jury. You want a settlement? I'll help clear your docket, but I'm not settling for peanuts."

"Tell you what, Edgar . . . I'll see you in court," Carver barked, knowing to negotiate with Hill was futile. Sharon realized Hill wanted to win the big one. She understood Judge Donovan had to go through the motions of a negotiated settlement for the sake of propriety. She knew, unlike most litigators, who dread litigating and rely on making a deal, Hill savored the chance to get in front of a jury. He thrived on his performances and would not settle unless the number worked for him.

Ron feared a scenario like the extreme jury awards that make the headlines, so he increased his liability coverage to four million dollars years before he ever met Jason. All of his personal injury attorney acquaintances told him one million coverage is plenty, and a four-million-dollar award is rare, a once in a lifetime fluke. Ron figured he would remain protected and never see his life ruined like people he knew. Ron read countless stories about doctors, architects, engineers, and most anybody who owned property who lost everything after an unfortunate professional result or ill-fated slip and fall on someone's front walk.

After the pretrial hearings, Sharon had to explain to Ron what might happen if he lost in court.

"Ron, I won't bullshit you. They're asking for six million dollars."

"Come on, Sharon, they can ask for anything they want," he replied in disgust.

"True, but they have big damages on their side. It's not altogether impossible for them to get a big number. Maybe not six million, but juries are unpredictable, and it could go even higher."

"But I did nothing wrong!"

"It doesn't matter here."

"Where are we, Sharon? Fucking Fantasy Land?"

"Come on, Ron. This is my job. Don't make me feel worse than I do. Don't make me acknowledge I work in the gutter. At least I try to make it better. I'm on your side. You'll be okay."

CHAPTER
NINE

FORTY PROSPECTIVE JURORS had to appear Monday morning at eight A.M. Each person filled out an extensive questionnaire querying such facts as: Did you ever sue a doctor? Has anyone ever sued you? Is anyone in your family a doctor? Is anyone in your family a lawyer? Do you have negative feelings toward lawyers that would make it difficult for you to decide a case without prejudice?

Once the bailiff gathered all the questionnaires, he distributed copies to the defense attorney, the plaintiff attorney, and the judge.

Sharon analyzed each page with her assistant. Ron watched as they scribbled hieroglyphic-like markings on the top of each form. The conversation between Sharon and her assistant seemed arcane and bordered on the mystic.

"For cause."

"For cause," responded the assistant.

They pulled these slips from the bundle of questionnaires and eliminated this group of perspective jurors based on answers to questions showing obvious prejudice.

Rules permitted each side to eliminate six people from the pool for no reason. This process made the analysis important, since there were always more than six people they wanted to eliminate without cause.

Like little kids about to trade and sell their most cherished baseball cards, Sharon and Edgar engaged in the procedure.

The racial mix of the jury pool was seventy to thirty, blacks to whites. The ratio was not a reflection of the city's raw demographics. Sharon explained.

"The white flight to the suburbs is just part of it. The unemployed and the undereducated don't mind coming here. They get eleven dollars a day and a hot lunch. Take the average middle class, or blue-collar worker, white or black, and they go to all lengths to get out of jury duty. Even if they get selected as prospective jurors, they know all the right answers to assure getting excused for cause. Now, add in the welfare recipients who by far live in the downtown boundaries. They love the eleven-buck stipend. And that's how you get this illustrious group. The fact is, Ron, we got a good jury, four high school grads, a nurse, and one who finished college, a valued commodity. Trust me, it could be worse."

Unlike criminal cases requiring twelve jurors in civil cases, the Philadelphia jury comprises between six and twelve participants. This jury of nine worried Ron.

It comprised three young black women, two of whom were high school grads, one worked as a secretary, the other two were unemployed. Two of the women with high school educations, well dressed, and attractive, seemed to doze during jury selection. Ron felt frustrated but realized he had no recourse.

I'd like to raise my hand and ask the judge to wake the two in the back. They don't understand how important the technical testimony is to my case, as boring as it might be. They can't understand the details if they tried. Where the hell are my peers? Why aren't they judging me? This is no joking matter!

Added to the mix, Teresa Bowdon, a twenty-four-year-old

white, cherubic, giggling, tenth grade dropout. She found a friend in Wesley Schilling, the white, short-order cook. He had one year of trade school and a job. He was in his early thirties and showed little interest in the proceedings. Concerned more with the ladies, during the jury selection breaks he flirted and tried to get close to the female jurors.

John Clydesdale, a minor administrator at a local hospital, was a well-dressed, white male, low-level executive involved in health care. In his late twenties, he would not have the level of experience and the knowledge Ron might have hoped, but he was the best thing going.

This guy will be my angel of mercy. He's the most educated. That'll be a real plus when they discuss anaerobic culturing and T-4 lymphocyte counts. For Christ's sake, he's got to be sympathetic. All hospitals get sued. He'll understand. I'm sure he will.

The sixty-year-old, toothless black woman, Nancy Barnes, worried Ron the most. She sat in the jury box rhythmically licking her edentulous upper arch.

Mrs. Barnes wore a silk dress that bore a floral pattern from decades past. She fanned herself incessantly with the *Daily News* she brought with her. Her animation gave life to the otherwise static group of jurors who slumped in their seats showing little interest in the proceedings.

Another hope, Ron figured, might be the elderly retired black gentleman, Ralph Samson. He arrived at the court early. He dressed in a fine suit and tie with a matching handkerchief folded into his breast pocket. The suit looked old, out of style, and a size too large, but it was clean and pressed. A collar bar held his tie in place, tight and crisp throughout the day. When he entered the building, he would remove his hat with rigid precision. He was old school. The neighborhood youth called him the "white man's nigger" because he was polite, followed the rules, believed in the system, and was a retired prison guard.

The final complement to this nine-member jury was Carol Grist, a twenty-nine-year-old reject from Fishtown. She grew up in the solid white, poor, working class neighborhood when it was solid white. While most of this population practiced and immersed themselves in tradition and prejudice, Carol grew up the rebel.

Through various redistricting plans developed by the City to encourage racial balance in education, Carol attended a school with a predominately black population, the result of busing. Despite the forced integration, strong racial prejudices kept the two groups apart. Carol, however, was one of the ever-increasing numbers who intermarried, and her family and friends shunned her.

To further alienate against societal dictates, Carol had tattoos in numbers exceeding that accepted as adornment. A nose ring and eyebrow piercing highlighted her body paint. The attention delighted Carol in that Ron and others could not take their eyes off the oddity of her appearance.

"I can't comprehend these violations of the flesh. What is she doing to herself? It's got to be a guilt-based mutilation. It must be punishment for some feelings of inadequacy. I don't understand this manner of living. What a fucking joke to have her hear my case and judge me."

Carol Grist worried Ron and Sharon the most. She was a reject, an outcast. Sharon always feared the downtrodden because they empathized more with the alleged victim, the plaintiffs. She learned they care little for the facts they didn't understand. They're more concerned with the injury of the aggrieved. This juror, she reasoned, was more likely to let emotion dictate her decision.

"Philadelphia is a plaintiff's town," Sharon explained to Ron. "This is a well-known fact."

"The reason we have problems with the Philly jury involves its makeup. Most of the jurors come from the poor, uneducated minorities. These are the two most revered qualities sought after by the plaintiff's attorneys.

"The older, less-educated black jurors are often religious people who have a heightened sense of the need for justice. Empathy grows from their history—seeing so many injustices to their people in the three hundred years on this continent. It's an internalized empathy that took generations to cultivate. It then takes but a few hours of manipulative talk to convince these jurors the plaintiff is a victim of an injustice."

"How do you know these details?" Ron asked.

"People write books on the subject. Companies do psychological profiling and sell the results. We read all the literature on relevant material. It's our job. We have to get the best jury we can. It's all based on profiling."

"What about the educated blacks?"

"They're more likely to be freethinkers, less prone to emotional pleas reigning over reason. They have the education and intelligence to understand the facts of the case and get past the emotional hyperbole.

"The more educated, the wealthier, the more successful the jurors, the more likely they identify with the defendant, especially when it's a professional on the gallows of justice," Sharon explained.

"Oh. Like the people who skip jury duty," added Ron.

"Exactly." Sharon laughed to acknowledge Ron's cynical humor. "But we try to get the best hand we can. That's why during the *voir dire*, that's what we call the picking and choosing process. The plaintiffs pick those jurors whom they perceive will be best for them, and likewise, we pick the best for the defense."

Jury selection is a routine matter for all litigation attorneys. The Philadelphia jury pool skewed in favor of the plaintiffs. That's what made Philadelphia ground zero for lawsuits. Hill and his ilk loved to bring their cases to court in this city. The same reason professionals at risk of lawsuits leave the city and move their practices to the friendlier suburban neighborhoods.

CHAPTER
TEN

THE COURTROOM LOOKED UNINVITING. Drab green, glossy, painted walls, harboring scuffs and stains, reflected the glare of too many bright fluorescent lights. A flag stood in each corner of the antiquated chamber offering the only semblance of ornamentation. A makeover never happened in this municipality with budgetary problems, the same as encountered in most big cities contending with ever increasing social service burdens.

"Hear ye, hear ye. This court is now in session. All rise."

Those in attendance stood as Judge Sean Donavan entered the courtroom. Ron's thoughts raced on about the incident which would play out in this court of law. The unfamiliar turf frightened Ron, and he expected it would not be a pleasant experience.

"Be seated," shouted the bailiff.

Ron sat in a daze. He stared at the American flag standing behind and to the right of the judge who fumbled with papers getting ready for the proceedings. Edgar Hill sat at the plaintiff's table with Mrs. Phillips. Ron and Sharon Carver sat at the defense table.

"Mr. Hill, are you ready to begin?" asked Judge Donovan.

"I am, your Honor," declared Hill in his impressive baritone voice

He stood, walked to the jury, and remained silent for a moment to set the stage for the show designed to shake Ron to his core.

"Ladies and gentlemen, I must tell you a story, a sad story, about how my client, Jason Philips, visited Dr. Ronald Rellick. He had a simple request. 'Doctor, won't you please help me?' Records and testimony will show Jason went to Dr. Rellick with a routine dental infection. In the days that followed, Jason's condition worsened to the point he had to go the hospital. His infection spread to his sinuses, then to his brain. Jason nearly died, my friends."

Ron shook his head in disgust as he had to suffer through the presentation made to paint the picture of incompetence upon his professionalism.

Like these people are your friends! I guess from his view, as a lawyer, anyone who holds the fate of millions of dollars going toward enriching his life is his friend.

Edgar Hill, known as the King of the Court, captivated every juror who saw him perform. His dress and demeanor exhibited power and wealth. Confidence attracted people to him. He intimidated with his stature and presence.

No one in the court was bigger than Hill. He dressed and groomed well. Like many men of fashion entering their fifties with thinning hair, he shaved his head, giving him the appearance of a defined manly dominance.

A dark shadow from a heavy beard made his aura more demonic as the day wore on. His eyes appeared alluring; a rare grey-blue, almost translucent. They caused people to stare, trying to understand how they could belong to this hulking figure.

No one better graced the stage of the Philadelphia courts. Hill did not have to advertise like the proliferating glut of plaintiff's attorneys whose names plastered the covers of every phonebook and barked for clients all day on the airwaves as they promised to "get you what you deserve."

If you had big damages, you saw "the King" and hoped he

would take your case. He only accepted prime lawsuits with the promise of a great reward. Damages had to be substantial enough to make it worth his time. Odds had to be in favor of winning.

The case did not have to be legitimate, just winnable. He had the ability to convince juries composed of the uninformed that awarding great riches to a sad soul was doing the right thing. It was Hill's perfect case. Jason's story fit the bill in every respect.

"Jason would have been better off had he died in the hospital," Mr. Hill spoke in a whisper while walking away from the jury box.

They leaned forward to hear his muffled words. He played them like puppets, skilled at pulling strings just in the right manner. When he had them at the edge of their chairs, he turned and came toward them. With each step, his voice transformed from whisper to thunderous roar.

"No! Jason pulled through only to have sickening neurologic damage. He lived in constant pain because his brain became so badly destroyed by the infection unleashed at Dr. Rellick's hand."

The members of the jury, their eyes opened wide, pictured manifestations of human suffering, and they fed upon every word. Hill turned away. He spoke in a whisper. It looked like one or two jurors would fall right out of their seats as they strained to hear.

"Testimony will show, for the next two years, my client, Jason Philips, saw every conceivable specialist in a quest to free himself from torturous agony."

With a slow cadence, Hill spoke the words "free himself from torturous agony" in the now silent courtroom. Everyone's eyes focused on Hill's back. He reached the corner farthest from the jury and looked into the wall as he spoke.

"Jason found no relief. He continued to suffer until his only hope came five years ago on Christmas Eve."

Hill paused. He turned to face the jury. A long silence set the jury's imagination wondering what reprieve rescued poor Jason?

"That night . . . Jason killed himself."

Hill pronounced "killed" with such a booming resonance it seemed to ignite the gasp of solidarity sounded by the nine jurors.

The "himself" was the product of a strained last bit of breath he forced out, emphasizing the "f" sound in self.

"Life had no meaning, only unrelenting pain. The doctors gave up trying. Jason could no longer bear his existence on earth. He took a handful of pills, his only solace in a world of unbearable suffering. Swallowing them, he understood the outcome. Death was his desperate attempt to find his peace. Death left Ann, Jason's wife . . ." Hill pointed to the plaintiff's table where Ann, now wept, synchronized by the orchestrating conductor. "Alone with a hurt so deep she no longer sleeps through the night. She's a woman whose memories of summer evening walks with Jason are fading images. Her companion for life . . . gone. His love, emotional and financial support . . . snuffed out like a flame in a storm."

"This guy should win the Shakespeare award for dramatic prose in the courtroom," Sharon whispered to Ron while the jury wore obvious signs of emotional distress.

Ron's face beaded with sweat. He felt the blood drain from his head, and his stomach sank to a depth he did not know existed. He doubted he would get a fair trial. The lynch mob stared at him like he was the agent of Lucifer, and they sat ready to pass judgment. Reason would never prevail. Ron's reputation, his home, even his life stood on the line.

CHAPTER
ELEVEN

BESIDES HILL'S DRAMATIC PERFORMANCE, many procedural processes allow a trial to meander and bore the most avid courtroom fan as many cases do. For the principles of the case, nothing seems boring. The experience took its toll on Ron's mind and body. At breaks in the proceeding, he ran to the men's room to swallow a Tagamet or Imodium. He felt a terrible burning in his gut as every meal traveled through him like water.

Ron no longer slept well. His day and night thoughts entertained an almost constant reincarnation of the court proceedings related to the experience with Jason.

Each night, all night, he'd lie awake and ponder how there is no justice. When slumber failed him, he turned to his bedside radio and listened to the local news.

"In the North Philadelphia section of the city, the court sentenced Hayward Huston to three years for manslaughter. He killed the three-year-old son of his girlfriend, Denise Johnson . . ."

Three years for manslaughter. What? I can't believe it. This is insanity. They rape and kill children, and there's no outrage, no punishment.

The radio played on.

"People gathered for an all-night vigil protesting the death penalty of James Bigley, the mass murderer scheduled for execution scheduled tomorrow evening."

Muggings, rapes, murder! Murder reported daily. It's become an expected occurrence, like a report on the weather. The violent death of a human soul no longer has any shock value. Has the world become numb, or have people become wrapped up in their own cheapened lives, too busy to care? What have we become? There's no longer logic in medicine, in daily life, in our existence.

It was two-fifteen A.M. when Ron glanced at the clock. A welcome commercial break from the chronicle of senseless mayhem played, and as if fated, the last thing Ron remembered hearing riled him, "Have you been injured by your doctor? Let me get you all you deserve. Call me . . ." He lifted himself into a sitting position and hyperventilated until he collapsed.

CHAPTER
TWELVE

RON AND SHARON understood the hoax Hill played on the jury. The private investigator they hired learned that Jason frequented gay bars for at least the past four years. The odds of him providing any conjugal comfort to his wife seemed limited.

Jason had a primary infection in his sinus, unrelated to his concurrent dental infection, before he ever saw Ron. Jason never told him about his immune deficiency disorder, Gardner Diamond syndrome, which complicated treatment.

Sharon had many records from a cadre of medical specialists treating Jason over the last eight years. They found out Jason was on total permanent disability. He received social security disability and lived off his two-hundred-thousand-dollar settlement from a lawsuit against his last employer. He claimed a fall he took while moving a desktop computer caused his arcane immune disorder, a medical impossibility, but it made no difference. The workers' compensation attorneys for the State learned there were no grounds for his claim, but the resolution was less risky than letting an uninformed jury decide the case. His employer's insurance company took the same way out by settling rather than allowing for a jury trial.

Jason worked for a small, local shipping and hauling concern. Black and blue arms and legs resulting from his fall took long to heal, and thereafter, he bruised often. It took several months for a hematologist to make the diagnosis.

While Gardner Diamond syndrome isn't AIDS, it's an immune deficiency with similarities. It's rare and almost never occurs in men, leading some of Sharon's consulting physicians to believe a few creative, sympathizing doctors used this little-known condition to hide an AIDS diagnosis. This way they protected patients from the stigma attached to an unpopular diagnosis inconsistent with their public lives.

"Let's show the jury he had AIDS. It's all there, the gay bars, the immune deficiency. He couldn't fight infection," said Ron at one of his meetings with Sharon leading up to the trial.

"Ron, this is a lot more complicated than it seems. Even if we prove AIDS, it makes this case a walk on broken glass. I have to be careful where I tread with the facts. A tremendous amount of sympathy exists out there. The gay community, ravaged by a plague, has victim status, and America loves victims. We can't victimize the victim in the courtroom.

"How can I declare or even hint that Jason had AIDS without sparking flames of the movie *Philadelphia*? How can I mention homosexuality without looking callous?"

"But it applies to his treatment," Ron pleaded. "We need to know the medical history, or we can hurt the patient. They can't keep these details from us."

"It's not how things work anymore. Doctors who understand the science of medicine don't judge you. You, my good man, get judged by lay people who emotionalize the case. Like it or not, that's the way it works."

Ron nodded in agreement, realizing the courtroom is a theater of drama, not a bastion of facts where logic prevails.

CHAPTER
THIRTEEN

IT WAS time for Sharon to present her opening statement.

"Ladies and gentlemen, we heard a most heart-wrenching story; Jason's story. A sad tale. Like most stories of conflict, if you only hear one side, you don't know the whole story. When you learn the *whole* story, you will see true sadness, and it will remain heart-wrenching. However, you will also see Dr. Ron Rellick had nothing to do with the desperate decision Jason Phillips made on that dark December night. Dr. Rellick did everything possible for Jason.

"You will learn Jason ignored Dr. Rellick's orders. Jason *continued* to deteriorate. He *continued* to ignore orders until his infection had the time necessary to spread beyond control. We will show you Jason never told Dr. Rellick about a disorder of his immune system, making it hard for him to fight infection. These facts *shall* come to light, and you will then be able to decide this case in a *fair* . . . and *just* manner."

Sharon's stage presence surprised Ron. She exhibited a dynamic driving force, unlike her mild persona at all previous meetings. Her presentation, though not as theatrical as Hill, proved professional. There wasn't a single hesitation or unjustified pause. Sharon prepared well.

"We shall see Jason had many serious health problems, not because of Dr. Rellick's treatment, not even because of the infection that brought Jason to Dr. Rellick. The full story will show Jason did *not* work for eight full years before he met Dr. Rellick. He, in fact, had a disability that caused him unrelenting pain for at least a year before he ever heard the name Dr. Rellick."

Sharon turned from the jury in a militaristic fashion as if to stress the last statement and joined Ron at the defense table. She looked up to the judge and waited for testimony to begin.

Ron felt a calm spread through his body after Sharon's opening statement. Perhaps reason would enter the fray and allow justice to prevail. The iron fist of angst gripping his chest released for the moment, letting him breathe easy.

The trial proceeded, and Ron felt uplifted. At other moments, his mind wandered into the world of recurring daydreams. He pictured losing the case and leading a life filled with strife. Each time this dreaded sequence occurred during the trial, Ron jumped in his chair, awakening from the bad dream.

"Are you all right?" Sharon asked after one episode.

"Yeah, yeah, sure," Ron stammered.

It wasn't the startled jump that worried Sharon as much as the pale coloring and perspiration forming all too often upon Ron's face.

"How about a beer after the proceedings today? We can chat a bit. What do you think?"

A long hesitation ensued. Ron never heard the question.

Sharon repeated, "What do you think about a beer?"

Ron returned from a distant place of deep thought. He looked around as if lost.

"I'm sorry, Sharon. Maybe another time. I have to get home."

FOURTEEN

HIS WATCH READ ONE P.M., but the door to the office remained locked. Always on time, it disturbed Ron when others were not. He paced another two minutes when the door clicked open to reveal a woman with a natural scowl formed by lips that turned downward.

Ron's first meeting with Steve Lagerfeld, after having killed Mittenberg, did not help as he hoped. The medication, the antidepressant, proved useless. Dread, guilt, and anger fashioned his daily existence.

He thought he would control his mood and feelings of despair with no need to seek more help. Like many discover, life doesn't always work as planned. He needed to talk more.

"Good afternoon. You must be Mr. Rellick."

"Yes, that's right. I have an appointment with Steve at one."

"That's Dr. Lagerfeld," the secretary stated with an attitude matching her expression.

"Well, I'm Dr. Rellick, and I was friends with Steve before he had his title, so you must forgive me for my lack of protocol. If I felt well, I wouldn't be here, would I?" Ron responded with an air of equal indignation and spirit of temper, never before part of his persona.

"Of course," said the secretary who now wore a blushed complexion, the result of the unexpected verbal assault. She led Ron to the inner office where his friend waited in his nest of books, journals, and scattered papers.

"Where do I sit, the couch or the chair?"

"Anywhere you like, Ron."

He hesitated, turned left, then right, not knowing where to take refuge. He chose the chair. He sat on the edge like a sprinter ready to launch.

"Relax, Ron. Please, sit back and relax. We're just talking here."

"Things rarely bother me."

"Everyone needs to talk to someone. Problems are like a puzzle. With all the pieces in the box, you can't solve them. You lay them out, and it all comes together as a clear picture."

"I have Susan."

"It's not the same. Close as we may feel to our wives, there are some things we can't tell them, and there are things we shouldn't tell them."

"I suppose you're right, Steve, but I feel . . ."

Tears pooled in Ron's eyes. He tried to hide them, but one escaped and rolled down his cheek. Steve reached for his tissue box and handed it to Ron. This act of kindness only opened the floodgate. Ron pulled the box to his face to hide from embarrassment.

"This whole situation is just ridiculous. I can't believe it's happening to me," said Ron while blotting his eyes.

Steve ignored the comment, knowing Ron was ready to open up to him.

"Talk to me, Ron. What's troubling you?"

"It's the system. It's driving me crazy. I just don't get it anymore. Everywhere I turn, all I notice are the negative things.

Violence is everywhere, no more values, and money is the god everyone seems to worship. The whole fucking world is going nuts, Steve. I feel like I'm losing control."

"Are you having trouble sleeping?"

"Not yet. Besides the dreams that you don't care about I sleep all right."

"How's your appetite?"

"Fine, and I can still have sex. I know where you're going. It's not depression, Steve."

"Okay, you had a bunch of psychology courses in your college days, but let's not forget you're a surgeon. If you remember back to Psych 101, you know denial is a strong defense mechanism."

"You're right. I'm sorry," said Ron. "I'll leave the diagnosis up to you, but I'm telling you, if it's depression, it's rooted in a world gone crazy. I'm losing control."

"Ron, you're the most renowned maxillofacial surgeon in town. At forty-five, you authored a leading textbook and hold a tenured teaching position here at the University. and you've built the best, most respected oral surgical practice in town. All this done through your superhuman drive. I know about your endless hours of work. You achieved your success ethically. The system frustrates a guy like you."

"It's more than frustration, Steve. In years past, the busier the day, the more the energy flowed. When I worked, I never wasted a motion. The world around me ran in slow time. I could think and react like lightning.

"It's different now. Since this court case, I daydream. Everything I do takes longer. I'm always running late. I have no control over what's happening anymore. I feel like the innocent man accused of murder. I feel like I can't fight the system. It's too big. I'm just being processed . . ."

Ron ranted on about the system. It was one fifty-five, and his session with Steve should have ended.

"What people don't know, is the cash awards in these lawsuits skyrocketed. Most doctors don't realize how vulnerable they are."

"And what makes you the expert?" said Steve with a tone of doubt.

"Since I got entangled in my case, I studied this kind of thing. You're like all the rest, Steve. Your head's in the sand. When it happens to you, I hope you'll find solace in knowing I warned you."

"Come on, Ron. Circumstances like yours aren't an everyday event. Your case is an exception, a fluke."

"Oh yeah? Do you remember Dave Jaspen?"

"The name sounds familiar."

"Dave, the endodontist. You met him. After practicing twenty years, he had his patient from Hell. A thirty-two-year-old teacher who needed a routine procedure, but she was the hysterical type. When he numbed her, her hands flew up, and she lunged forward. Dave didn't want to pull out the needle. On a hysteric patient, you don't want to inject them a second time. These are the problems we deal with every day."

"So, what happened?" asked Steve, now showing more interest.

"In her suit, she claimed he assaulted her."

"What?" Steve responded with amazement.

"You wouldn't believe the charges lawyers claim. It's routine to put in as many violations as possible, figuring some will stick. She claimed she tried to leave, but he pushed her back into the chair. Her attorney said because he continued the injection, she became permanently numb."

"They didn't fall for that, did they? They don't think doctors are assaulting patients, do they?" asked Steve.

"I didn't believe it either. This gold-digger claimed she could no longer work. She was a teacher, and the 'permanent' numbness to her lip prevented her from speaking properly."

"Can that happen?" asked Steve.

"Look, I don't care how numb you get when you go to the dentist, you can still talk. Hey, facts don't matter. The jury fell for it. They claimed permanently disabled because of Dave's treatment.

Wait, that's not the worst part. The award? Four million, one hundred thousand dollars!"

"You got to be kidding!" said Steve with eyes wide open.

"That's not what Dave said. He couldn't believe what he heard. He jumped up from his seat in the courtroom and yelled, 'Are you fucking crazy?' The judge started banging his gavel. You know, like they show on television. Dave repeated himself, and he started walking toward the jury. All eight of them jumped out of their seats and tripped over each other trying to leave the jury box. They thought he would kill them.

"Dave is a big guy but gentle as a lamb. He wouldn't hurt a bug. He dedicated his life to helping people. It was the deceit and manipulation of facts that twisted this jury. By the time the lawyer finished, they thought some doctors are out to assault their patients."

Steve shook his head in disbelief. He sighed as if holding his breath throughout the story.

"Mr. Murphy, the judge's bailiff, an old retired cop, had to restrain Dave because he then stepped toward the hired gun sitting in the courtroom.

"The what?" interrupted Steve.

"The hired gun. They're the expert witnesses who'll testify to anything the lawyer needs said to win their case. They buy their experts. It's big business."

"That's sick. I find it hard to believe these shenanigans go on. We have to be thankful we have insurance for malpractice."

"Oh, we do? Dave's insurance coverage was for one million dollars like most everyone. He was responsible for the rest. By the time the plaintiff's lawyer gets done playing the jury, they believe these evil doctors are too rich and need punishment. That comes out in the penalty phase of the trial where they show the fees charged and estimate the lifetime income of the defendant."

"Come on. They don't do that."

"Oh, yes, they do. Lawyers have forensic accountants testify how much you make. They know what the plaintiff would have made in her lifetime if she had no injury. It's unbelievable what they do to come up with these numbers. So, what's the big deal if they hand out an outrageous award? Dave had to turn over his life's savings and sell his vacation home to come up with the money. Serves him right. The sadistic son of a bitch shouldn't have a vacation home. His attorney got him to hide some assets, and they couldn't touch his pension funds. The courts haven't let the looters take retirement plans yet, but I suspect the trial lawyers lobby is working on it too."

"God, he lost it all. Does he work for someone now?" asked Steve.

"No. Dave left practice and does photography. It was his hobby for years. What a loss. One of the finest practitioners lost for good."

"That's some story, Ron, but let's put it in perspective. I might believe everyone suffers from depression based on my work. You may think everyone has infections. The mechanic reason every car needs fixing. If we look at the world through our personal stories and experiences, we can become jaded. You're researching lots of these cases, but they're the exceptions," explained Steve.

"It doesn't make it right just because it hasn't affected everyone yet. The personal injury lawyers are raping us, and until it hits enough of us, are we just supposed to take it?"

"What can I say, Ron? Injustice has always been with us. It's the human condition. We can't act on every evil to keep them from affecting the masses."

"Well, it's happening to me. It's affecting me. I feel I have to do something. I find I have trouble breathing, like I'm being strangled."

"How did the medicine I suggested work out for you?"

"Nothing. I threw those pills away. Useless . . . they were useless."

"Ron, your trial is in the past. You're over that now. We can't change the past.

It's time to move on. I'd like you to start on some old-school meds, Xanax and Prozac. Sometimes they work better than the new stuff. It's all about finding the right medication to control the feelings of anxiety and depression. That's why you have breathing difficulty."

Steve handed Ron the prescriptions. He stared at them with a look of disgust.

"I can't do this psych med thing. I'm stronger than that," he said with his voice gone flat.

"It's not about being strong."

"No, it's how I feel about our nation becoming a bunch of zombies on all of this crap. I can't believe how many of my patients take this stuff, and they become the living dead."

"Come on, Ron, these are wonder drugs. They'll help you feel better, then we'll wean you off them."

"I'm sorry about being a pain in the ass, but I can't do all this psych drug thing. I'll go with the Xanax for the breathing, but I have to pass on the antidepressant. I'm not depressed."

"Okay, Ron, but just take the Rx with you, and if you change your mind, go for it."

"Jesus, I can't even go to my neighborhood pharmacy to get this prescription filled. They'll think I'm a nutcase."

"Once you get through this, you'll be fine. Trust me."

CHAPTER
FIFTEEN

RON KNEW litigation horror could happen to anyone given the right circumstances. He would not place his security in jeopardy. Ron planned with great foresight and caution. He mortgaged his homes to the hilt, leased cars, and had his office real estate owned by a family limited partnership. Most of Ron's wealth remained liquid, made up of securities, gold, diamonds, and a horde of cash.

Ron earned much more than the interest due on his mortgages through a steady income stream. He serviced his debts with ease. His planning afforded the security needed should a catastrophe hit as it did for his friend, Dave Jaspen.

Many thoughts composed the daydreams played out in Ron's head as his trial progressed. He remembered the day he met with his estate attorney, Paul Stansberry.

"Paul, you know how upset I am over this case against me. For the past year, I expected you to find out what I could do to protect myself against a catastrophic lawsuit. What's been taking so long?"

"Ron, I've researched this area for you and several other clients, and for myself. I'm happy to say, if you have a problem, we'll cash you in as fast as we can. You know, before they can attach your assets, and I'll see you off at the airport. It'll be a trip to Tahiti where you'll spend the rest of your life in paradise."

Ron laughed, thinking Paul was kidding. He was not!

"They can attach anything you own, which means if they can't find it, they can't get it. In the simplest case, they put a lien on your home, your bank accounts, and brokerage accounts. We must cash you out before the liens come down, and you'll leave town. Get things out of your name. We'll set up some limited partnerships, trusts, and those types of measures."

Ron could not believe what he heard, but he knew Paul was the best. He set up his affairs based on this conversation to escape the possibility of destitution should the unthinkable become his nightmare as it seemed to get closer to his reality.

CHAPTER
SIXTEEN

DR. JONAS OLEN, Jason's primary physician, treated his autoimmune problem for the past eight years. In the natural course of treatment over such a long period an attachment often develops, which was the only explanation Sharon found for Olen's rabid testimony against a fellow professional, unless he received money to prostitute himself.

Under Hill's direct examination, Jonas painted Ron as incompetent. He claimed Ron misdiagnosed Jason and prescribed an inadequate dose of antibiotics, allowing the infection to "get away."

Jonas provided good testimony. Like the doctors on television, he exuded intelligence, warmth, and professionalism . Confident, good looking, and suave, he turned and made eye contact with the jury each time he spoke.

Gray temples and reading glasses perched at the tip of his nose gave the appearance of wisdom. While all attorneys coach their clients and experts, Hill did not have to prepare Jonas. His cool demeanor troubled Ron.

"He's really good," Ron murmured.

"Hush!" Sharon snapped in a soft whisper.

Sharon became absorbed in Jonas' testimony. At each pause, Sharon wrote notes. She would not allow Ron to ask a question or make a comment on the proceedings as Jonas spoke. During the other witness testimony, Sharon could listen and talk with Ron and never miss a word. Now, she could not entertain him as she devoured Jonas' every word with an intensity Ron did not see before.

Sharon seemed eager to attack. Her time came. She pushed her note pad away, stood and lingered in place for a moment. Her slow-paced trek toward the witness stand brought Sharon to an arm's length from her prey. She looked down at the floor, then lifted her head to confront the witness.

"Dr. Olen, when you told us of your credentials earlier, I noticed you are board certified in internal medicine with a sub-specialty in gastroenterology. Is that correct?"

"That is correct."

"Can you tell us precisely where the scope of gastroenterology begins and ends?"

"I don't understand," responded Jonas with an air of innocent perplexity to imply that perhaps Sharon did not understand her own question.

Sharon continued. "What do you treat? Do you treat ulcers?"

"Yes, of course!"

"Do you treat diverticulitis, colitis, and the various inflammatory diseases of the colon and small intestine?"

"Of course!" said Jonas with unbridled confidence.

All along, Ron feared Jonas would crush Sharon using his expertise to destroy their case. That Sharon had some apparent medical knowledge and did her homework impressed Ron.

"Doctor, do you treat diseases of the gallbladder, such as cholelithiasis, as they may relate to the digestive process even though these glands do *not* reside in the gastrointestinal tract?"

"Yes, I most certainly do!" said Jonas, looking around uncomfortably to see if anyone else realized the complexity of the question.

———

Jonas seemed surprised, and a bit intimidated. He believed Sharon could not joust with him on medical knowledge because she was a lawyer. All lawyers research their cases. But, Jonas reasoned, he would make Sharon look foolish in due course. However, the display of confidence with which Sharon charged forward unsettled him.

"What I'm asking Doctor . . ." Sharon spoke in a slow, precise manner, as if to imply maybe she was going too fast. The emphasis on the title, "Doctor," made Olen's defensive hairs spike. "What exactly is your scope of treatment?"

"Madam, my field of treatment includes the entire gut from os to os. That's Latin for opening to opening, which means from mouth to anus. I treat auto-immune diseases that can show up in the oral mucosa—that is the mouth—and travel throughout the esophagus, the stomach, and the entire length of the intestines."

To better prove his prowess, and in his attempt to upstage Sharon, he went on for several minutes naming every area he could think of that he treated. His strong, cool facade crumbled. It became obvious the previous, well-rehearsed examination testimony elicited by Hill contained no hurdles. Now, under pressure, Dr. Olen lost his epitome of cool in the line of fire. Jonas ran out of areas he treated, yet he held up his fingers as if to count. He looked toward the heavens as if divine intervention might shower down one or two areas he may have forgotten.

"That's fine, Doctor. I believe you covered most, if not all, of the scope that defines gastroenterology."

Sharon paused and, looking down at her feet, playing coy as if almost too shy to continue, she asked, "Doctor, do you fill teeth?"

"Why, of course not!"

"Do you pull teeth?"

"No!" Jonas responded with a tone of indignation. "Did I mention I'm a dentist?" Jonas said with utter sarcasm.

"I'm the one asking the questions, Doctor!" Sharon scolded.

"Did I say I pull teeth?" said Jonas, ignoring the admonition and sinking into the quagmire of lawyer trickery.

"Doctor, I'm the one asking the questions here!" Sharon's tone became stern and condescending.

Jonas looked up to the judge.

"Your Honor, can she—"

The judge cut him off. Just as stern and condescending he chided, "Doctor, she asks the questions."

Now, rattled, Jonas' salivary glands shut down, and his tongue felt like dried board. Having trouble swallowing, he loosened his collar and tie.

Sharon read all the signs of a wounded adversary and resumed her attack.

"Dr. Olen, are you practicing, or did you ever practice dentistry?"

"Why that is—"

"Answer the question please!" Sharon drilled with a slow cadence and emphasis on the "please!"

A gruff response, "No!" echoed from Jonas's parched throat. "Your Honor, I need some water," he muttered.

"The bailiff will provide water for Dr. Olen."

The court agent presented a glass of water, and Jonas worked again to loosen his tie before he took a long sip. Sharon did not wait for the quenching effects to take place before she marched forward with her examination.

"Do you now, or did you ever hold yourself out to be an expert witness on dental matters?"

"You don't have to be a den—"

"Doctor, I will ask one more time. Do you now, or did you ever hold yourself out to be an expert witness on dental care?"

Jonas sat flustered and silent. He waited too long to respond. The judge, now showing impatience, scolded him again.

"Doctor, answer the question without commentary."

Hill could not object or rescue Jonas without highlighting the poor showing. He would attempt damage control on redirect. Hill felt distressed that Jonas, so well prepared and a natural in the courtroom, allowed his pompous ego to clash with the likes of an experienced trial attorney. Sharon trained well and knew how to dice and slice opponents on protocol. She was a master.

The day dragged on. Sharon Carver held steady with a constant upbeat persona. In contrast, Ron became more depressed, even though Sharon performed so well. The unpredictability of jurors troubled him.

No reason existed for jurors Theresa and Wesley to whisper and giggle during the proceedings. They did not take the trial seriously, and it showed by their disrespect for the process. Several times the judge cleared his voice to break up the chatter. Finally, he admonished them in open court, explaining he would hold them in contempt and fine them if they did not get their minds right. It worked.

Whenever any witness' testimony became heated, Nancy Barnes, the toothless juror fanned ever more vigorously. Her brooding bothered Ron, and he called it to Sharon's attention.

"Well, I imagine this woman had bad times at the dentist. Will she take out her experiences against me?"

"She's a recovery center nurse. Ron, she may be your last, best hope in understanding the medical issues. I'd guess she's probably one of the two people on the jury who can understand what's coming."

"Yeah, but the missing teeth, the fanning . . ."

"Big deal. Her denture doesn't fit, and this courtroom is warm and stuffy. In the summer the air conditioning system strains. The winter heat doesn't let up. This is city government. They try to keep the civil court civil but never get it right. Be cool and stop the worrying. When we get finished, you can find her a good dentist to fix that denture." Ron smiled for the first time.

At about three P.M., Hill approached the bench and asked the judge for a conference.

"Sean, I need an extension," Hill told Judge Donovan.

"Come into my chambers, ladies and gentlemen."

The judge motioned the attorneys toward the huge mahogany door behind which many off-the-record meetings take place.

CHAPTER
SEVENTEEN

"SEAN, I have a problem. My expert oral surgeon canceled on me for Monday. He was the key to my case. I will have to get a sub, but I'll need a day to prepare him," Hill pleaded.

"Jesus Christ, Edgar, when did you find out about this? When did he go south on you?" responded Judge Donovan in an aggravated tone.

"I just got this fax, Sean. What do you expect me to do?"

"Let me see that," said Sharon.

She stared at the transmission with inordinate curiosity, and her puzzled look turned to a glow.

"What's so intriguing, Sharon? What's the problem?" the judge asked twice, noticing the look of elation on her face.

"I'll tell you what the problem is, but first let me note this is Edgar's problem, and it's a big one! Look here at the date on this fax, his expert sent before the trial started."

Judge Donovan took hold of the fax for examination. His brow furrowed, adding to the look of confusion. He responded, "This didn't come in today. What are you trying to pull?"

Hill stiffened, grabbed the fax, and studied it for a moment while he thought of an excuse to cover for this most slipshod deception Sharon discovered.

"This fax must have been sitting on my secretary's desk for a week. I can't believe this. She handed it to me this morning. How was I to know?" reasoned Hill.

"Sean, the date of transmission is on the fax. It never came today. He can't substitute an expert if he had notice of cancellation *before* the trial," Sharon exclaimed with an expression bordering on rage in her voice.

Hill stood to set himself in a position of authority before he spoke.

"What kind of law are you practicing, Sharon?" he demanded.

"Meshkov versus Leone, 1989, upheld in Superior Court, 1992, and again in the State Supreme Court, 1996," responded Sharon haughtily.

"You sure?" the judge responded with a look of uncertainty.

"I am."

"Well, it won't be hard to find. And if that's the case, you better persuade your original witness to show up Monday or be ready for dismissal with prejudice."

"What are you talking about, dismissal? Olen already established the malpractice. Let the jury use his testimony," said Hill in a state of disarray.

"He's your corroborating expert. He's not an expert in the same field as Doctor Rellick. I believe Sharon made that rather clear out there," said Judge Donovan, whose tone revealed a loss of patience.

"This is absurd. Let's review that caselaw right now. If Sharon's right, I'll yield. If I'm right, I'll have my new witness in court bright and early. No matter what, I damn well expect today's testimony to stand as expert."

Sharon rolled her eyes, and Judge Donovan returned the gesture.

For the next hour the three of them read through all the pertinent caselaw on LexisNexis contained within their mobile devices and verified in the wall of books at the back of the judge's chambers. Sharon was right; not that it stopped Hill from making threats to challenge the law.

"Edgar, how about you bow out gracefully on this one? We work out a settlement right now. I'm willing to stay for whatever time we need. You'll cover your expenses, Sharon will save the insurance carrier from the big one, and the challenges you would bring, and Dr. Rellick won't lose his shirt. Your expert witness doesn't have to get hounded all weekend hearing how he'll ruin your case. And if you don't have your original witness Monday, as noted, I must declare a dismissal with prejudice . . . you get nothing. My way, everybody's a winner. How about it?" said Judge Donovan.

Hill ignored the offer, grabbed his briefcase, straightened his tie, and stated, "We shall resume on Monday. Good day, sir." He ignored Sharon and stormed out of the judge's chambers.

Friday court sessions in Philadelphia end by four-fifteen at the latest; however, three-thirty is more common. Not privy to either of these statistics, when Hill asked for the conference in the judge's chambers, and they returned at five P.M., it did not seem unusual to Ron.

Face pale and hair disheveled from playing with it throughout the day's proceedings, Ron appeared worn and emotionally drained. Sharon walked over to him. In deep thought, Ron barely noticed her presence.

"Monday should finish things up," said Sharon. "More than likely, we will have a dismissal with prejudice."

"I think I'll go to the shore for the weekend to recharge," Ron confessed with little interest in Sharon's statement.

"I guess you didn't hear me, or you don't understand what I said. Well, in either case, after next week you'll be spending some great days at the shore."

"You are rather upbeat here at the eleventh hour," said Ron with an element of brooding in his voice and facial expression.

"Ron, we nailed their medical expert." Sharon laughed.

"We're home free, my friend. Unless Hill comes up with a miracle, he will lose this case. The judge will throw it out.

"I established they couldn't use Jonas as an expert on the dental-surgical aspects of the case. By law, to win a malpractice case, you must show malpractice took place, and you must show the malpractice resulted in the claimed injury. You can't prove malpractice without the testimony of an expert, and the expert must be from the field in question. Olen is an MD. That's as useful as if he were an accountant. His testimony won't cut it. They need a maxillofacial surgeon to make their claims of malpractice against you."

"And they can't get one to testify for them?" Ron asked sarcastically.

"They can. They have networks of experts bought for any field, to take any side, to say anything needed said. However, they may not."

"Let's just cut the riddles and tell me what you're talking about," exclaimed Ron.

"So far, Hill has yet to produce a witness who testified you did anything wrong, other than Olen. Right?"

"Yeah."

"Olen says you did everything wrong. However, we've established he's not an expert in your field of oral surgery. They have a medical doctor who presented well, at least until I put him under the gun.

"Without an expert in your specific field, the judge will have to discharge the case. Monday, they planned to put Harold Delaney, their oral surgeon, on the stand. He canceled on them because he knows you did nothing wrong. We all knew Edgar was having trouble with Harold based on his deposition. It appears he had second thoughts about testifying. When Edgar came out and told us Harold canceled on him, the judge turned red. Sean hates to waste time."

"Who's Sean?" asked Ron.

"The judge! Pay attention here. It gets good. He likes to keep his court moving. He'll do anything to close out a case, to empty his docket. Well, it turns out Harold canceled *before* the trial started, and Hill knew it. He faked like he didn't. The date printed on the cancelation FAX proved when the notice came. He tried to blame his secretary. Doesn't matter. He's captain of his ship, and caselaw forbids substituting an expert if you found out your guy went south *before* the case started, and you don't notify the court. Hill learned about the cancellation in plenty of time, but he must have figured he wouldn't get caught. And if discovered, he'd be able to convince Harold to show up when push came to shove.

"Harold is a good oral surgeon. He knew you didn't commit malpractice. And who knows, maybe his conscience got to him. So now, Hill is scrambling to get a new expert witness admitted to the case, but he's not allowed. So, come Monday, this case will get thrown out if Harold doesn't show," explained Sharon.

"To make it an even sweeter victory, Hill turned down a chance of settling to cover his expenses right there in Sean's chambers."

"And you mean you would have given them money even though they have no case?" Ron asked in amazement.

"You bet your sweet-ass I would. Ron, you know they have no case, and I know they have no case. They even know it, for Christ's sake, but that's not how the system works. Though it's a long shot, I don't like the possibility Harold might still show up, come Monday. If we settled in chambers now, we would have had closure. No risk of appeals later. It's all a game of odds."

"It's a fucking game? Do I hear you right? It's a damn fucking game. Don't you know, this is my life, my reputation, everything I ever worked for, and to you guys, it's a fucking game, with me as the pawn?"

"Ron, hey, nothing personal. It's a game. Please understand, we have to do what makes sense. If we could walk away paying out a hundred g's and avoid risking the unknown, we would have to play that hand. It would have paid for Edgar's expenses. He'd get some pocket change. The only loser would have been Jason's wife since expenses come off the top. Sure, she would get a few bucks but not enough to finance her retirement as she expected. Now, she'll wind up with nothing. Have a great weekend, Ron, and lighten up a bit."

Ron felt annoyed as he watched Sharon walk off, knowing this day and the proceedings were no big deal to her. She'd get paid no matter the outcome. If it worked out as she described, the insurance company would keep her on high retainer for the great performance. He expected Sharon would jump into the air and click her heels at any moment, but it never happened. Ron remained still as he watched until Sharon faded from view. He blinked several times to clear tears coating his eyes, walked to his car, and headed to the shore.

It now appeared the trial would last six working days, an eternity for Ron. A ruling would come on the seventh day.

CHAPTER
EIGHTEEN

SUSAN LOVED the spontaneity of Ron's occasional call to meet him at their Margate beach house. It meant good food, a romantic walk on the beach, and great sex. The shore provided time together without the interruptions of life's petty callings. These moments delivered the spark and excitement too often missing from decaying relationships.

Susan lived for romance novels and used seeds from her readings to drive a great imagination. Every time Ron reached out, she'd go through a ritual. It started with a shower. She donned a seductive bra and panties, then spent at least an hour doing makeup and hair to compliment her natural beauty.

Ron arrived at their Margate home well before Susan. A walk on the beach offered him the solitude he needed to think. The sand felt cold and unfriendly in contrast to the invigorating warmth generated on summer days. It molded to his feet and spawned an uncomfortable chill as he walked closer to the surf. Fall presented Ron with a private seaside since the summer residents long abandoned the shore's edge. He stared at the most majestic cloud formations in the sky as the horizon eclipsed the sun. The feathered wisps of blue and white melded into the hues of magenta and crimson red. Nature's canvas was forever changing, and Ron considered it God's art displayed in an ever-present celestial museum.

Artists have tried to capture the beauty of nature, yet here it is for all to enjoy if they would gaze upon the heavens. I haven't seen this magnificence for way too long. Some never see beauty in natural surroundings.

The omnipotence of the sky and ocean sparked a nostalgic joy of past seasons in Ron's life. He missed the splendor of this most recent summer as it passed by without notice.

God, how I long for all of this! I spent the last three months indoors reading depositions; every fact, every accusation, and every statement. I had to know it all. I had to make sure I did nothing wrong. I had to know it cold, or they would make me look foolish to the jury, my peers. My peers, right!

The torment of his thoughts faded as he walked closer to the water. The sound of the surf worked its soothing magic on his clouded mind. He wandered on in a trance until the chilled water of the incoming tide, not yet frigid from winter winds, startled him. The cold water stung his toes and rode up upon his ankles. Susan approached.

"Ron!"

She knew where to find him. Running to embrace, she met with his grasp of desperation devoid of the expected romantic desire.

"Are you all right?" she asked with concern in her voice.

"Life! God, what's it all about?" Ron muttered.

"Everything will be all right, honey!"

Susan grabbed his arm, and they strolled farther along the shore's edge.

"I never tried to hurt anyone. We all seek happiness and pleasure, but it can't be at the expense of others. Why do they do it?"

Susan understood Ron did not expect an answer, and she did not have one.

"It's all pleasure; hedonism. That's it. Some seek pleasure and don't care who gets hurt along the way."

"Ron, it's our turn for some of that pleasure."

Susan pulled Ron close. His arms went limp, and he fell to his knees. She knelt to comfort him. Ron began sobbing, and Susan felt helpless not knowing how to provide strength for her mate, who never showed any weakness. He too felt the uneasiness of his sorrow.

Ron regained his composure. The scene seemed humorous to this rock of stoicism now reduced to jelly before his lover. He fell into a manner of laughing. The laughter escalated into a hysterical amusement. He could not speak nor catch his breath. The oddity of his reaction was contagious, causing Susan to join in the laughter, overcome by a bizarre mix of fear and joyful hysteria.

When the hilarity slowed to an occasional sputter followed by a few seconds of silence, Ron pulled Susan into his arms and kissed her. They tasted salted tears while groping each other's bodies. They shared their love on the sand, filled with a grand zest for life. It was Ron's night to have some pleasure, to become one with nature, to savor all his senses could devour and show gratitude for these gifts.

The same forces buffeting the nearby surf, yet so capable of roiling a storm, could rile the emotions and actions within the soul of this man scorned.

CHAPTER
NINETEEN

DR. HAROLD DELANEY WAS A HANDSOME, charismatic expert witness for hire. At thirty-four years old, he sported a celebrity flare highlighted by a year-round tan. Though he only stood five feet, six inches tall, he carried himself in a grand manner. He wore custom tailored and impeccably appointed clothing. Straight black hair slicked back, and not a whisker out of place on the beard outlining his angular jaw line, defined the pride he took in grooming.

A strong ego and expensive tastes made up for his height, and he broadcast a bold stride wherever he traveled. The Bentley he drove about town conveyed an exuberance for wealth and distinction. From peripheral vision exclusively, he rejoiced at the stares of the common folk. He dared not let them know he basked in their envy.

In depositions, Harold Delaney made several allegations of malpractice against Ron. He hoped his deposed testimony would be enough to force a settlement without ever appearing in court. Harold was the best at playing Monday morning quarterback. After Harold Delaney reviewed a case and based on his stinging reputation, defense attorneys advised settlement at much more than the insurance companies they represented wanted to pay. The victims of his savvy called his dreaded case review the "Delaney Report."

Delaney showed every nit-picking flaw of treatment. If assigned to grade a master carpenter driving a nail, he could make the carpenter look like a hack. He uncovered every conceivable technicality, expanded on and implicated it in whatever favor he so desired. Harold usually didn't testify at trial, because he was so effective at the deposition. He was the expert to hire for the "big buck" cases, and Hill used him often. Having dual medical and dental degrees, personal injury lawyers called Harold for many types of lawsuits.

At first review, Harold called Hill and turned down the Phillips case.

"What do you mean, you can't take this case, Harold?" asked Hill in a most disgusted tone of voice.

"It's just not good enough. There's too much risk. This guy is too meticulous. He documented everything. It will cause us all grief if they don't settle early. Get someone else to work this case."

"I need you on this one, Harold. I could get a dozen other experts, but you present better than any of them. How about we abate that risk with a guarantee of a hundred thousand dollars and five percent of the final settlement?"

"You've got to be kidding. You can't give an expert a piece of the action. And a hundred thousand guaranteed? We'll all go to jail."

"What's to worry? Who will find out? You'll never see jail. You'll see just about a half million dollars to ease your conscience."

"You're making it awful hard to turn down. What's going on? What aren't you telling me, Hill?"

"I need this case. It's huge damages. The type you read about in the papers. A potential record breaker. What do you say?"

"I don't know," Harold said.

"Look, guy, you owe me. I keep food on your table, and don't you forget that."

"Five percent of the take?" Harold queried with a touch of greed in his tone.

"That's what I said. I play tough to win. I do whatever it takes, and I expect the same from my people."

"All right, I'll do it, but you better get a fast settlement and keep the easy ones coming my way. I don't like the smell of this case."

"You got it, Harold. Nothing to worry about," said Hill, and he hung up without further comment.

Harold could find fault with anyone's treatment when he looked hard enough. Even in no fault cases, he would blind the unsophisticated jury with a cloud of ambiguity. Ron's case did not lend itself to the usual "sign me up" upon Harold's initial perusal.

Harold knew he should not have taken the Phillips' case. All of his accusations at deposition appeared poorly grounded. He did, however, claim Ron committed malpractice on several accounts, hoping Ron and his insurance carrier would settle.

Harold knew Hill expected a huge award on this case, but he did not know Hill desperately needed a big win to ease financial troubles related to his fast lifestyle. He never expected Hill would forgo a quick, decent settlement.

It mattered little to Hill if Harold perjured himself or ruined his reputation by making unfounded accusations in open court. Beyond protecting his reputation, Harold worried about a lawsuit for libel if he stepped beyond the bounds of what happened. In the end, Harold bailed.

When Hill found out he could not use another expert, he was livid. The fate of this case remained contingent upon convincing Harold to testify. He called him the moment he returned to his office after Friday's session.

"Harold, you're a dead man, and I mean dead. If you leave me fucked on a limb, you won't live to regret it."

Hill almost never lost his decorum. Harold recognized his life would never be the same.

"I told you before this wasn't a good case. You don't have to get hostile with me . . ."

"I'll not argue with you now, Harold. I expect you in my office, nine tonight."

"Tonight? Are you out of your mind?"

"Oh, I'm crazy out of my mind all right. But I do mean tonight."

CHAPTER
TWENTY

AT NINE P.M. Harold Delaney exited the elevator on the thirty-fourth floor of the Land Title Building. The entire floor belonged to Edgar Hill's firm.

By night, the interiors of these morgue-like, high-rise buildings cast an eerie pall, devoid of the bustling activity giving life to the structures during the day. An empty reception desk greeted Harold once he passed through the massive plate glass doors.

Harold called out to the darkened corridors, "Edgar? Edgar? Hello?" No one responded.

He knew the general direction to Hill's private office, though he only met with him in various conference rooms over the years. After wandering through the maze-like hallway, he came to the epicenter of the firm.

Under the nameplate on Hill's door, he saw a typed note: "Harold, go to the public men's room to the left of the elevator." Curiously it ended with, "413."

He approached the men's room, and understood the hidden meaning of 413. Many of the public restrooms in urban high-rise office buildings had locking doors. Here, the 413 was the combination to gain entrance.

Over the years thugs and rapists gained entrance into the buildings, hid in the restrooms, then attacked unsuspecting men and women. Personal injury lawyers held owners of the buildings responsible, and they lost millions of dollars. The misguided blame brought about various security measures like locked bathrooms, security cameras, and alarm systems.

It will not be long before we see an armed security guard on each floor. The violence, the corruption; it's everywhere, thought Harold upon seeing the security lock. It reminded him of the possibility of becoming a victim of a crime and made him uneasy.

After entering the lavish lavatory, he laughed and shook his head at the ridiculous cloak and dagger game.

An unrecognized voice bellowed, "Greetings," in unison with the door closing behind Harold. He jumped at the peculiar nature of this unwelcome reception. The device used to hide witness' identities distorted the voice. Too macabre for Harold, he turned to leave.

"Don't do that, Harold! We must talk!"

"What's with the spy game, Hill? Where are you hiding?" asked Harold with discernible nervousness, causing his voice to crack. Perspiration beaded on his entire face. He reached to loosen his tie. Now commanding every bit of his attention, the specter continued to address him.

"What we'll be discussing can put us both in jail. I'm too smart for that. You'll never be able to testify that you and Edgar Hill had this conversation. As far as you're concerned, Harold, you're talking with the ghost of courtroom chicanery. You're playing with fire, my friend.

"When you take one of my cases, must come through. You can't just live on your reputation of big-time, easy settlements and never expect to testify. Sure, we've had many easy cases over the years. That's why you live the good life, but when it gets a little rough, you can't bail out."

"You don't seem to understand," said Harold in defense of his actions. "Rellick did nothing wrong. He's too thorough. I can't even second-guess him. He documented every fuckin' detail like a man possessed. I told you this before I ever got involved. We'll wind up losing this case, then get sued for slander. I'm out of here."

Harold turned to leave, but the voice challenged him. "You choose death over life?"

"Don't fuckin' threaten me, Hill! We're professional men, or did you forget?" Harold shouted in a shrill, defensive voice.

"Harold, let me explain. If you don't come through, I'm ruined. If I go down, I will take you with me. You're the sole obstacle to success in this case. They've established that Jonas can only corroborate your testimony. He laid down the groundwork in stating how Rellick screwed up, but his hotshot defense attorney neutralized him. As it now stands, Harold, the ambiguity is in place. I need to have the right expert to tie it all together, and that's you! Without my expert, the jury never gets to decide, because the case gets thrown out. I need you to say he did something wrong, anything. Then it's in the bag."

"Get someone else if this is such a great case. There're plenty of guns for hire out there. For what you would pay me, you'll have no trouble finding a new expert."

"I can't," was the thundering response. "You canceled on me too late. Once the trial starts, I can't get a substitute unless you were to die. Don't make that an option."

"You wait just a second. I gave you plenty of notice. I sent my notice well before the trial started. It's you who fucked up. Don't blame me now."

"You don't understand the strategy in a lawsuit. If I told them you canceled on me before the trial, it would have weakened my position. Everyone would wonder why you wanted out. I expected I would convince you. I thought you'd come through for me."

"Well, you thought wrong."

"I don't think you understand, Harold, I need you to be there. You can't back out."

"Even if I lied and said Rellick committed malpractice, his expert will refute it. Any jury will know I'm lying, and we'll lose.

Then, Rellick will come after us. I know the statistics. Most doctors win their cases, but they almost never counter sue. He'll have a case against us, and he'll fuck us."

"And that's because for them to win a slander case, they have to show blatant, malicious prosecution after they win the malpractice case. I don't have to tell you, the master of ambiguity. It's nearly impossible for them to prove malice. We'll be fine, but we will not lose this case," Hill stated with authority.

"What am I going to say? He used the wrong antibiotic. He used a dose too weak to control the infection. Hill, you may know the law, but you know shit about medicine. These are the only arguments I can make, and they'll blow them out of the water. They'll make me look like an idiot on cross-examination. We'll lose. Then I'm finished. You're not the only one who uses me as an expert witness. I'll never work again once we lose this case."

"We won't lose! I own the jury," echoed the eerie voice.

"You can't be serious. We'll all end up in jail."

"I'm goddamn serious, and just remember, you tendered your soul for diamonds the first time you came on board."

Harold now understood why Hill maintained all the secrecy. Beyond the illegal expert witness compensation, this case involved jury tampering. Hill explained he had two reliable connections, one in the voter registration office and one in the jury selection business. These two folks participated in Hill's hefty cash payroll. They fixed the system on any jury involving Hill's less than ironclad cases. They made sure Hill's trained professional juror for hire landed on his jury. The panel member was an articulate, persuasive plant; a hand-picked Trojan horse who always made it through the jury selection process. Once on the jury, with little effort, he always became the jury foreman.

Hill only needed to use his connections eight times in the last ten years. His people assigned a different alias to the golden juror for each case. The judge, the defense attorneys, and the insurance companies, whose pockets got picked, always had to be different.

He left nothing to chance. No flaws survived to bring down this elaborate scam.

Hill was a careful man, and this case was the first one he had to bring an outsider to the inner sanctum. He did not count on Rellick's meticulous attention to detail or Harold's reluctance to risk tarnishing his reputation, or worse, losing a slander suit. He had to bring Harold into the scheme.

By guaranteeing the outcome of the trial, Harold could rest assured Rellick would not sue him for slander. He understood all it takes is one convincing, dominating juror to control the sheep and lead them down any path. They would win this case if Hill's plan played out as expected.

When Harold left the building, he knew he had to perjure himself come Monday. He felt dirty and ashamed. Money became his addiction. The power and respect wealth engendered served as his aphrodisiac. He was not any better than the greedy advertising attorneys. He was the same as Hill, hiding behind an illusion of respectability.

Harold did not doubt that Hill, the consummate personal injury attorney, would have him killed if it became necessary. The stakes and his personal debt arose too high to accept defeat. Money and greed ruled all of their lives. It was the golden calf to which they all bowed.

Harold reflected upon how he abhorred the organized crime families he read about in the news.

Those people never lead a normal life. Now I'm in the same predicament. How can this be? I wasn't selling drugs, loan sharking, pimping, or involved in any murders. It's just some insurance fraud. That's all. Nobody's supposed to get hurt.

Afraid, Harold now realized people without respect for laws kill other people for money.

CHAPTER
TWENTY-ONE

HAROLD DELANEY MADE his appearance Monday. He performed as directed. It was apparent to all his testimony failed. After two hours of deliberation, the court waited for a final verdict.

"This is it, Ron," said Sharon with exhilaration as they waited for the decision. "We nailed the son of a bitch. Harold's days as an expert are over. He won't be able to show his face in court after that bullshit testimony. Once word gets around, all the plaintiffs' attorneys will avoid Delaney like the plague. This hired gun had better hang up his six-shooters. The best part of all, you'll get even."

"What are you talking about?"

"You'll be able to sue for malicious prosecution. You'll get payback for your time in hell."

"Oh, so I sue them. I get to continue this infernal game. That's what it's all about?" said Ron.

"Shush! Here they are. Get ready for Hill to jump up ranting he wants a retrial."

"He can get a retrial? What about double jeopardy?" asked Ron in utter surprise.

"Double jeopardy is only for criminal matters. They can always ask for a retrial in civil cases, but it rarely happens. These guys are smart enough to know when to cut their losses."

"I sure as hell hope you're right because I don't think I could go through this nightmare again."

The jury completed their procession into the courtroom wearing solemn faces. They avoided eye contact as they always do before the pronouncement that will lift one party yet shatter the lives of the other side.

"Have you reached your verdict?" asked the judge.

"Yes, we have, your Honor," answered the jury foreman.

"And how do you find?"

"We find for the plaintiff, your Honor."

Sharon did a double take. Her smile of confidence became a contorted look of dismay.

Ron got caught up in the confusion of the legal jargon. Finally, it hit him; he was not the plaintiff. He assumed the jurors made a mistake.

"They meant they find for the defendant. Don't they?" Ron said to Sharon, loud enough for the judge to tap his gavel.

Judge Donovan displayed the wide-eye open look of shock like everyone else following the case. In an unusual move, he asked the jury foreman to point to the plaintiff's table. He, too, assumed the foreman confused the plaintiff and the defendant. There was no mistake. It was all part of a well-choreographed dance on the scales of justice.

Ron never felt emptier than after losing his case in court. The dreaded hollow of mourning carved a void in his soul. Letting a material issue gnaw at his gut to such a level seemed even more disturbing to him. He understood his reaction was foolish, but deep inside he felt defiled, tormented by the system.

Every case has a winner and loser. The losers couldn't all feel as badly as I do. It makes no sense at all. Just get on with life. Why am I letting this incident destroy me?

Antacids and aspirin became a staple to contain the constant headaches and heartburn that developed since trial began. Ron no longer found humor in anything. He did not express love to his wife or children. Work became work. He doled out care without caring.

Several weeks after the trial, Ron's phone rang one evening while he stared in front of his television, something he never used to do.

"I have some bad news for you."

Ron did not like to hear Sharon's voice any longer. Nice as she was, she reminded him of his legal fiasco. She called periodically to discuss the chances for an appeal, so the introductory pronouncement of "bad news" only made this call more repulsive.

"What do they want now, my soul as part of the judgment?" asked Ron.

Sharon dealt kindly with Ron's cynicism because she understood the sentiments plaguing him.

"As you know, the judgment was unprecedented. The actuaries made a good case for the twelve million dollars, but we never thought the jury would capitulate. The judge always knocks it down. I've never seen this happen. Sean wouldn't budge. I'd think he was on the take if I didn't know better.

"The insurance company has little to gain from a retrial. I'll explain in a minute. First, understand how insurance companies think. To them, it's all dollars and cents. They play the odds game. They had this case written off years ago by putting dollars in reserve. They'll just raise premiums on all their insureds, and it gets passed along to everyone. It's called spreading the wealth to the connected. When you think about it, we all pay.

"The big thing they fear now is a suit from Jason's wife against them for prolonging her grief. It becomes a punitive damage claim. That can mean more money than they can afford. It's meant to punish.

Since the courts came out with this concept, plaintiffs' attorneys use and abuse it to force settlements. The insurance company now wants to end it and get out."

"What's the bad news?" asked Ron, with the tone of abject disgust in his voice.

"Early in the case, you turned down an offer to settle before Hill entered the picture. Their first attorney was an amateur. Your insurer offered him a hundred thousand dollars, and they were willing to take it."

An awkward pause ensued.

"This offer was before Jason killed himself. You told them, 'no way.' It was eight years ago, Ron. You knew you never committed malpractice and didn't expect a jury to find against you. That's how you felt back then."

"So?"

"Your insurance policy has provisions. They all do. If you don't settle when the plaintiff accepts an offer, the company will only pay up to the amount of the offer. Then you're left holding the bag. They even sent you a letter explaining this risk, and we discussed the details years ago. I forgot all about it, but it's in your file. They're getting out of this situation for one hundred thousand dollars. They didn't even realize it until the actuaries went over the case with a fine-toothed comb. They have no reason to support a retrial. It would put them at more risk."

"You mean Hill will come after me for the whole twelve million? You mean all my insurance will cover is one hundred thousand dollars? And there's no retrial or appeal?"

"Well, you can appeal at your expense for legal representation, but—"

Ron began laughing. It started in a normal manner but progressed to the point of hysteria. His uncontrolled laughter left him near breathless. It was a cathartic release, for he no longer saw the humor in anything but the absurd.

"Ron . . . Ron, this situation isn't a laughing matter," Sharon called out with some urgency. "We can still try for an appeal. I believe we have grounds for the appeal, but you must pay the legal fees."

"The hell if I'll go through an appeal. The system doesn't work. I'll have no part of it," shouted Ron. "Sharon, just because the insurance company is getting out of their share doesn't mean I have twelve million dollars to hand over to those pricks. It doesn't matter, because I don't have eight million dollars above the four-million-dollar insurance policy I had to cover this judgment either.

"If they want to attach my wages so I can give these whores ten to twenty percent of my weekly earnings, I'll fuckin' retire. I have enough money to get by. I'll live on what I have. They can't touch my house or other properties because they're not in my name. My Family Limited Partnership owns them. It's out of their reach."

"That's the bad news I'm calling about," said Sharon in a somber voice.

Another awkward silence came about, only longer. Sharon hoped Ron would break it, but he did not.

"Hill petitioned the court to declare fraudulent conveyance of property."

Again . . . a long silence.

"Let me explain, Ron. The various estate-planning vehicles you set up are excellent ways to protect your assets from these predators. But if you set them up *after* an action against you, they can claim you set them up intending to shield these assets from forfeiture. That's what they mean by fraudulent conveyance. It means the courts can get to those assets. Hill is out to get every penny of that twelve million dollars. He's going for the brass ring—your properties, investments, future earnings, bank accounts, everything!"

Another killer silence deafened the phone. Sharon heard a click at Ron's end of the line and never again saw or spoke with him.

Except for Susan, no one communicated with Ron after he lost his case in Philadelphia and Mittenberg's murder in Florida. The note she found at their beach house contained her last contact with him.

"I can't take it anymore. All the bullshit! This world is full of injustice. It's only a matter of time until anarchy rules. A distinction between right and wrong, good and evil, used to prevail. Now anything goes. Money is power. Morality doesn't matter. We've lost all of our properties except for this beach home, which we put in your name before the suit filed against me. There's enough cash in the fur closet to take care of you. They don't know about it and don't tell them. I love you and the children more than anything. I just hope you can find a way, in time, to forgive me for my actions. Until we meet again when the world turns around, I will always love you! Ron"

The next morning's television newscast featured an ominous lead story: "Prominent center city attorney, Edgar Hill, found murdered in an elevator at the Society Hill Towers. Rather short on details, authorities stated that similarities to a Florida murder prevented them from discussing the matter further. Hill was a well-known benefactor of the Art Museum where he was a regular patron."

Susan felt a wave of nausea embrace her as she listened to the report. She realized Ron had to have lost his sanity and in some manner taken part. She knew he had always been obsessively principled. But it was beyond her wildest imagination that he would take his obsession to the point of giving up his freedom, allowing the forces of evil and greed to defeat him.

CHAPTER
TWENTY-TWO

DETECTIVES SHOWED up at eight A.M. to begin their investigation. Susan sat in the plush easy chair that became Ron's favorite place to nap once the system drained his energy. Across from her, she faced the leather sofa where detectives launched their interrogation.

Susan felt groggy from the previous night's interview with the police. She reported Ron missing and gave his farewell letter to the officers, who delivered it to the two detectives now about to question her.

"Did he show any signs of depression, any recent deaths or business problems?"

Susan did not want to reveal much. Ron always kept their private lives private and drummed this concept into the family. Though she offered some insights, she tried to keep them generic.

"He's a principled man, and he finds much frustration in lots of things."

"I'd say that is the theme of his note here," responded Detective Murphy sarcastically. He presented as the gruff, disheveled, nervous partner.

"Can you be more specific?" asked Detective Lane, the good-looking, groomed type. A kindness in his voice worked well to gain confidence after the brusque assault by his partner.

"I'm sorry I can't talk now." Susan broke into sobs and stammered as she tried to pose the question she needed to know since Ron left her.

"Is this a suicide note?"

"Mrs. Rellick, we have to level with you," the gruff Murphy replied. "This is a goodbye note. They almost always end with the recovery of a body."

The bluntness of his answer and the cold presentation pierced Susan's heart, and she called out, "Oh God, no!" Her sobs continued even louder.

Lane stepped forward and sat beside Susan. He put his arm on her shoulder as if to shield her from his partner's callousness

"Be more specific about his state of mind. We can sometimes intervene before any loss of life," Lane said with compassion.

Sussan responded to his kindness, and desperate for any chance at saving Ron, she opened up between gasps for air to keep her words flowing.

"He lost a huge malpractice case, and he couldn't deal with it. Please find him before he does anything foolish. He's my life!" More uncontrolled sobbing followed.

The veteran detectives understood they had to let the reality of what happened take hold. Interrogating emotion would not get any useful information. They would wait for another day.

By circumstance of the investigation, only twenty-four hours passed before Lane and Murphy returned with more answers than questions.

"Mrs. Rellick, we may have some bad news. We'd like you to sit down," Lane said in a compassionate tone knowing he delivered the words everyone dreaded.

Susan resigned to the situation and expected the worst. Certainly they suspected that Ron killed Hill, she did not need to sit.

"What happened?" she demanded.

Murphy broke the news. "Yesterday, someone murdered Edgar Hill, a prominent Philadelphia center city attorney. We believe your husband, Dr. Rellick, committed the murder."

"Hill was a despicable man," she countered. "Anyone could have done it. People like him have lots of enemies. You don't think Ron would kill him."

Susan knew Ron had a strong motive to get even with Hill, making him a prime suspect. It did not matter to her. She lashed out in his defense.

Lane took charge. "Please, Mrs. Rellick, there's more to this story. It appears the murderer then killed himself."

It didn't take long for the words to register. Susan went numb. She stumbled to the couch and sat still, once realizing the gravity of the declaration.

"The investigators found a body at the bottom of the elevator shaft. It was beyond recognition. We'll need Dr. Rellick's dental records to determine if this was him."

Though she appeared to be listening with a gaze fixed beyond the confines of the room in which the detectives stood, she never heard the rest of the report. While she learned the rest of the story days later, the last thing echoing in her mind became a recurring chant, "We'll need Dr. Rellick's dental records."

They found a body crushed to pieces. Upon further investigation, they determined after killing Hill, Ron opened the elevator doors at the twentieth floor and jumped to his death. Having removed the elevator safety, the car hit bottom, pulverizing the corpse several times before the building management realized what happened. The dental records checked out. For Lane and Murphy, the determination of murder-suicide closed the case.

96

CHAPTER
TWENTY-THREE

UNSHAVEN AND DISHEVELED, the anonymous traveler scribbled an indecipherable name into the guest register on the ash-littered desk. Cigarette butts littered the lobby. A few tattered magazines dressed the table next to a stained sofa offering refuge to the maid who chatted on her cell phone in Spanish while on break. This fleabag lodge, a far cry from the classy midtown hotels, housed the sotted drifters who had not yet lost the ability to seek shelter from the ravages of delusion and inclement weather. The stranger checked into the St. Epps Hotel in the Village, often a chosen lodging for the temporary vagabond. He pulled out six hundred-dollar bills and told the clerk, "This is for November."

Without looking to see the newly acquired tenant, the clerk said, "See me in December." He tossed a key onto the counter and went back to his newspaper.

The new arrival rode the rickety elevator to the fourth floor. Upon exiting, he bumped into an attractive, expensive looking woman who would adorn the halls of an upscale hotel. She looked more the part of a high society hooker. Her presence seemed out of place. The accidental contact resulted in an awkward embrace.

They held each other for a moment, locking eyes fixed upon faces of equal parts despair and longing. They excused themselves, and she entered the elevator without further comment.

Ron walked along the hall and stopped in front of the door to his room. Upon entering, he became one with a world of misery. The sheet upon the bed provided the only point of light able to reflect the dim fixture hanging from the ceiling. It offered contrast against the shadows that cloaked the rest of the modest furnishings.

For the next many months, Ron felt bitter, lost, and lonely. Food had no taste, music no melody. Bleak emptiness best described his world. Beyond the confines of his darkened room, the city too looked like a collection of gray shades underscored by the natural gloom of winter months.

While the Hill murder investigation closed back in the Philadelphia region, some unexplained occurrences remained. Ron killed Hill, but it was not the passion killing described in the press. It was not the impulsive revenge killing the detectives authored for the official crime report. He planned well, thought out, and executed with precision. The murder was undeniably first degree by design.

Ron had access to the medical school morgue. The bodies, some donated, were usually those of homeless people, that ended their days lying upon cold stone slabs in anatomy classes. Students and staff came and went into the anatomy lab at all hours to catch up on their dissections. The security guards never requested an ID, even though the University required such precautions. If those entering looked like they belonged in the lab, the guards let them come and go as they pleased.

Once inside, Ron made an illicit requisition for a fresh body of his choosing. He needed a fresh cadaver, not yet embalmed. For his plan, he needed a corpse of a specific size, weight, and bone structure, but most important, it had to have an intact dentition.

Ron wore his white lab coat and wheeled the requisite body on a sheet-covered gurney past security.

"Where you going with that?" asked the disinterested guard.

"They need parts up at podiatry. I'm making the delivery. Professor Snodgrass has the requisition papers. Should I to go back in and get them?"

"Naw. All good."

Ron traveled half a block to his waiting car and, with much difficulty, loaded the dead weight into the trunk. It would be another month before the inventory of the departed would reveal a missing corpse. With no friends, family, or loved ones to claim these bodies, no one cared. Herman, the lab mortician, would write it up as a miscount which he often did to cover his black-market dealings in body parts. Ron knew Herman answered to no one.

***

Ron brought the body to his office where he took x-rays of the anonymous soul's jaws. He then placed the films into his own electronic dental records. He made several sets of x-rays with different dates to give the appearance of routine, periodic examinations. Ron did not have any restorative work since his days at dental school. No one provided him with dental care to have any conflicting records. Ron drilled several new cavities into the cadaver's teeth and placed fillings to give the appearance of change over the years. He replicated his restorative history and added a few small fillings to make the x-rays look authentic.

When the investigation began, Susan knew where to find Ron's dental record. She directed the detectives to his office, and the staff obliged by providing the requested x-rays. The savviest of detectives would never guess these weren't films of his teeth. The sophistication of Ron's scheme stumped the most astute forensic experts who became involved in the case.

Ron drove the body to the Society Hill Towers before the evening guard came on duty. The elevator key was easy to get. Like many buildings, managers attached it to the wall on the lobby floor for use by emergency personnel and the fire department.

In the basement, Ron dumped the cadaver into the open elevator shaft. He released the safety switch, allowing the elevator to descend into the pit that lay ten feet below the basement floor. He learned about elevators observing the one at his three-story shore home, where it was much smaller but worked in the same manner. During a repair, he saw the technician bring the elevator car into the pit. He said to Ron, "You don't want to be down there when we lower this baby. I've seen what it can do to a body. Not nice."

Having remembered that incident, Ron used the high-rise elevator to provide the crushing forces needed for his scheme. A few rides down into the pit would do the job of making the cadaver unrecognizable, except for the teeth.

Ron waited in the basement, hiding behind huge boilers where no one ventured. By two A.M., he summoned one of the uninhabited elevators to his basement refuge and he set the emergency stop. No one would miss or notice it at this late hour. He needed assurance that Hill would be on the only other lift in service when summoned. Ron rode to the twelfth floor and by cellular phone made the call. It was a big gamble, but he had to do it.

Hill answered his phone half-asleep. "Hello?" He tried to sound alert while clearing his throat from the stagnant congestion of slumber.

Ron announced in a whisper-like voice, "I have information about the Rellick case that can put you in jail."

"Who is this?" Hill demanded while rising to attention.

"Let's just understand I'm a friend who needs a favor. I'm in the lobby, and I must talk with you."

Hill did not like drama outside the courtroom, and he became agitated.

"Are you fuckin' nuts? You expect me to come down in the middle of the night?"

Ron interrupted, "Listen up, Hill. With what I know, I gotta get out of town quick, so I'll need some cash. Get down here, and I'll explain."

Ron hung up the phone. He hoped his bluff had some element of truth. At least, he hoped he piqued Hill's interest. Now, Ron watched the floor marker lights waiting for Hill to summon the elevator to his floor.

Stunned by the hour, and by the content of the call, he had to find out what the mystery caller wanted. A setup for a mugging was his first thought. Hill stood at six feet three inches and was an imposing man. Not too many muggers would prey upon him. He weighed in at around two hundred and sixty pounds and was far from being a slouch.

While capable of defending himself, he still maintained caution in a world gone crazy. Raw instincts made him reach for his Seecamp thirty-two caliber semi-automatic pistol from inside the night table. At four inches long, this was one of the smallest powerhouse weapons made, and it easily hid inside Hill's massive enveloping hand.

In anticipation of this encounter, Hill felt the veins in his neck pulsating, along with a level of agitation, as he waited for the elevator. The familiar adrenalin rush caused this sensation he experienced often in court when going for blood during cross-examination. He stepped into the elevator having no clue as to his fate six floors beneath him.

Upon seeing the elevator called to eighteen, Ron pressed the down button from his observation perch on the twelfth floor. If the door opened and anyone other than Hill, and Hill alone, was on the car, Ron would walk away. To carry out the assassination he had to be alone with Hill. Sprayer in hand, and hand off to the sidewall, out of view from the opening elevator door, Ron stood with a quirky smile dressing his face.

Hill vaguely recognized Ron but not as a defeated opponent. Hill smiled back as a courtesy to what he assumed was another nameless neighbor embarking on a vertical ride in the night.

Unexpectedly, the pepper spray rained its fury of fire into Hill's face. He could not make a verbal sound, though he tried. Gasping and gagging, he reached for his burning eyes. Hill fell to the ground with a car-shaking thud and dropped his weapon. Ron picked up the gun, held it to Hill's head, and grabbed his throat with his other hand.

"You piece of shit. How many lives have you ruined?"

Hill whimpered between sibilant rales as he tried to get air into his paralyzed lungs. Ron snapped Hill's larynx like a plastic spoon, shutting off any airflow. The gasps and the grumbling came to an abrupt end. Hill's pawing to get free from the irreversible death sentence continued for but a short while. Soon, all that remained of Hill's animation were reflexive spasms of his arms and legs. They persisted for another thirty seconds.

Ron locked the elevator car between floors and forced open the door. With Hill's stiffening body propped to the wall, he shoved a one-hundred-dollar bill into Hill's mouth and lifted himself to the above floor.

Into the fire tower, down the steps, to the basement he ran to free up the elevator car that lay upon the unknown cadaver. After a final crushing impact to the mangled skin and bones in the pit, he rode to the lobby.

Ron waited in the shadows until the security guard wandered off to relieve himself. Ron disappeared into the night.

CHAPTER
TWENTY-FOUR

UNLIKE ANY SMALL TOWN, Manhattan offered Ron an exceptional level of facelessness. It was hard to stand out among the diverse mix of people. The suits walked in stride next to the freaks, students, blue collars, shoppers, and the homeless. The enormity of the setting allowed one to disappear. In New York City, anonymity was a reality for most. For Ron, it was his goal. The impersonal nature of modern society made it easy to hide physically, emotionally, and spiritually.

How did I get here? How did I get into this mess? Every problem has solutions, logical solutions. I know this. God, how I know this! The ruination of my existence has unfolded. How did this happen to me? I have too much to offer, too much principle to become a lost soul. My life must have purpose, or it's not worth sustaining. I can't shrivel and die on these streets—in my wretched room. I must live life to the fullest. I must seek pleasure to avoid the pain. Oh, how I long for some semblance of pleasure. I can't describe the pain by words. The pain; the emptiness is overwhelming!

Ron devised a plan conceived in his defeat. Determined to rise from the ashes, he wanted to fix the world. He questioned himself over the months since the Hill incident. Did he accomplish any good by his acts, or was he acting out of vengeance? He knew vengeance was wrong, and it should not define his motive. After denying that he perverted his thoughts, and searching his innermost self, he decided his actions were just.

I could turn myself in for the Mittenberg and Hill murders. Right! Go to jail and rot. They'd never kill me. We're kind to our murderers. The death penalty? What a joke. The odds are slim I'd die by the hand of society. I would live out my days trapped in some cell, not much different than I am now, but without my freedom. I couldn't do it. Maybe I could. Three meals a day, recreation, hanging out, drugs, sex, just about whatever.

Ron wandered the streets of the Village. He watched the truants play all day, preparing for a life of poverty and crime. He ventured to the Bowery and walked along Canal Street where merchants pawned their goods to the poor who had enough to buy the latest in technological innovations.

Look at them. These people love welfare. They thrive on it and claim perpetual oppression, victims with anger feeding justification for their plight. They use government handouts to supplement their black-market earnings. The suckers in America are the people who live right and work hard. They get shit on by the system. They try to make ends meet. They do without, and they pay their taxes to a system that hands their blood and sweat to the looters.

He explored and observed the seedier side of life. Integrating within the diversity offered a glimpse of how unstable and dysfunctional the world had become.

Help thy neighbor is proper. Are they helpless or hopeless? They're all looking for a free ride. What happened to honesty, integrity, and hard work?

Ron walked the streets, whereupon he came to a bridge on the East Side overlooking cars flashing by on the busy road. This perch served as the exit point for many despondent souls over the years. On the concrete facing, scrawled upon the wall, he read, "We miss you, Tara," with some withered flowers and a shredded teddy bear laying nearby.

I could jump. End it all right now. Never think about my fate again.

Maybe the world would be better. No! I can't do it. That would be senseless.

The immediacy for Ron to end his life vanished by the realization of how easy it would be to accomplish. The depths of his depression did not reach the level of finality, for he still reasoned there must be some meaning to his plight, which he would never know if he ended it all now.

Look at the lunatics who kill the innocent for a cause. The terrorists; they're the worst scum. Why don't they go to the source of their discontent? No, they kill the guiltless for glorious cause. Well, I went to the source. I got to the cancer and cut it out. And now I'm lost. I can't see my loved ones ever again. I'm lonely, but I'll go on alone.

The day Ron left his life behind, he filled a backpack and suitcase with provisions for all the expected complications of becoming a man without an identity. He took no clothes, no toothbrush, and no razor. Instead, he stowed away cash and diamonds to buy all the things he would need. He could sell the sparkling gems along jewelers' row, and they would sustain him.

Ron learned much from the wealthy immigrants he treated as patients over the years. They explained they used gemstones as the best way to make wealth portable. Easy to hide and few questions asked when cashing in several thousand dollars at a clip made jewels the perfect vehicle. Diamonds gave Ron the fuel upon which to live. His soul was the engine. He had a plan, and it would become his mission. He already defiled his moral base, lost his family, his position and his stature, offering nothing more to lose.

CHAPTER
TWENTY-FIVE

JADE GREEN SLABS of marble lined the elevator. They matched the flooring in the lobby with each tile configured for unique color and design. Everything in the building exuded a garish opulence. When Ron stepped out of the elevator, rich hardwoods, oriental carpets, and a most attractive receptionist greeted him.

"Can I help you, sir?"

"Is this the Monroe Corporation?"

"You want the thirtieth floor. It's two floors above us."

Ron smiled, looked around, and stepped back into the elevator. He presented himself to check the physical setup of Norman Kaplan Associates, the most media identifiable, personal injury firm in Manhattan. Recognizing Kaplan would be no problem. His face and irritating voice showed up on television for years telling the public about their terrible doctors, defective products, and evil employers along with what rewards they deserved.

The challenge involved learning Kaplan's behavior, habits and idiosyncrasies. Ron had plenty of time to stalk him. He needed to know his hours, hangouts and where he lived. It took about two weeks.

Kaplan stayed in the office late on Tuesdays and Thursdays to enjoy the services of a masseuse, not for a bad back as much as it was for a bad marriage. Twice each week a young woman would arrive at seven P.M., engage Kaplan in a relaxing hour of massage culminating in some form of sex depending upon his mood, stamina, and level of erectile dysfunction.

After his encounters, Kaplan waited until the young lady left, and precisely five minutes later he took a different elevator car, came to the lobby, and exited the building. His habits made easy prey for criminal types, psychos, and terrorists.

Ron did not want his homeless persona used for his daily routine to become his sole alter ego. To get Kaplan, he needed to join society. On the final day of stalking, he needed to get closer to his prey.

Ron left the St. Epps wearing his everyday uniform of tattered jeans, a flannel shirt, and long unkempt hair. Brown bag in hand, he traveled uptown and visited the lavatory of a fast-food restaurant. He shaved and changed into shirt, tie, and slacks, giving him the respectability needed to check into the Ritz Carlton. He didn't need reservations, as a twenty-dollar bill went far with the desk clerk even at the upscale hotels. The gratuity stuffed under the clerk's hand established a two-night stay paid for in cash. Ron now assumed the look of a well-groomed business executive allowing him to blend into the midtown crowd.

From the Ritz location, as a registered guest, Ron spent one day, Wednesday, again watching Kaplan's movements. On Thursday, Ron arrived at Kaplan's office building by six-thirty in the evening. He signed in at the security desk using an innocuous 'Raymond Stone' as his alias.

At eight o'clock, Ron waited on the nineteenth floor. At precisely eight o'clock the elevator floor markers showed a car, the hooker's car, summoned to the twenty-eighth floor. This night, it was the fourth car farthest from Kaplan's office. Five minutes later, Ron watched and waited as the eighth positioned car, the one he and Kaplan both called, sped along the cables to get them.

Ron stepped onboard at nineteen and greeted Kaplan with an outstretched hand from the shadows of the tiny cable supported chamber.

"Hi, Norm!"

Not sure who offered the greeting did not surprise Kaplan, knowing how his advertisements allowed most New Yorkers to recognize him. A constant barrage of media featuring his face provided him with a minor degree of celebrity. They shook hands, and Kaplan offered a friendly smile.

Without warning, a blast of pepper gas stabbed his eyes like daggers. He tried to gasp for air and scream in pain, but his lungs froze. The constriction of his throat muscles fighting his need to breathe produced the sounds of an asthmatic's visit with death.

Having experienced the reactions of this type attack twice before, Ron knew in a matter of seconds more audible whimpering and muffled screams would surface. To avoid hearing those sounds of suffering, Ron grabbed Kaplan's throat and snapped the vulnerable cartilage like a cracker. About four minutes from death, Kaplan could do nothing to save himself once the broken fragment blocked his airway. He grasped at his throat in a desperate attempt to breathe, while all energy drained away until he remained lifeless upon the floor.

Ron stuffed a one-hundred-dollar bill into the mouth of the corpse and exited the elevator at the eighth floor. He took the fire tower stairs to the ground level, and in less than a few minutes from the time of the murder he blended and disappeared into the still busy streets.

The morning papers have always reported violent crime, but when one of the bourgeoisie gets murdered, it makes front-page news.

"Police found Norman Kaplan, New York's most recognized personal injury attorney, murdered in the Manhattan building where he practiced law. The authorities ruled out robbery as a motive because they found jewelry and a wallet on his body."

They made no mention of the one-hundred-dollar bill.

Ron checked out of the Ritz Carlton and boarded a train to Connecticut by the time police started the Kaplan investigation. He used the same method as he stalked and attacked the most prominent advertising personal injury attorney in city after city.

Ron checked in and paid for the rooms in cash. He lived a different alias in each town. Once in his room, he turned on the television and within an hour had his prey picked out. The phone book was always good confirmation. The bigger the ads in the phone book, the bigger the ads on television. The more repulsive the manner of the written piece, the more disgusting the television clip.

In some cities, Ron found it difficult to pick his victim due to the efforts of each lawyer vying for that coveted title of television's most noted ambulance chaser.

In many a nameless hotel room, Ron sat in bed perusing the local yellow Pages. The listings for attorneys seemed endless. The full-page advertisements galled Ron in their tacky pursuit of the next big case. The advertisements served as a trail to each victim.

These ads are expensive, but they get results. Though abhorrent, they appeal to more people in recent years. These are the people who live on the bottom of the dung heap, willing to perjure themselves, cheat, and steal for their chance to win a few bucks.

Ron worked hard for several months. He crisscrossed cities up and down the eastern corridor with regular back tracking to give the appearance of multiple perpetrators. He created a rather ingenious path that resulted in fractured investigations by many jurisdictions. Soon a dozen fewer personal injury attorneys practiced their trade.

Ron expected the national wire to pick up the story of his deeds after two-dozen terminations. When he completed half that number of murders, it surprised him to hear the evening report on television.

"Everyone knows a good lawyer joke, but could the animosity created by the negative reputation of lawyers be the seed for an elaborate campaign to destroy them? We'll be back with this story next."

Isolated murders rarely get much national attention, but when a conspiracy theory comes to pass, the media jumps. Now, with twelve personal injury attorneys murdered, the press joined the case.

"Twelve murders of prominent, flamboyant attorneys have taken place in six states along the eastern United States. The one trait in common—how these attorneys advertised their trade. They became the most recognized among their peers by their rather brazen, often offensive advertising."

While the reporter spoke, the background showed the ads of one victim after another.

"At an emergency meeting, the National Association of Trial Lawyers today petitioned the attorney general to set up a special task force to address fears of a conspiracy aimed at their members."

They cut to an interview with Attorney General Janet Aims.

"I spoke with the President, and he met with his top advisors to take this most serious problem to task."

The news report continued. "In other developments, detectives from six states have been comparing notes in their search for the killer or killers."

CHAPTER
TWENTY-SIX

JANET AIMS WALKED to the podium.

"Good morning, one and all. For anyone who hasn't met me this morning, I'm Janet Aims, Attorney General. I hope we'll find time to get acquainted after our formal meeting today."

Elite attorneys representing the political wing of the legal profession came to meet with CEOs of several industrial giants. Representatives of some of the largest and most prestigious law firms also attended. Even these most respectable blueblood firms earned much of their wealth from the litigation arena. They too felt threatened.

In her own right, Janet Aims was the consummate politician. She rose to the top through many years of networking and endorsing quid pro quo with her connections.

"We invited all of you to this conference to take part in the task force set up to solve the terrible problem facing us involving the senseless killing of many members of the legal profession. To fill you in on the details, I'd like to present Sam Rodman, President of the Trial Lawyers Association."

After making a vast fortune in personal injury practice, Sam Rodman chose the political route instead of retirement to some tropical island like many of the rich members of his profession. Money no longer gave him a rush. He needed power to fill the void in his life.

Many of his colleagues let conscience get to them for having made such enormous amounts of money in ways that made them feel uneasy. They often became involved with philanthropy to assuage their guilt. Sam felt no guilt for his success and moved on to higher stake games.

Sam stood and walked to the podium. He was about to speak when the double doors of the conference room opened and in marched James Howard, President of the United States. His entourage of six Secret Service agents and two "yes" men accompanied him.

"I'm sorry to interrupt. Please go on, Sam. Hi, Janet, John."

The President nodded and gave the high sign to just about everyone in the room. He recognized them all, except the phone company executives in attendance. This president supported the personal injury lobby and they reciprocated. He vetoed every attempt to change the system, to limit liability, to limit the bounds of class actions suits. Everyone understood he sold his political influence to this group of powerful attorneys. They rewarded him with many millions of dollars in political contributions.

Sam continued. "Good morning, ladies and gents. Thank you for responding the way you have. A special thanks to Janet Aims, our attorney general, and you, Mr. President, for setting up this task force, without which we wouldn't be so able to attack this demon threatening our way of life. As of this morning, there have been fourteen attorneys murdered."

Chatter erupted in the room. The count, as shouted from daily papers around the nation on the previous day, numbered twelve.

Sensing the tension, Rodman explained.

"I'm sad to report there have been two more incidents, one last night and one early this morning. We cannot overemphasize the seriousness of this situation. Intelligence, based on investigations sponsored by my lobby group, the Trial Lawyers Association, in conjunction with local police departments, believed there was one and only one perpetrator. The M.O. was distinctive. Certain characteristics and specific physical evidence led our people to this conclusion.

"This morning, word from our investigators tells us the last two murders were not the work of the same psycho to whom we've attributed all previous crimes. Last night's incident occurred in Houston, and the early morning incident took place in Los Angeles. Aside from the incredible difficulty of being in both cities in such a short time frame, investigators told me the physical characteristics in these two killings were different from each other and from the East Coast killer.

"Folks, we need a new theory. The one now being developed is that we have a serial killer on the East Coast and copycats, probably two, on the West Coast. Should this phenomenon continue, my friends and colleagues, we could all become targets."

"I beg to differ with you, Sam," protested Alex Furman, a conservative representative of the plaintiffs' bar.

"From the accounts I read, the targets are the most blatant advertisers of our profession censured until the Federal Trade Commission deemed their advertising legal, many years ago, leaving us no power to govern professionalism within our ranks. I hate to say it, Sam, but it looks like someone out there isn't happy with the seedier members of our profession . . . if you can still call it a profession."

Alex waited for the predictable murmur in the room to subside and continued as if he was answering the collective voice.

"We've become big business, putting wealth ahead of virtue, money, and power above justice, ignoring things that are right and embracing that which is wrong."

"Alex, for many years we've heard your views at our conventions, and I shouldn't have to remind you the democracy of our organization chose me to represent the members. You're living in the past, Alex."

———

Alex relished provoking Sam. His words were an acerbic reminder of what they had become, even if they wished to forget or deny their mode of practice. Some recognized he was right, and he was ever present holding up a mirror to the faces of the others.

"Let's get back to the issue. I'd like to introduce Howard Kenyon, Commerce Secretary," said Sam with authority.

———

Howard Kenyon fawned over the many CEOs present. He was in search of a cushy job for when his term would expire. They would call upon him when they needed political favors or a direct conduit to the President's ear.

"Several of the phone company executives representing the eastern states have contacted me. Their concern relates to the recent rash of killings. It's rather odd how so many things tie together in commerce. I'll let Graham Knowles explain."

Graham was one of the bluebloods in attendance. The CEO of Bell East, he was a corporate leader, well respected by his peers and competitors alike.

"Aside from the personal tragedy each family of the murdered attorneys has experienced, the events have grave consequences for all Americans. Our company alone must brace for a hundred-million-dollar loss of income."

Another buzz reverberated throughout the room as Graham lifted a Yellow Pages phone directory and tossed it onto the conference table. Rigged to open to the lawyers' listings, it landed with a resounding thud.

"My friends, this is the Philadelphia Yellow Pages. In here we have ninety pages of listings for lawyers. Each full-page ad represents forty-thousand dollars a year in revenue. In just one market, in this case, Philadelphia, we will lose over four million dollars a year if these advertisers cancel. There are thousands of these markets. You can do the math. Nationwide, we're talking about a multibillion-dollar industry between our books, TV, radio, newspaper, and internet advertising. The entire market is in jeopardy. We have cancellations from attorneys coming in at an unprecedented rate compared to the vast increases we used to get from their group.

"You may think our concerns are self-serving, and you may figure we make plenty with our well-diversified business interests. The fact is, we will survive, but there are thousands of jobs involved from sales, printing, manufacturing, and distribution that depend on this advertising.

"We were very much surprised, as I'm sure you were, when we ran the figures. Lawyers saturate the media with advertisements more than any other group. Look here at the number of pages of advertising: physicians, fifty-seven pages; dentists, twenty-two pages; plumbers, twenty-one pages; electricians, eleven pages. For crying out loud, the massage parlors only have six pages in here."

These little-known facts coupled with his last comment provoked nervous laughter that swept through the room.

"No one advertises at the level seen among attorneys. The effect of a lost market will ripple down and hurt hundreds of thousands of people. A lot of jobs have already disappeared.

"We set up a program to keep our accounts by contacting the lawyers leaving our ranks as advertisers. Financial assistance is also available to solve the mystery behind these dreaded killings."

The time arrived for Sam to end the meeting. He stood up and turned toward the President.

"This debauchery is much worse than we ever imagined. Look at the innocent people affected by this barbarism. It's with this calamity in mind I make a plea to you, Ms. Aims, and to you, Mr. President. Please come to our aid."

After Sam's appeal, the President took his cue and rose from the table.

"Sam, I don't have to tell you how much I respect you and your organization. Your members are well aware I'm in their corner. Go back and tell your members I'll support your request for help with the full powers of the United States Government. We will not allow some sick mass murderers to cause you to live in fear like so many other victims of violent crime. Janet will handle the details. I'm sorry I can't stay to hear the rest of the facts about this tragedy, but I'm late for another meeting."

The President turned and walked away with his attendants. He never had to worry about some lunatic stalker. An army of Secret Service agents shadowed and protected him.

It was Janet's turn to make her closing remarks.

"Sam, as you heard, you have our full, unwavering support. This is a civil rights issue! These killings affect all the people. We'll mobilize a team from the FBI to work with your group."

CHAPTER
TWENTY-SEVEN

A MONTH PASSED with little accomplished in halting the murders. Teams of FBI agents worked on many cases stretching their resources to the limit. The lawyers pursued all their connections to get the job done.

Janet Aims shuffled papers at her desk when her secretary's voice announced the guest over the intercom.

"Mr. Grey has arrived."

"Send him in."

Through the door entered a confident Agent Grey with his outstretched hand forging the way to an introduction.

"It's so nice to meet you, Ms. Aims. I'm Rupert Grey, Special Agent from the Philadelphia office."

"The pleasure's mine," responded Janet. "I've heard a lot about you. Heading up the insurance fraud unit in the northeast region is an accomplishment. You must lighten up on the heavyweights."

Grey looked at her with a confused stare.

"Some of our people have shown concern about the legality of FBI sting operations. Look, Grey, the interstate fraud rings are the real villains, but the private practice accident attorneys shouldn't have to worry every new client could be an undercover agent.

These lawyers support our party in a big way with their time, money, and influence."

"Ms. Aims, you can't mean that's an excuse for illegal activities?"

"Grey, I'm the last one in the world who would condone any illegal activities. I'm referring to the bread and butter personal injury game. A client comes in with a legitimate claim and perhaps the attorney has to embellish the injury a bit. For Christ's sake, Grey, they're going up against the insurance companies. They've got more money than God. An equalized playing field is a good thing. So, they have the client see the doctor longer than needed. Who's to say? That's what the Scales of Justice are about . . . equalizing."

"Ms. Aims, with all due respect, fraud is fraud."

"Just watch your step, Grey. Some influential, unhappy groups of people out there are getting edgy with these lunatics killing their members."

"That's why I asked to meet with you," said Grey. "I believe I know the man who's committing these crimes."

"You mean men, don't you?"

"Well, yes. We have some copycats on the West Coast, but the East Coast murders are being committed by one and the same. I believe he lives in New York City."

"You know who's committed these murders?" she exclaimed.

"I'm almost certain, and I know the way this man thinks."

"Then let's lock him up. What's the delay?"

"I don't have the resources. Our villain is in hiding, and it will take more resources and money to take him out."

"Then go to your division head and get the funding," suggested Aims with a thread of anger and frustration in her voice.

"Until I have some concrete proof, my people aren't listening to me," he said.

"Then why should I?"

"I find I work better independently. With your help, I can maintain my autonomy in this investigation and crack the case."

"You mean you can take this guy out covertly?" asked Janet, with a tone of excitement.

"Ms. Aims, I'm talking about capture, not an assassination. The FBI doesn't work that way. We have to follow the letter of the law."

"It's the letter of the law that's making it so difficult to deal with these nuts. Sometimes we need extreme measures," exclaimed Aims, trying to assert her authority.

"That's not how I operate, ma'am. What I need from you is special funding if I'm to work through my theory. Our team has too many agents on this case with an overloaded budget. They declined my request. They think I'm looking in the wrong places."

"And what makes you think I agree with your 'one man, living in New York' theory?"

Grey looked into her eyes with a fixed stare and stated, "You don't have to agree. Why not take a gamble on me?"

Aims, felt uncomfortable with the cold gaze. She turned away and asked, "What's in it for me?"

"If I'm right and I get this guy, and I will, I'll see to it you get all the credit. You'll be on the map. Your name and photo will get plastered on every news outlet. It will put you on the political high road."

Janet Aims smiled. Grey knew he had his funding.

CHAPTER
TWENTY-EIGHT

"HI, STRANGER," Gary's coarse voice bellowed over the cacophony of conversation and loud music being ignored by all.

The tavern had the smell of musty beer and the dim lighting of similar bars found in most old neighborhoods. Small for a New York establishment, it mostly remained half-filled with an assortment of patrons ranging from friendly chatterers to those who lived in silent melancholy. Ron graduated from the depths of despair to seek a means of conversation. Unable to stare at four walls daily, and in desperate need of company, he looked forward to visiting this tavern.

Realizing the need for anonymity, but succumbing to the desires of companionship, Ron allowed Gary to befriend him on a superficial level. Gary seemed a lot like Ron intellectually, which was surprising, because his dress and demeanor were one step away from that of a street person.

He walked with a subtle but discernible limp and wore an oversized dirty and wrinkled trench coat. On the lapel he sported a medal of sorts, unidentifiable to Ron, who understood nothing of military matters.

Gary's topics of discussion always centered on his frustrations with government, crime, politicians, and a host of aggravations familiar to all city-dwellers. Ron liked the conversation as they shared similar views, however, he had to maintain a distance to protect his dark side.

"Haven't seen you for a couple weeks. I missed you," Gary lamented.

"Been away on a job," Ron replied.

Gary remained out of work on a medical disability. He had not worked for years. Ron never pursued the issue but thought it was most likely a mental disability. He reasoned the twitch, the constant lifting of his right shoulder, resulted from some stress or trauma Gary experienced leading to his inability to work.

When Ron once asked what he used to do, Gary told him he did not like to talk about it. While that kind of answer turns off many prospective friends, it made Ron feel safe because he too had no desire to visit his former life. During their relationship, Gary never discussed the past, his or Ron's.

"Do you believe it? The count is up to eighteen, Ron!"

"What are you talking about, Gary?"

"Fewer assholes, my friend. Less pricks in the world."

Ron's face spoke of confusion. Gary pointed to the television that delivered news all day long from the wall above the bar. Ron turned around and strained to hear the story over the endless patron chatter. He almost choked on his drink when he saw the report of six more murders he did not know occurred. They happened on the West Coast and in the southeast over the last two days.

The next story described a high-profile plaintiff's attorney being stalked and killed.

"In a related case, Los Angeles Police today reported the murder of Ann Marie Levinson. You may recall, Miss Levinson received an award of four million eight hundred thousand dollars in a sexual harassment suit against the Bunning Company two years ago. Authorities reported she had received several death threats over the last month, and one indicated a stalker was out to get retribution 'for a system out of control.' Investigators are now looking for any links to the rash of plaintiff attorney murders and this case."

Dumbfounded, Ron did not believe what he heard. In a perverse manner, he wanted to jump for joy, but the chain on his conscience tugged just enough to let guilt suppress any manifestations of pleasure.

He turned to Gary and replied, "Look, there are a lot of jerks in the world, but it doesn't mean you kill them all."

"No, you don't understand. This is justice. When the system fails, when institutions stop policing themselves, the people have a right to revolt. That's what's happening here. This is evolutionary change by revolutionary action."

Gary twitched in an excited manner, and Ron loved every minute knowing someone shared his views. At least a few others felt like Ron, but they were mostly homicidal and sociopaths.

"Man, if I had the guts to change the world; to live and die for a cause," said Gary with remorse in his brooding voice.

"Yeah, right, Gary."

They stared at each other, minds waltzing down similar paths, Ron flashing back to his acts of murder while Gary relived his actions on a battlefield from a long time ago. The background voices, music, and TV faded far from their reality as they became captivated by repressed thoughts brought to the fore.

After a startled awakening from an explosion in his past halted his mind's journey, Gary muttered, "We eat, we sleep, we read, we watch TV."

"What are you talking about?" Ron responded as the intrusion aroused him from his secret deliberations.

"What's life all about, Ron? I've analyzed it to the extreme. What's it all about?"

Tears filled Gary's eyes, and for the first time since he had met him, Ron noticed the twitch went silent.

"What's the problem, Gary?"

Gary started gasping for air. Ron jumped to his feet to assist, but Gary motioned him to sit. After a few labored deep breaths, Gary relaxed.

"I suppose you were ready to do some CPR," Gary said in jest. After a long sip from his vodka over rocks and a deep exhalation, he continued. "Just a little anxiety. Gets me every once in a while," he confessed as another sip finished the libation.

"What are we doing here? What's life all about, Ron? That's the problem. What purpose do I serve? I look at this nutcase killing greedy people. He's sick, or is he? Right or wrong, he has a purpose for his existence. He's putting his life on the line for a belief. God, it makes me jealous.

"What about me, Ron? What am I here for? I wake up, I take a piss, I eat, I shit, I read the paper, I watch TV, and I go to sleep."

"Stop it, Gary. Stop tormenting yourself. Don't analyze life. You're here for a reason. It's way bigger than you can imagine. Each person you come in contact with has the potential for meaning. Every connection we make can change lives. The world is a product of these interactions. Just enjoy this American Strangler in the news reports if it makes you happy. Savor the meals you eat. Just live life for the pleasures."

At night's end, Ron walked back to his room thinking how Gary trivialized existence. It made him feel more alone than ever. Riding the elevator, he hoped he would run into his neighbor, the woman of the night. He paused outside her room and listened for a moment. Ron heard nothing from within, only the siren passing by on the street below. It was one A.M., and he expected she would return in an hour. He often heard her footsteps from night's labors and wondered about her life.

Gary's confessions of meaningless existence weighed heavily on Ron. He wanted to reach out to someone. The social discourse he found with Gary had meaning, but it could never gratify the longing for a physical embrace, a union of affection. Ron felt alone and lonely for the first time in his life.

CHAPTER
TWENTY-NINE

RON WANDERED the streets aimlessly over the next few weeks. He couldn't resume his mission, the result of overwhelming despair and loneliness. He drifted further into the darkness of seclusion. The light of his origins without sin grew ever more distant. Conflicted feelings over his acts of violence as a means for change brewed somewhere in his psyche, resulting in a deepening depression. He occupied most of his time with mundane activities and found no purpose to his existence.

Every morning he listened to the news. More killings of all sorts reported, but nobody seemed to care. Violence had become an accepted part of the culture.

Ron's early excursions to the tavern became more common. Gary strolled in around eleven that morning.

"It ain't fair!" said Gary as he tossed the morning paper to the table where Ron sat staring at a half-emptied vodka and orange juice.

"What's the latest to rustle your feathers, Gary?"

"They got away with killing Mr. Jacobs."

"Who?"

"The deli guy, Izzy Jacobs; you know, around the corner. Know the place? It was cold-blooded murder."

Ron picked up the paper and read in silence while Gary continued his rant.

"This is disgusting. Everyone's oblivious. Where's the outrage? Where are the protests, the politicians? What happened to the cops?" asked Gary.

Looking up from the newspaper, Ron tried to answer him. "Nobody cares because there are too many murders."

The simple explanation did not quench Gary's frustration.

"They're more worried about protecting the rights of the criminals. Remember that mugger? The one the cops shot while he was running away. The courts awarded him two million dollars and painted the cops as the bad guys. How in the hell does any lawyer with a conscience take that case? They've tied the cops' hands. The cops just as soon let the creeps run away now, and the bad guys know it," Gary bemoaned.

Ron, engrossed in the newspaper, paused to comment.

"Prosecuting the guys who killed Izzy was a game. Another fucking game."

The news article described how Robert Belman, a criminal defense attorney, got Jamal Asadd a "not guilty" verdict on charges of first-degree murder. His aunt turned him in knowing he committed the crime with two of his friends. It was her word against his since there was no physical evidence. Jamal, a veteran street hood, knew rubbing the gun with oil removed the prints, and tossing it into a dumpster uptown assured a cold case without the evidence of a weapon.

Jamal never had to testify. The only thing he had to discuss about the proceedings occurred when he walked out of the court. A reporter asked him for a comment.

With a glare in his eye and a haughty air he told him, "It ain't no big deal if they would a convicted me. I'd get to be wit my boys on the inside. No big deal. See what I'm sayin'."

The article described how Belman, in a separate case, got Jamal's brother off on first-degree murder charges as well. He did not walk free like Jamal, but his punishment did not include serious jail time. An off-duty cop caught him in the act of killing Jinsuk Oh, a Korean grocer. Belman contrived the defense that his client acted in self-defense when the grocer pulled his gun. It worked, because that is, in fact, the law. He served five years of a ten-year sentence for second-degree murder. The felon served the mandatory five years for using a gun to commit a crime concurrently, allowing him to go free in much less time than the actual intention of the sentence.

After reading the article, Ron became upset. He threw the newspaper onto the table.

"How can a robber have rights?" he shouted. "How in Christ's name can a holdup man claim self-defense when he puts a gun in your face? Are we all mad?"

"Izzy Jacobs got the death penalty," exclaimed Gary in a most agitated manner. "So did the grocer. They saw no commutation of their sentences, no reprieve from the governor, no fancy-talking lawyer to bring them back. There weren't any of the vocal opponents of the death penalty out there praying for those poor guys. Where's the outrage for the victims?" he demanded.

"The Jacobs and the Ohs are no longer detached from the discourse of human suffering. Their lives, like the lives of an ever-growing pool of victims, became indelibly scarred. For them, the sanctity of life, liberty, and the pursuit of happiness, as guaranteed in our constitution, died along with their loved ones," said Ron.

"Their families were at least spared the death penalty, but they didn't get off all together. They got a life sentence with no chance of parole. For the rest of their lives, they will grieve. The survivors will feel emptiness beyond description. They'll serve some hard time and never recover. They'll never escape from the pain, the incarceration of their souls. Their sentence *is* for life."

Ron stopped his rant as he noticed Gary's eyes fill with tears.

"Until tragedy strikes home, these stories are just one more atrocious event after another. Every story seems to be distant, fuzzy, and almost surreal after a while," said Gary, waiting for a reply.

A numbing immunity encumbered Ron's thought as he no longer listened to what Gary had to say. He said nothing more.

God! How each family of a victim suffers, yet we never give it much consideration. He's right. It's just another news story.

CHAPTER
THIRTY

ANOTHER EVENING of senseless wandering ended for Ron, and he returned to his hotel. With his mind devoid of any particular thoughts, he rode the elevator to the fourth floor. Upon rounding the corner of the dimly lit hall, he saw the silhouette of a figure sitting against the door of a distant room. Sobs echoed through the corridor, heightening Ron's guard.

The building had no security. At two AM, the chance someone would gain entrance to rob a tenant for a few drug-habit dollars remained real.

Ron walked forward and soon recognized the dark silky hair of his nocturnal neighbor. She wept and never noticed Ron until he began his quixotic approach.

"What happened?" he asked in a horrified manner after seeing fresh blood under her nose and swelling over her left eye.

She answered with sobs muffled by the hand held to her mouth. Ron leaned over to comfort her. She grabbed his kneeling frame and cried uncontrollably. He held her close as the joining gave him a spark of desperately needed warmth. Ron felt ashamed his craving somehow superseded hers. Her firm embrace upon his shoulders lent a wonderful sense from his faded past.

"I'm so sorry," she said, embarrassed she now involved Ron with her troubles.

———

Despite her injuries, she needed to explain her predicament. "I'm so incredibly stupid. This kind of thing has never happened to me," she confessed through her sobs. "I was walking home when this homeless creep came up to me asking for some change. I always slip by these jokers. It's New York, so I get plenty of practice dodging them. When I sidestepped him, he grabbed my bag and pulled me toward him. The next thing I heard was a crack, and a shooting pain filled my eyes with tears. He took off with my bag, and my nose started gushing."

Ron shook his head in dismay.

"How does anyone do this and live with themselves? I guess we can thank the ACLU for bringing us together," he added sarcastically.

She stared at him with a look of confusion.

"This joker was considered soliciting for charity. At least that's what the courts said when they threw out the vagrancy and panhandling laws. Never mind me. I like to vent."

Ron raised his brows, and she returned the gesture with a stunted smile.

"Let me help you to your room."

"I wish it was that easy. My keys are in my purse."

"Come with me. We'll get you cleaned up."

"I'm Jill," she said.

"I knew a name went with this story. I'm Ron."

He helped Jill to stand and escorted her to his room. Having washed the blood from her nose and lip, he attended to her injury with ice packs. Jill shivered from the traumatic event, and the ice magnified the chills, causing her teeth to chatter.

"I'll make you some hot tea. We'll get rid of those shivers just like that." He snapped his fingers, eliciting a smile from his forlorn guest.

While Ron stood by the stove and stared at Jill, the room transformed from the gray, gloomy haunt of the past year. The scent of her perfume dissolved the musty, foul odors that defined the decline of Ron's life. A warm glow and aura of tranquility competed for Ron's senses, and for the first time the decrepit stench of his recent life left him, replaced by memories of better times.

Jill sipped at the brew, and all the while Ron transfixed his gaze upon her beauty, not knowing if it was that he had noticed no women for so long or that God sent a goddess to awaken his sensibilities. She wore skin without flaw. Her angelic face looked radiant as framed by dark silky hair. Her every feature was like clay molded to perfection. Each time she spoke, her full lips defined sensuality.

"Would you mind if I stay the night? I can call a locksmith in the morning," Jill said.

"No way! I'll to have to throw you out."

She smiled.

Ron walked to his closet in search of a robe, a pillow, and a blanket.

"Here," he said as he tossed her the sleeping gear. "Get some rest. You take the bed. Isn't that what the hero says in the movies?"

"No! No! I can't."

"Come on, do you think I'd let you sleep on the floor? Gentlemen don't treat ladies that way."

She was quick to respond, "And ladies don't let their problems ruin even one night of a gentleman's sleep."

"Look, lady, you're my patient. Until I say different, you get the bed."

"Okay, Doctor, I give."

With that exchange, Jill lifted herself and walked to the bathroom, robe in hand. Ron turned down the scant covers so the bed might invite Jill to a night of slumber. He propped the tattered pillows from the sofa onto the floor and made himself comfortable.

Heavy eyes began their descent even against the exhilaration of meeting Jill.

When she exited the bathroom, the glimmer of light awakened Ron. Her silhouette stood out from the backdrop of soft light and appeared dreamlike. His eyes followed her movement, but he couldn't speak a word.

Jill did not take the bed. She curled up next to Ron, facing him, and closed her eyes. He looked down at her cleavage exposed from the loose-fitting robe. For the first time in a year, he felt the swell of passion.

"Would you hold me?" Jill whispered.

Without words, he pulled her close. Tears streamed down her cheeks. Ron hugged her and kissed her forehead. Fatigue paved the way to slumber, and he remembered nothing more of that evening.

***

Jill's shadow interrupted the warm amber glow of morning sunlight embracing Ron's face. He yawned and opened his eyes. Startled at first, he needed a second to remember why Jill was in his room.

"You're the first person who didn't try to take me in this kind of moment. I didn't think men like that exist."

"If I were a whole man, I would have tried. You're beautiful," he admitted as his face flushed with embarrassment.

"I'm sorry. You don't like women," she stated as fact rather than a question, making it easier for Ron to respond.

"Oh, no, that's not it at all," Ron maintained. "I've just had some recent problems."

Her eyes widened in distress. To move away from the sensitive subject, Ron stated in jest, "I didn't see you taking advantage of me last night either."

"I could have," she replied.

Jill's eyes filled with tears. Ron reached for tissues to offer her comfort.

"I'm a prostitute, but I'm sure you knew."

Embarrassed by her confession, Ron tried to console her.

"Well, no, I, not really . . . You help people," he finally said. "So, it's noble, whatever you do. You don't have to talk about it."

"I want to."

Ron remained silent as he did not know how to respond. For Jill, the pause served as an endorsement to continue.

"I don't help people. The cheap hooker walking the streets, she helps people. I hop into bed with wealthy men who can't get it on with their wives and don't want to start over with some gold-digging sluts."

"You don't have to share your tale. You don't know me," said Ron, trying to deflect and feeling evermore embarrassment for the confessor.

"Maybe that's why I feel I can talk to you. I have no one else. You're different, I can tell. You don't belong here."

"Sure. Go on," Ron offered.

"I'm in this place because of my marriage. Taylor and I met at Baker and McKenzie, the investment banking firm . . . love at first sight. He was handsome, manly, and everywhere he traveled things seemed to light up. Everyone wanted to be around him.

"Early on, our love was like a fairy tale. I never realized he had a drug problem. I couldn't believe the energy he had. He'd set up deals at all hours; burned the candle at both ends. He was the best producer for the firm in the five years he worked there.

"Almost every night he had client meetings at our apartment. They'd last until two, three in the morning, and he still had energy for love. Animal lust would be a better description.

"Well, he couldn't hide a habit like cocaine forever. The hours took their toll on Taylor, and his production fell. The smaller paycheck cramped his style. He loved the good life and had no intention of seeing it disappear. He needed to make more money at any cost.

"It was about a year into our marriage when Taylor started wooing Henry Booth, and he brought him home for dinner."

"*The* Henry Booth?" Ron queried.

"Yes, *the* Henry Booth. Taylor had to close this deal. It meant a huge bonus, and it would put Taylor on the charts with the big boys, the players. When you travel in those circles, deals come your way. Everyone throws you money. He wanted into that circle.

"After dinner, I excused myself and left them to conduct their business. Around two A.M. I heard the bedroom door open, as expected. I was ready to let Taylor drain his libido so he'd be able to go to sleep.

"That night things were different. Instead of the usual animal attack, a hand gently caressed my neck with a soothing, almost timid, up and down motion. It was the touch a woman wants."

Jill stopped her tale, and Ron recognized the image of dread in her expression.

"Go on," he prodded, realizing this story needed to be told.

Her lips trembled. She could not go on. The memory of a brutal event branded into a part of the mind that suppresses its expression silenced her voice.

While she could not speak of the incident, she remembered the soothing touch that explored her neck. She remembered how the hands slipped her nightgown from her shoulders to expose her breasts. The contact felt soft and teased an approach to her nipples throbbing with desire she longed for but never experienced at the hand of Taylor, who pawed and grabbed his way to pleasure.

The hands wandered lower on her body and went into a circular massage causing her skin to rise with goosebumps as each wave of touch moved closer toward her groin. She remembered how she thought this night she would not have to feel the frictional burn of a too anxious lover like all other nights.

After a minute of exploring her inner depths, the tone changed. The hands became strong and grabbed her legs. Like a piece of meat, she was twisted violently, spinning her body a hundred and eighty degrees. Now, upon her stomach with rear exposed, she felt this stiff, rock-hard, anal violation. Taylor never acted this way. In the past, he expressed disgust of sex in this fashion as degrading to women.

Pounding away with every stroke more forceful than the one before, Jill found herself locked into a foreign experience of pain, inexplicably bound up with pleasure. At the height of animal ecstasy, they both screamed out in unison. It horrified her upon the realization it was not Taylor's voice. Henry Booth and Tyler, by consent, took part in defiling her body, mind, and heart.

After reliving the repulsive scene in her mind, Jill realized she could not deny Ron. She told him the abridged story without the lustful details and could tell no one how she felt. It troubled her that she found pleasure in such a reprehensible act.

"It ruined me. I couldn't leave our apartment. I never returned to work. Taylor got the contract and the bonus. And then he continued to use me as a prostitute for his habit, for his ride to the top.

"I stayed with him for another year, pleasing every wealthy client he brought home. They loved it. These men were mostly pretty conservative and would never get involved in this kind of play, but Taylor had a knack for exciting their wildest fantasies. They threw deals his way, and he became the total player.

"Repulsive as it was, I loved Taylor, so I rationalized I was helping him. Then he stuck the money up his nose and bought more toys. He became a slave to the drug, a mindless imp. I had to leave.

"I left and took his client list. I went out on my own. I kept my costs low, so I could get out of this game quicker. That's how this hotel became my home. I can't afford to meet anyone I know. This is the perfect place to hide from my world. Now, I visit the heavy hitters who need the spice they can't get at home. I make enough to provide for food, shelter, and savings for when my looks fade."

She welled up with tears again, but she continued. "I feel so cheap, so ashamed. I can't believe I'm telling you this story, but I had to get it out. Please forgive me."

The confession disturbed Ron. He felt an odd bond to Jill. He, too, felt defiled. He, too, stooped to disgusting acts, even worse, to survive his violation.

"People do bad things sometimes to get by. You can't see it through your guilt! You gave uncompromising love, and Taylor used you. You have no reason to be ashamed."

She wiped tears from her cheeks and felt cleansed, having confessed her horrid past.

To reciprocate, she asked, "Who are you? A guy like you doesn't belong in a dump like this. What's your story?"

Ron's kind smile faded. She realized, too late, she should not have inquired into his life.

He shook his head, placed his hands upon his eyes, and replied, "Oh God! I wish I could tell you."

"I'm so sorry. I didn't mean to pry."

"No need to be sorry," said Ron. He turned and walked to the bathroom.

After having slept in his clothes and now recalling his past, he felt dirty and cheap. He removed his shirt and pants and turned on the shower. He removed his underwear and looked into the mirror to see the naked remains of his still manly figure.

Ron lamented being devoid of the relations he so desired. Jill reminded him about living, something he had not done for too long. He stood inside the shower with his head hanging. The water spray coated his body with a warmth not noticed since his ordeal began.

The door to the shower opened, startling Ron. Jill stood with her robe hanging open, allowing Ron to see her breasts and the shaded dark of her groin. The light behind her diffused the steaming haze, creating the image of a halo surrounding her figure.

"Jill!" he called out in embarrassment.

"Shhh." Her soft reply silenced him.

Jill dropped her robe to the floor, revealing the perfect body. She entered the shower, stepping behind Ron, pressing her body against his. The steamy water felt like velvet against his skin. Her arms wrapped tight around his chest. She began kissing his back with the passion he so desired. His heart pounded as his longing for this woman he barely knew consumed him. Jill stepped around to face Ron and dropped to her knees. He felt the kisses, the long sensuous strokes of her tongue and the nibbling bites pulling at his flesh. The blood drained from his head. A euphoric encumbrance seized Ron's being. He had to brace himself against the tile wall to keep from collapsing in ecstasy.

Her hands now massaged his thighs, moving closer and closer to their target. Ron moaned in anticipation of climax. Being so long deprived of pleasure, he welcomed it but feared its end. Jill sensed his fear.

"Sit down here, next to me," she beckoned.

Ron needed no prodding as his legs were about to fail him. He sat with Jill in the pool of steaming porcelain. Their lips made contact. It was fleeting at first. She teased him with soft bites that morphed into long, passionate kisses.

Jill stopped her seduction and stared at Ron. He looked deep into her eyes. Without a word spoken, she placed her hands to his face, kissed him, released, and kissed again.

Ron pulled away to stare at Jill's beauty. She opened her eyes, and for a moment they gazed into each other's hearts.

Jill waited no longer. She pushed Ron back against the wall and climbed on top to mount him. The penetration was deep. The union traveled from body to soul. Jill gyrated methodically, guiding them toward a unified ecstasy. She panted while Ron's heavy breathing became utterances of pleasure.

Without comment, Jill stopped her every motion and clung to Ron in a manner that halted all animation. The climax was of an unbound intensity, causing him to be in perfect harmony with her, and it bordered on transcendence.

Jill fell back to take pleasure in the coolness of the tile wall as a welcome relief from the heat of their union. Ron could not move. They sat motionless as droplets of water cleansed their souls. At that moment they united as one. They had reached heights seldom experienced but for the synergism of lust and the deep-seated emotion of souls searching for a connection. The mist-filled shower became Ron's paradise. If he died, at that moment, he would have had no regrets.

CHAPTER
THIRTY-ONE

SHAVEN AND WELL GROOMED, Ron strolled through Tiffany's bronzed doors to enter a world of splendor. The contents of each display case glistened from gold, silver, and multifaceted gems. The extraordinary exhibit of color and gilt reflected kaleidoscopic patterns from the ornate light fixtures hanging above him.

There were many beautiful objects to choose, but the task seemed daunting. The result of long-lost interest in material things made this selection process a rebirth of appreciation. Ron felt both excited and perplexed. Within minutes, the bean necklace drew his attention away from the opulence. It was plain compared to the costly jewels in the many cases nearby. A sterling silver lima bean on a necklace fascinated him. Although simple, he felt an affinity for this charm representing the bonding seed of a new life.

"I'll take it," he announced to the saleswoman assigned to him. She smiled with approval. "Oh, would you please wrap it extra nice?"

He fixed his gaze upon the packaging process. The clerk tucked white tissue into the sky-blue signature box. She placed the tiny bundle, gracefully bound by soft white satin ribbon, into a small sky-blue shopping bag with a handle.

The anticipated visit each Wednesday touched a primal chord in his heart. By the fourth week Ron, sapped by the hunger of his anticipation, could wait no longer. Instead of the usual eight P.M. arrival, he stopped by at seven.

The streets presented a new vitality. Ron noticed things always present but below his consciousness. The icy evening air feathered his hair as he walked onward with purpose. His pace was brisk.

The much-expected knock required no question as to whom it might be. The door opened, and Ron gazed upon his redeemer.

Jill was not ready. She sported an oversized linen man's shirt, revealing a lace-trimmed bra. She pulled her hair back and wore no makeup but still appeared as pure beauty.

Upon seeing Ron, Jill leaped into his arms and hugged a long-lost lover kind of embrace cheek to cheek. Her face, draped with a smile and eyes closed, looked pure and innocent. She pulled his face to hers and kissed his lips, gently at first, followed by an attempt to devour his mouth. She moved her head side to side, engaging his lips and tongue. Ron ran his hands over her shoulders, caressing and molding the tenderness of her skin.

A kiss never before drove Ron so wild. It was not just the kiss. Her hands communicated an intense passion in their movement upon his face, neck, and shoulders. Together, they strove to reach a closeness undefined by physical boundary.

Ron grabbed Jill by her waist and pulled her to the cold, hard floor. Holding her hands in his, he began massaging and kissing her fingers, wrists, and arms. He pressed his body upon her pelvis, and her hips rose and retreated in a rhythmic motion with an ever-increasing tempo. Finally, with great force, her body surged forward, and she pleaded, "Ron, I can't wait. Please, I need to feel you inside me!"

He wanted the moment to last forever. Every touch, every caress, every taste of flesh filled his senses with desire. In the heat of passion, they tore at each other's clothes until they lay nude upon the floor. Jill wrapped her legs around Ron in such a manner that he could sustain no motion. He experienced the most unusual release, cerebral, emotional, and more focused than any physical union. From the silence of the motionless embrace, both Ron and Jill felt their spasmodic contractions binding them to one another.

Jill taught her fading warrior many things about love, offering him a new life. That evening they joined body and soul two more times. Each encounter brought with it a higher degree of intensity. Ron loved every minute of their moments together, and more important, he loved Jill.

When the evening's end approached, Ron presented Jill with the gift he so carefully selected. She tore away the wrapping and removed the necklace.

"Ron, this is the nicest thing you could have done for me!"

"I'm sure it's nothing compared to the gifts—"

Jill stopped him mid-sentence.

"No. This necklace means more to me than you can ever know," she replied.

"This charm represents us being together."

Jill rubbed the object like an irreplaceable treasure.

Ron smiled. "Can I stay tonight?" he asked sheepishly.

She replied with a hug.

While they slept side by side, Ron awoke in a sudden terror, the product of an anxiety attack. He dreamt of his Uncle Eli who died many years ago. He had not seen this uncle for thirty years.

Uncle Eli outlived seven sisters. Never having married, they all lived together since they were born. Ron visited them throughout his childhood as part of a boring, weekly ritual dinner.

The years marched on, and all the siblings died, except for Uncle Eli. He moved far away and lived alone. Ron's parents kept in touch by phone and visited with him on occasion. They told Ron how Uncle Eli lived out his remaining years. He learned about how his eyes failed him, how he could not hear well, and how arthritis kept him from getting around in his already limited confinement. In spite of the infirmity of body, they always marveled at the sharpness of his mind.

A great mind getting stuck in a feeble body wracked with pain, isolated from the world as all senses faded, troubled Ron. While he never thought much about death and decline in years past, this dream became an ever-increasing reminder of the failings corresponding to longevity.

Uncle Eli lived to his ninety-second year. Ron did not remember how he died, fast or slow, painfully or peacefully. He never visited him in the last years, being too busy with school and his social life. Now, he lamented his long-gone uncle and questioned his recent bouts of anxiety as the product of either selfish fear of being alone too, or a display of unfettered compassion.

Ron's heart beat fast and heavy, making his loneliness worse. He wanted to wake Jill, to hold her, to gain attachment to another soul, but he would not allow her to see him this vulnerable. Sharing such deep feelings risked exposing his secrets.

To break the grip of this anxiety attack, Ron focused on other things. His thoughts drifted to his children. When they were young, he tried to play with them as much as he could. He envisioned playing trapeze, where he balanced them on his knees and lifted them into the air. He thought about the fun they had play-wrestling, pretending he could not find them when they ran behind his back. They played many silly activities, and the memories helped to ease his angst.

Ron did not remember the details of a favorite game he created. The lapse in memory frightened him. The anxiety heightened, and he hyperventilated.

What the Hell was it we used to play? I'm losing my mind. I know it. Their faces seem distant. I can't see them clearly any longer. What's happening to me?

Having refrained from murdering any more lawyers since his

attachment to Jill grew, he felt a sense of lost self-esteem. He missed the purpose he derived from his mission.

In the bout of emotional turmoil, Ron walked to the kitchen and pulled out a phone book. His thoughts no longer fixated on his failings and isolation. He now relished an overwhelming pride as he thumbed through this year's yellow pages. The legal listings read like an era past with only names and numbers listed. It was a haunting difference from the preceding years when glitzy advertisements filled page after page.

The only advertising under the lawyer heading was for corporate law and criminal law. Ron's mind flashed back to the local news headline about the killing of deli owner, Izzy Jacobs. He flipped the page, and there it was, "The best for criminal matters." A dose of adrenaline whisked through his vessels. Instead of feeding his anxiety, it had the opposite effect on Ron. A manic sense of worth, of purpose and well-being, filled his mind.

It was four A.M., and Ron reclined once again at peace. His back brushed against Jill's arms, and she nestled close to him. He smiled and closed his eyes.

From that night forward, Jill realized she could no longer continue seeing the men who supported her. She returned to executive secretarial work.

Jill did not want to tell Ron of her decision, because she did not want him to feel obligated to her. She would continue to look forward to Wednesday nights without commitment or obligation. For their moments together, she experienced gratitude. Their future remained uncertain.

THIRTY-TWO

TOM ASH, chief judge of the Philadelphia Court of Common Pleas, addressed the membership.

"It's damn spooky, gentlemen. We have no backlog, and we can't fill all of our dockets."

So began a special meeting for the judges and judges pro tem, the lawyers who act as judges to help with the overcrowded court system. The tone and intensity of Tom's speech escalated.

"It's unprecedented! That's what it is! It's a disgrace! The dawn of the twenty-first century is here. We live in the greatest democracy the world has ever known, and our profession is under siege by a mass murderer. I can't understand it. It makes me sick! It's outrageous!"

A deep voice from the back of the room interrupted Tom from his ranting.

"It's like Shakespeare has come back to haunt us with his charge to kill all the lawyers."

The voice belonged to Andrew Byer, Tom Ash's nemesis, and one of the few defense attorneys to become a judge in Philadelphia. His legal decisions showed fairness to defense teams, unlike the rest of the judges who did all they could to help their pals, the plaintiffs' attorneys.

The judges identifying with the plaintiffs, the overabundance of lawyers, and the large pool of sympathetic jurors made Philadelphia the litigation capital of the world.

"Maybe Billy Boy was more perceptive than we'd like to admit, Tom," Andrew added, again referring to the Shakespeare admonition.

"Why don't you keep your disgusting opinions to yourself!" protested Carl Pearlman, the heir to the chief judge, after Tom Ash's expected retirement that year.

The "old boys' club" had a few thorns like Andrew, who excited them to incivility. Once engaged, he riled them as long as they played into his dialogue.

"Wake up, Carl! Look around you. Reputations and stereotypes have some truth as much as we may like to deny that fact. We need to change the system to get the people's respect."

"Look, Andrew," roared Carl, "this is still the best system anywhere."

"So that means we shouldn't fix its flaws?" countered Andrew. "I'm appalled at what the courts have become. Everybody is suing everybody. They have nothing to lose."

Carl, face flush with anger, jumped out of his chair. "Who's doing all of this suing? It's the same damn people complaining about the system. They're all whores, you self-righteous son of a bitch."

"No, Carl, everyone isn't prostituting themselves like you might like to think. All I know is I take the heat whenever anyone finds out I'm a lawyer, and worse yet when they find out I'm a judge of this fucked-up system.

"For too many lawyers out there, it's all about building bank accounts with this easy money. Gentlemen, these tainted dollars are now darkening all of our lives. Get used to it!"

"That's bullshit. Everyone loves the money we make. I set up a charitable foundation at my church, and they put me up on a pedestal. I won a ton of money for all sorts of people injured by doctors and faulty products. I'm a fucking hero."

"It's amazing how you believe such crap. I know a dozen doctors who left this state to practice elsewhere and another dozen who'll do everything they can to avoid treating a lawyer. And if they have to, they run tests on them till they glow in the dark to prevent second-guessing lawsuits. You just don't get it."

An awkward few seconds of silence settled on this room that played non-stop host to verbose combatants.

Tom had to regain control.

"Gentlemen, gentlemen, let's get back on point," he pleaded. "I want to present some facts. The number of active litigation cases has plummeted over the last six months. By settlements and outright withdrawals, we've lost all but a handful of cases that remain active. New cases just about dried up. What this slowdown means to all of us is some well-deserved vacation time, and you won't have the strain of court sessions lasting until five P.M.

"We must let the pro tem judges go. I'm sure that's music to your ears."

A rumbling surfaced in the room. The pro tem judges professed their discontent.

Hal Brenner jumped up, out of order, and shouted, "Maybe a few months ago we would have welcomed your offer but not now that our practices are folding. When you needed us, we were there for you. When you had cases piling up in the halls, you thought nothing of pulling us out of private practice, taking us away from the real money. Now you want to dump us. I don't think so. We'll sue the city over this, Tom!"

Andrew chuckled to himself. No one else in the room saw the irony of the threat or the self-serving motivation behind it.

"Hal, please, let's not overreact," said Tom, visibly upset. "I'm scheduled to meet with the attorney general in a special strategy session. They will end this nightmare.

"The count is now eighty-four. Most of the recent victims were no longer doing any advertising. It's like someone out there is going through last year's phone books looking for their next victim. Let's face it. The TV ads are non existent, and there are no more radio spots. I can't see this disaster going on much longer. I give it another six months, and it will be past us. And you know what I will do for you, Hal? I will pay for your televised ad, and I'll bask in the pleasure of seeing it every time it plays. It'll be well worth it."

Hal smiled and took his seat.

CHAPTER
THIRTY-THREE

AN IMPORTANT MEETING in Washington took place to deal with the ongoing murderous situation. Many important people in politics and law enforcement gathered to learn the latest in the ongoing investigations.

"Judge Tom Ash, I'd like you to meet Agent Cheryl Levin. Ms. Levin is with Justice. She's in charge of special investigations and reports to Janet Aims. And Mr. Ash, here, is Chief Judge of the Philadelphia Court of Common Pleas."

One of the young interns made this introduction. Tom never traveled in such circles and meeting the "who's who" of the Criminal Justice Department made him feel important. Being involved with the local city courts in Philadelphia meant he rubbed elbows with State members of the House of Representatives and State Senators when an occasion arose. The national political figures remained familiar faces many tables away at fund-raisers. Both groups preferred isolation, doing their own thing with their own agendas, but this event created an unprecedented union.

After a lull in the investigation's progress, leadership expected some important announcements, and anticipation filled the room with a buzz of excitement. Janet Aims entered the Great Hall of the

Justice Department and walked toward Tom. Having elevated his importance in his mind, he smiled, and thrust his hand in her direction.

"Hello there, I'm Tom—"

To Janet, Tom did not exist. She pushed away his extended hand as she passed through the crowd on her way to the podium. Her face appeared contorted and angst-filled. Darkness spread under her eyes as a visible reminder worry occupied her every waking moment.

The Grand Hall accommodated a sizable capacity, not like the small conference room meeting used for the earlier strategy session. This congregation included a multitude of members of the House of Representatives and Senators, the ranking Commerce Department staff along with their entourage of constituents, and all the representatives of the Justice Department involved in the investigation. Attendees included a large contingent from the FBI and many Secret Service agents.

The only group conspicuously absent was the press. As much as they tried to gain entrance, the pretense of national security barred them.

"The bad news is the body count. One hundred and sixty-four," Janet stated without introduction at the beginning of her update.

For those in the know, that tally conveyed terrible news. This number meant there were eleven new murders overnight.

Janet continued. "Rather than present the latest facts second-hand, I asked Special Agent Grey, heading up the investigation, to come down from his New York command center to fill us in on the latest."

A murmur of discontent from Grey's superiors followed her announcement. His appointment surprised them, and the favors he received from Aims became contentious. He maneuvered himself to the top of an investigation on several occasions.

Grey rode on the fast-track career path grounded in hard work and back door dealings. He walked to the podium. After placing a folder filled with papers in front of the microphone, he began his report.

"The coordinated efforts of the FBI and Secret Service have brought to light some interesting facts. We've determined we're dealing with approximately thirty-eight perpetrators. A deranged doctor on a personal vendetta carried out the first two murders. A new assailant carried out the next twelve cases."

Grey had no intention of revealing all of his theories. He wanted to solve the entire case with inside information he shared with no one. He continued.

"The deeds of this second murderer seemed to have set off the wave of copycat killings. We attribute thirty-five different copycat killers with each having two to four victims, the average being three. The biggest problem is assailant number thirty-eight. Here we seem to have a valid serial killer with forty-five homicides attributable to him alone.

"The good news we've all been waiting for is in just a matter of hours we plan to make an arrest. Through tireless efforts, we are on the brink of eliminating what has been the single most significant threat to our system of justice.

"One Osborne Judge appears to have committed all but the last of forty-six murders."

A distinguished looking suited gentleman approached the podium and whispered into Grey's ear. He smiled.

"Osborne Judge is now in custody!"

With the announcement, thunderous applause filled the hall. All in attendance stood for a resounding ovation. The handshaking and hugging would lead one to believe law enforcement rounded up all thirty-eight killers. Grey did not share their joy.

Tapping upon the live microphone to regain attention, he continued, "Let's not forget where we now stand." The room went silent. "Thirty-seven assassins remain unaccounted. In our favor is the fact that the MO shows a distinct two or three kills for each of these deranged copycats. Then they stop, never to act again. Our forensic psychiatrists are confident these represent isolated cases; cases of individuals making a statement or perhaps having a personal vendetta against attorneys who may have done them wrong, then calling it quits.

"Our people also expect the elimination of the multitude of tacky personal injury advertisements will help to mend the terrible reputations that have plagued all lawyers. Since litigation has pretty much stopped, it has afforded the public a break from such unfavorable news stories regarding multimillion-dollar awards to irresponsible people. On all fronts, this has been a good day."

Members of the gathering shouted questions as if at a press conference, but Grey picked up his folder and left the stage entertaining no inquiries.

Pleased by the report, Janet went back to the microphone.

"We'll break up into groups so we can analyze the statistics and brainstorm remedies to our plight based on your individual expertise. Those discussing commerce issues please go to room 119. The judicial panels will meet in this hall. Law enforcement will meet with me in my office. I thank you all and hope to see an end to this melee soon."

After Tom Ash and the chief judges from the ten largest metropolitan jurisdictions presented their statistical data, they had ample opportunity to develop ideas on ways to deal with the unforeseen overabundance of judges and the dearth of cases left for judgement.

THIRTY-FOUR

JANET AIMS TOOK a late flight to Los Angeles. She flew a military jet whose full-time crew was at her disposal by executive order from the President. He and his advisors spared no cost in efforts to solve the mass murders.

A young blonde flight officer trying to make conversation as he catered to Janet's every need presented in a most polite Southern drawl, "The word has it you going to announce a big break in the American Strangler case, ma'am."

After the first several months, the serial lawyer-killing phenomenon garnered a media name. They gave the assassin a title.

"That's right, young man, we have one culprit in custody, and we'll be putting an end to this national disgrace!"

"Ma'am, with all due respect, there's a lot of talk the national disgrace happened long before the American Strangler thing ever began."

"How can you say that, boy?" chided Aims, her tone condescending and abrasive.

The young officer responded, "Ma'am, the word on the street is things are getting better for the little guy."

"What in God's name are you talking about?"

"Ma'am, my sister lives in Philadelphia where all this started. Why, she's paying half as much for car insurance than she paid just last year. All the articles in the newspaper are talking about how if this goes on another year or two, the cost of health care, consumer goods, and most services will become affordable."

"Don't be naïve. The world doesn't work that way."

"Ma'am, the little guys' world works that way. He can't take part in the stock market gains or the upside of being a business owner in the good times. He can only engage in the markets priced by the policies of government and big business."

His logic and presentation sounded more sophisticated than his drawl let on. In obvious disgust, Janet picked up her magazine to let the young man know their conversation ended.

Brad Anderson, the top-ranking Justice Department attorney from the Los Angeles District Court, met Janet at 5:30 A.M. They entered the stately Secret Service limousine, the one reserved for presidential visits, and drove onto the highway.

"Ms. Aims, it's so nice to meet you finally."

"The pleasure is mine, Brad, and please call me Janet."

"Sure thing. We're heading to the Police Administration Building in downtown LA. We should be there in twenty minutes."

While traffic in Los Angeles made travel stressful for most, the police escort provided made the hour trip in fifteen minutes. A victory over the historic psychopathic phenomenon merited extreme accommodation to speed the process.

"Brad, the President expected us to make our announcement at the Federal Building. It's guaranteed to generate more media hoopla. Why are you putting this story on the local stage?"

"We haven't charged Mr. Judge with any federal crimes. His killings took place in the same city. In reality, this case is an LAPD matter," he explained.

"Do you mean to tell me, in the course of the investigation, you couldn't elevate his charges to the federal level?"

"No one told us to."

"You weren't told? Do we have to spell out everything?" she spewed in utter disgust. "This our most important case! What about the *denial of the victims' civil rights*? We use that charge all the time. It worked rather well against the cops acquitted in the Rodney King beating. It brought them to justice after they went free at their first trial."

"Janet, I have a problem with that approach. It twists the law to place people into double jeopardy."

"Brad, there are no truths in the law, just interpretations that can change, get twisted, reversed, or canceled based upon the needs of the times. If you don't understand that, you're in the wrong business.

"It shouldn't take much effort, just a little creative thinking for a team of prosecutors from the Justice Department to change the jurisdiction."

Brad lowered his head, ending eye contact with his unwelcome superior.

"You better get your act together," she added. "We'll make our announcement at the Police Administration Building for now, but I'll expect your team to have federal charges filed before the day ends."

He lifted his head, gave a cold stare, and replied, "Yes, ma'am, whatever you say."

Inside the Police Administration Building, a towering black man greeted Janet and Brad.

"Ms. Aims, this is Chief Simpson of the LAPD," said Brad. "He'll be standing by your side when you make your announcement of the arrest."

Janet shook his hand but dispensed with the amenities of

greeting.

"Gentlemen, this story has already leaked to just about everybody. Based on the FBI psychological profiles of the other perpetrators, they feel the show of authority now taking control is an important step in maintaining the present dormancy of the other killers. That's why we need to sound the trumpets for this official announcement today," explained Janet.

"I understand," said Brad. "Word came down from Washington before you arrived, so I can assure you we're well aware of the situation. Crowds have been forming all morning. There will be plenty of press."

Brad smiled gratuitously. He never liked the arrogant attorney general, and this experience confirmed his aversion, but he had to do her bidding.

A top brass officer entered the room and stepped to Chief Simpson.

"Sir, we seem to have a problem developing on the steps out front."

Instead of excusing himself to get briefed, the Chief was eager to move on. He knew the more sensational the press coverage, the more national exposure he could earn for the benefit of his future.

"What's up?" he shouted.

"Some protesters are arriving."

"Protesting what?" the Chief stated with annoyance in his voice.

"Well," he responded timidly, "they want us to let this guy, Judge, go."

"The problem we have today is no one is discreet, inhibited, or deterred from speaking out or protesting anything!" the Chief declared.

"Hey, it's the first amendment. That's what we swore to defend," Janet responded haughtily.

"I understand what the Chief is talking about," added Brad. "It's not the first amendment rights as much as it's the lack of dignity and respect. It's like letting the Klan or the Nazis spread hate under protection of the first amendment."

"Everyone has the right to protest. We live in America!" Janet stated boldly.

Chief Simpson looked at Brad, then to his watch, and said, "It's showtime! Put more men on the steps."

He motioned for the messenger to do his bidding.

They exited the ominous steel doors guarding the grand granite façade, where they happened upon an unprecedented wave of demonstrators. Rows of signs with messages that read, "Free Judge," "Osborne Judge Rules," and "The Strangler is hope for America," danced about in waves of protest.

The media members got jostled, and the apparent lack of crowd control now worried Chief Simpson. Turning to his lieutenant, he yelled, "This mob is more than *some* protesters, you fool. Deploy additional units. Get every available man down here."

Undeterred, Janet stepped to the podium decorated with microphones from every news service. The crowd erupted into massive jeering and booing. She cleared her throat, and to her expectation, the crowd quieted down to listen.

"From your reception, and the signs you wave about, I'm appalled."

Her scolding brought forth a roaring cheer followed by calm.

"You people have a right to protest, to speak your mind. I fight for that right. I, also, have that right, and I can tell you . . . you are a bunch of deplorable people!"

They chanted in unison, "Free Judge! Free Judge!"

At that moment, Chief Simpson's team lost control. From stage left, a glob of slime lobbed to the podium landed on Janet's tailored white suit. The look of shock and exasperation on her face caused Brad to laugh the laughter that denies courtesy when someone trips and falls and looks humorous. His laughter became uncontrollable, further insulting her.

Janet looked toward Brad and barked, "You insolent pig!"

She turned around to retreat from the podium and got slimed

again with the mass directed at her back. The crowd continued chanting and roared in approval as Janet walked away.

From out of nowhere, baton and shield-wielding riot police formed a barrier for the dignitaries, allowing them to get back into the building unscathed.

Once inside, Brad saw Janet crying with her head in her hands. He walked to her side, offered a handkerchief, and in a most sincere voice said, "I'm sorry! I didn't mean to laugh. It was rude. However, I'm sure you've been in a situation where you laughed . . ."

She blotted her tears and responded.

"I accept your apology, but that's not why I'm so upset. I can't believe these people. They're ready to defend a killer . . . a serial killer!"

"No, Miss Aims, it's deeper. They're ready to defend an end, and they're justifying the means to that end. You need to get a pulse on the mood of the nation. Your white tower in Washington is shielding you from the real world. The lawyers and politicians abused the system for a long time. The people got fed up and angry."

Janet responded as if she heard nothing Brad stated.

"I've got to get the details of this arrest report back to the President."

At the very least, she did not understand his caution. She blotted her eyes and runny nose, looked at her soiled suit with disdain, and walked away.

CHAPTER
THIRTY-FIVE

THE PRESIDENT and his advisors observed the mood of the people on live television. They responded, as did Janet Aims, with contempt and disdain.

"Animals! Fucking animals!" shouted Secretary of State Warren Anderson.

"They may be animals," responded the President, "but they have the right to vote, and about half of them do."

His political advisors understood this all too well, and they already figured out ways to distance the White House from the developing fiasco.

Sheldon Brooks, the President's chief strategist, presented his assessment.

"Jim, I've spoken with Janet by cellular, and I don't know how much help she'll be. She's been up for the past thirty-six hours and sounded half-coherent."

"Does she have anything to offer?" the President asked.

"Not really. We already received the interrogation transcript by secured transmission along with the video footage. I shouldn't have to remind you, the power brokers, all those personal injury attorneys who helped get you elected, are steaming mad. We all saw the grassroots display this morning. You will walk on eggshells at this press conference. Make everyone think you're on their side. Tell them whatever they want to hear and make excuses behind closed doors for the pronouncements they didn't want to hear," advised Brooks.

"This performance can become touchy. I don't want a wimpy opening in this speech. I've got to be in command," demanded the President.

"I couldn't agree more. Our best people wrote your speech, but the press is hot for this story. They will replay Janet being humiliated by that mob a hundred times before you go on. With your lack of support for tort reform over the years, this situation isn't good for you, but we worked on the wording the best we could. We ran it by Sam Rodman from the Trial Lawyers Association. We didn't want to rile his feathers, and he's all right with the content.

"You'll make no promises, ignore your record, and most important, give the appearance of concern that will lead to action. People buy it every time, and those who don't, they soon forget, they're in the minority, or they don't vote."

Brooks adjusted his tie and grumbled something inaudible, venting his disgust for the masses. He came from a middle-class home but moved up to the elite class by working the political system to his advantage. He couldn't care less for those folks he left from his past life.

A few hours before the press conference, Janet returned to the White House. They ushered her into the Oval Office looking beleaguered and feeling the same.

"Mr. President, I can't describe the horror of today's events. We would have never guessed—"

The President cut short her statement.

"Janet, maybe we've been listening to our colleagues, the insiders, too long. Maybe we haven't been spending enough time monitoring the mood out there. It'll be different now. At a press conference we control the environment. This office will not succumb to mob rule tonight!"

CHAPTER
THIRTY-SIX

THE PRESIDENT HURRIED into the staging area with the aura of a confident general entering the "war room." He greeted the press with a hearty, "Good evening!" He did not perform his usual perusal of the crowd, nor did he stop to shake hands and nod hellos. Though adept at schmoozing, he wanted his commander-in-chief persona to take precedent over elbow rubbing.

Arriving at the podium, he took his signature pose looking to the floor waiting for the room to settle. He cupped a hand to his mouth, cleared his throat, took a deep breath, and began with a statement.

"We're living in difficult times, confusing times, where right and wrong get reversed on occasion. The motive is often benevolent while the actions may be corrupt. Today's un-American display of vitriolic fervor by a mob was a prime example of misdirected patriotism, not unlike the sick actions of the depraved individuals among us who committed murderous acts. In a civilized society, we will not tolerate unlawful acts by criminals, nor the part of citizens involved in misguided deeds of violence."

He turned away from the microphone and cleared his throat once again. Beads of sweat formed on his brow, and he knew this appeared weak, but he refrained from using the tissue box at the podium.

"We must recognize the problems that led to these crimes. We need to understand the emotional support for such an embarrassing assault on the very institutions that make America the greatest country in the world. Our courts offer all people the opportunity to get redress, to right the wrongs, to make whole again. Our Department of Justice is not an institution up for radical change. Ours is not a system to alter without forethought and planning.

"In conjunction with the attorney general's office, we will work with Congress to develop a blueprint for modifications to make our system of justice . . ." He paused for emphasis. "Even more just."

The opening statement, while strong, made no concrete promises. Now, the members of the press looking for big promises responded.

No less than twenty correspondents crowding the pressroom called out, "Mr. President." The loudest voice got a response as usual.

Kate Bloom from the *Boston Globe*, the only woman baritone in her high school choir, received the nod. The voice did not fit her appearance. She looked somewhat asexual as a middle-aged, petite, homely woman sporting a short, conservative hairstyle that matched her unadorned outfit.

"Does this experience mean you'll support tort reform?" she asked.

"It figures. The first question, and the wolves are already looking for promises, real changes. He won't satisfy them with 'modifications,'" commented Sheldon Brooks to one loyalist standing on the side of the podium where they watched the proceedings.

Being a lawyer, the President knew well how to parry the assault with carefully chosen words.

"We will take the appropriate steps to see that the House and Senate have the initiative before them so they can debate the current system. As I stated, we cannot change the best legal system in the world without in-depth analysis."

Kate continued the attack. She had impeccable timing and began her next sortie before the other aggressive interrogators could enter the fray.

"I believe the American people are looking for some commitment. In the past, you vetoed legislation placing caps on injury awards and punitive damages. You vetoed all changes in the tort law that have come to your desk."

The President could not believe the actions of a few madmen raised arcane issues of law to the level of national conscience. It seemed the pent-up anger just needed a catalyst to become an explosive issue.

"Kitty," he said, looking directly at her, attempting to work the bonds he always strove for with the press. The President made it a point to know all of their names and what their friends called them. "Please don't push me into the corner on such an important issue."

He liked to put his "friends" on the defensive to attenuate the attack.

"We'll take a serious look at the issues and run with it."

Another robust voice took center stage.

"Mr. President, if we look at our ancestors across the sea in England, we find the loser in civil court matters has to accept some responsibility for the legal costs of his opponent. Fiscal risk would act as a deterrent to the unmerited, malicious, and frivolous lawsuits clogging our courts. It would reduce the billions of dollars in costs to all of us, and the emotional trauma to those ending up sued in court. Mr. President, are you aware that on a two-hundred-dollar high school football helmet, one hundred dollars of the cost is for the liability insurance needed to protect the manufacturer from lawsuits?"

The President detested Amos McDermott and would never call on him at press conferences. His piercing voice and pushy manner worked in concert as the only way he got to ask a question. An arch-conservative with the gift of being able to get in great points fast and furious, he frustrated the President.

"Amos, many of our ancestors left England for a better world, and I don't have to tell you what you can do with statistics."

Steve Freed, from the *Philadelphia News Corp*, jumped to his feet and forced his question.

"Mr. President, punitive damage awards can run into the millions and even billions of dollars. These incredible sums go beyond compensating the victims for all their losses, including pain and suffering. While they're meant to punish the perpetrators, they reward the lawyers to excess. How about some legislation that would take all the punitive awards and use them to cure cancer, feed the poor, or help make the world a better place instead of buying some lawyer his private island and jet plane?"

"It's not so simple, Steve. If there wasn't a big reward, the lawyers wouldn't have the funds to go tackle the big corporations."

The President countered all the questions. He selected the "just right" moment to excuse himself and walked away to the frenzied calls for more answers.

The press took over the next half-hour, doing a sensational job of beating up on the President in their post-press conference analysis. They addressed the real issues, armed with real statistics, and the President was no longer present to counter with evasive answers.

Tom Morris, a senior correspondent of ABC News, did a thorough discussion of the British tort system of shared responsibility. He countered the usual argument that if a loser has to pay legal fees, it blocks access to the courts for the poor. He offered a simple formula to let even the poorest pay what they could afford if they were to lose their case, still providing them with the ability to sue big corporations.

"This would get rid of the 'I have nothing to lose' attitude inundating the plaintiffs today," he said. "No more free ride. The lawyers would also be liable for some costs in frivolous cases. This responsibility would send a message to prevent all the wasteful cases draining the lifeblood of this country."

They presented a better case for legal reform than ever before in front of the American people at prime time. The press did a masterful job in presenting opponents of change, then having proponents destroy their arguments. Distinguished professors from prestigious law schools opined, as did retired judges and CEOs from major corporations.

When the CEO of Primary Pharmacia Corporation, Malcolm Lynch, reported on the shortage of DPT vaccination in years past because of the outrageous lawsuits, the magnitude of the message became apparent. As a crusader for tort reform, his impassioned statements unnerved the parents watching the discourse.

"Mr. Lynch, can you tell us what it was like before the era of vaccines?" asked Morris.

"It was terrible back then, Tom. The sickness, the suffering, the oft times fatal endings caused by such scourges as diphtheria, whooping cough, and tetanus had parents and doctors alike looking on as the children suffered extraordinary pain leading to the most heartbreaking end."

"How did it come to pass we nearly lost these lifesaving vaccinations?" Morris continued.

"Two out of one hundred thousand patients have severe reactions to these vaccines through no fault of the drug companies, yet lawyers developed the novel theory someone has to pay for all damages. They won these suits so often the vaccines neared extinction.

"Who would be stupid enough to continue making lifesaving drugs if in the process it risked destroying the company? Suicidal CEOs are far and few.

"If the laws didn't change to protect the drug companies like they eventually did, millions would have suffered to benefit the lawyers and the unfortunate few who had allergic reactions exploited by the greed of lawyers. They've created a doctrine in America that you must find someone to blame for acts of God."

"And how did the laws change, Mr. Lynch?"

"The solution was to set up a catastrophic loss fund to pay the unfortunate children who were injured by the DPT vaccination."

"And who pays for their suffering?" asked Morris.

"The public pays sixty dollars for each dose of vaccine that used to cost two dollars. Most of that cost goes to the catastrophic loss fund, and it took the lawyer's fee out of the equation. Now, all the money goes to help the injured party. This way it also provides equal compensation for each person injured. Before, the individual who had the clever lawyer and generous jury received a bigger cash settlement than someone with the same injury and circumstances but a lesser lawyer and less generous jury."

"You don't think the lawyers do what they do so well to make the world a better, safer place for everybody?" Morris asked.

"How ironic," mused Lynch. "The plaintiffs' attorneys are the most capitalistic sons of bitches on the planet, yet they use socialistic doctrine to get their capital from every deep pocket they can pick. Rather than creating a damn thing, they redistribute wealth, taking thirty to fifty percent along the way. The lawyers want it to appear under the guise of altruism. My opinion . . . it's unadulterated greed."

Malcolm Lynch became sought after for business seminars because of his ardor in attacking the archenemies of business.

Playing devil's advocate, Morris described the wretched existence of a child affected by a severe reaction to the DPT vaccine. He hoped to put Malcolm on the defense.

"That's the game they play," said Malcolm. "They use a touching argument to get sympathy for life's sad events, then blame someone. Any disease, accident, or drug reaction can cause tragic consequences for human existence. They use this tragedy to garner sympathy from jurors. They play upon emotion, which throws reason out the window. Sure, these kids suffer, but how would you like to pay them compensation out of your pocket, Tom?" he asked, placing the burden to answer into Morris's lap.

"Mr. Lynch, why that would be ridiculous. I had nothing to do with the injuries of these kids!" Morris replied.

"Well, neither did we!" Malcolm responded.

"Yet you and I and everyone watching tonight are paying! Sure, it's spread out, a few dollars here and there, but it's eating into our quality of life. Startup companies with fantastic ideas, new technologies, new drugs, and cures have to deal with such a quagmire of regulation and fear of lawsuits that many will never come to market. That's costing America plenty more than dollars!"

"Thank you, Mr. Lynch."

"Thank you, Tom."

Putting kids at risk always moved the American people into action. The White House knew it well. Those strategists in the Oval Office planned damage control as the special news report aired. The President and his close advisors watched as the press vilified the administration.

Reports from high-level cabinet officials and a few strategic leaks gave the appearance that action from the dictates of the President himself already began.

The President readied himself to leave the Oval Office, and addressed his staff one more time.

"From all of our sources, I expect this insane affair will now end. The capture of Judge and the ongoing investigation should stop the killings. Our top people have projections and psychological profiles pointing to a close. We've reached the peak of bad press tonight. We're now coming down the other side of the mountain. Just give it a few weeks. Let's get some sleep, ladies, and gentlemen."

The President rose from his chair with difficulty. He tried to hide the worry in his expression. Swollen pouches of bloated skin under his eyes showed evidence of the ongoing strain. He exited the Oval Office sporting the gait of a beleaguered soldier.

THIRTY-SEVEN

FOLLOWING HIS ENCOUNTERS WITH JILL, Ron found a renewed purpose to life. The sullen feelings he sported for too many months faded into a subconscious space, allowing him to do everything with more vitality. Even his dark side energized in the new light. He picked up his phone and dialed.

"I'd like an appointment to meet with Mr. Belman."

"Certainly, sir. May I have your name and number?"

"I'm Joseph Fairchild, and my number is 201-622-8551, but I'm rarely picking up because of personal matters."

Ron gave a carefully selected number to the secretary. It belonged to Fairchild Communications. By perusing the bankruptcy notices and making a few calls throughout the week, he found a company phone no longer answered but not yet disconnected.

"What's the nature of your business with Mr. Belman?"

"The city brought fraud charges against me for billings involving several contracts with them—"

"Hold, please."

Excitedly, and with purpose, the secretary acted. She knew a worthy case required setting up an appointment with haste.

"Mr. Belman, I have a new client on the phone. It's regarding fraud charges. He said the city is coming after him. I noticed you had nothing scheduled for this afternoon."

Belman's eyes lit up. He loved white-collar cases, especially where the government would be his adversary. It was a welcome break from his usual dealings with street thugs. The criminals he defended, and the nature of their crimes wore thin on his nerves. He feared a drug addict or an armed robbery client would turn on him. The fears became more tangible as the clients he attracted through referrals exhibited ever more sociopathic personalities.

Belman bonded rather well with the low-life culture because of his shtick, but he hated being near them. While they paid well, and often in cash, if he could find more respectable cases, he would climb out from under his rock.

When Belman defended a client against government fraud charges, it was a golden opportunity. The government, having unlimited funds to pursue fraud cases, allowed him to bill for a massive number of hours on behalf of clients feeling the wrath of Big Brother.

At the initial meeting he would learn if the client had the bankroll necessary to buy his time.

"Have him come over today at three."

"Sure thing, Mr. Belman."

Returning to the stranger on hold, she announced, "Mr. Fairchild, Mr. Belman can see you at three today."

"Is it possible to see him in the evening? Perhaps I could be his last appointment."

Ron did his homework, as usual. Belman always stayed late on Tuesdays. He would see one or two clients. His secretary, Marisa, left by six P.M. Belman exited no later than seven, escorted out by the last client.

Following a light dinner at the corner tavern, Belman would play racquetball at his private club until ten P.M. If Ron timed it right, he would never have to meet Marisa.

After a brief hold, during which time she made sure Belman would let Ron take the evening appointment, she came back on the line.

"Sure, Mr. Fairchild. Mr. Belman can see you on Tuesday evening at six-thirty. That's the fifteenth."

"I do believe that's the Ides of March," said Ron.

"If you say so," said the young secretary giving no significance to the date.

Belman worked out of a small but plush office. Ron arrived on time, walked up the four steps to the entrance, and grasped the brass handle of the majestic eight-foot mahogany door. It opened and closed with masterfully fitted, precision found in Old World craftsmanship from a bygone era.

When Ron entered the richly appointed reception area, he felt blood drain from his face. Unlike in the script he authored, instead of an empty office, two imposing toughs sat in stately, high-backed, leather chairs speaking to each other.

He didn't expect or want a challenge. After twelve assassinations, he left no physical evidence or witnesses to implicate him. The most any investigator got was his mode of operation. With nothing more concrete, the detectives remained baffled after each of his murders.

Turning around now would imprint a suspicious mental picture in the minds of these two characters. Ron was much aware of the forever intensifying FBI and Secret Service investigations. Thoughts of getting caught overwhelmed him.

The possibility these men represented a stakeout was slim. Ron recognized there were not enough resources to watch the tens of thousands of law offices all over the country. While the news accounts spoke of these surveillances, the chance of walking in on one was not likely.

Being a great judge of character and the consummate logistician, Ron decided these thugs did not belong in government employment. He ruled out the stakeout scenario with a reasonable level of comfort.

From the way they appeared and interacted, they looked more like the bodyguards of one of Belman's mob clients, still engaged in a meeting running late.

Ron felt intimidated as he took a seat across from the behemoths. Though they wore suits, he noticed massive underlying bodies. The bigger of the two had a scarred face, a large keloid on his left cheek extending from his ear across his sideburn to the corner of his mouth. The other man exhibited a broken nose that never received an appropriate setting.

I don't imagine the foes who placed their marks on these two inhabit this planet any longer, thought Ron as he assessed the situation.

Huge jaws and jutting forehead protuberances made their dark inset eyes look cold, almost evil. They both had small waists with thighs bulging from beneath trousers too tight for their bodies.

God, these muscle-bound goons look like they could run me down and tear me apart with little effort. What the hell can I do? I can't leave now.

In mid-thought, the door from the inner office clicked open. Behind the door, Ron saw a hallway lined with paintings in hand-carved gilded frames. The display of wealth stood everywhere, from the dense pile carpet to the elaborate sconces casting soft light upon the walls and custom tiled ceiling.

"Mr. Fairchild, won't you please come in?"

The friendly voice bellowed from the gregarious Mr. Belman. He held out his hand to welcome Ron.

Ron rose from his chair and stepped forward, not knowing what to expect or how to act. A disgustingly clammy paw swallowed Ron's hand in the greeting.

Belman was a large man of a genteel composition bound with more fat than muscle. He did not conform to the dictates suggesting a jacket and tie for business meetings. Instead, his wide-open collar revealed a soiled neckline. Sweat grew upon his brow and upper lip, and the underarms of his shirt displayed dark blue pools on wrinkled azure linen. Belman's disheveled appearance contrasted with his most stately office.

"It appears I'm early. I see you still have some clients ahead of me. I'll wait, or I can come back," Ron volunteered.

"Don't be silly. These thugs are no clients. Rick, Barney, say hello to Mr. Fairchild."

The two hulks nodded and offered courtesy smiles.

"These good fellows are my new bodyguards."

Belman laughed heartily, producing a grotesque snorting sound

.

"This American Strangler phantom got to me. Call it paranoia if you will. The Justice Department sent our profession a letter telling us our chances of becoming a victim are minuscule to allay our fears. The way I see it, Joe . . . Do you mind if I call you Joe?"

"No, no, not at all," said Ron.

"The way I see it, if you're the one in a million victim, it's one hundred percent for you. You're gone, and you're not coming back."

How repulsive coming from the guy who puts killers back on our streets, thought Ron.

Belman escorted Ron to the inner sanctum and motioned for him to take the plush client's chair. Ron recognized the Vasarely, Miró, Chagall, and Picasso paintings crowding the space behind the oversized desk.

How many murderers, drug dealers, and other assorted scumbags sat in this chair, gazed upon these walls covered with blood-stained trophies?

"Quite a collection, isn't it?" said Belman, noticing Ron's attention to the artwork. "These aren't the signed prints found in better galleries. These are original oils. Every painting here is worthy of hanging in museums. I don't like to collect anything but the best. If you don't buy quality, why buy at all?"

"They're impressive," replied Ron. "Just the other day I read a news report about how a prison established an art collection to provide the inmates with some culture. Maybe you could make a donation."

"Well, isn't that an irony," said Belman. "Instead of hanging murderers, they're hanging pictures."

Belman laughed and snorted once again while pointing to his artwork with pride.

"It just goes to show how far we've come in the world of law. We can keep just about anyone out of the gas chamber. That's even if we go to trial in a state that has the death penalty. Life in prison without parole? Not likely. I can get them an easier sentence. I can drag out their cases so long the witnesses either die or stop coming in to testify."

Ron wanted to jump out of his chair and tear out Belman's heart. He contained himself, knowing that heart would soon stop beating if he remained calm.

"Tell me about your problems, Joe. Let me see if I can help you."

Ron explained his concocted tale. It was so well constructed it hooked Belman in less than five minutes. He made his sales pitch chattering a mile a minute in his effort to have Ron contract his services.

As fast as Belman's mouth flapped, Ron's mind moved faster. He listened to nothing Belman said. He just nodded when appropriate. Ron had a plan and needed a diversion to set it into motion. It came about six minutes into Belman's pompous monologue.

Ron knew how Belman, like many lawyers, would use fear and the joy of having found a savior to clinch the relationship. Ron also expected that at some point Belman would rise from his seat, turn his back to him, and search for a text from the wall-to-wall books all lawyers sit in front of intimating their scholarly omnipotence.

He could not use Pepper spray this time. Rick and Barney might hear muffled shrieks or the sound of the big man falling to the floor. Strangulation was also out. Belman's hands were too large. Ron could not risk his grip failing, allowing Belman the opportunity to call out or fight back. In addition, his neck was so fat, Ron might not get to the vulnerable anatomy fast enough to silence the big guy.

For backup, Ron always had a piece of piano wire coiled in his coat pocket. It had a handle of steel on each end, producing a most grotesque weapon.

The moment to act came when Belman turned his back and retrieved a legal tome to explain his defense strategy. Ron leaped forward and, with the grace of a nimble athlete, wrapped the garrote around the thick neck of his prey. Ron spun around to position his back to Belman's. The tension on the wire produced bulging veins set to explode.

Having never executed this technique, Ron was not sure what to expect, but based on his vast knowledge of neck anatomy, he knew it would do the job.

In the first instant, he noticed the minimal resistance of the larynx. It produced a snapping sound as the wire severed cartilaginous rings. A simultaneous whooshing of air escaped, the last breath of air in Belman's lungs rushing from the space created by the wound. The extreme change in the pressure gradient emptied his chest with an unexpected hissing sound.

The severing of the carotid arteries and jugular veins was imperceptible from a tactile sense. Visually, it resulted in a display beyond anything Ron expected. Seven liters of Belman's blood sprayed over the room in a matter of forty-five seconds.

While the deluge of gore exploded, Ron felt the steel wire meet Belman's spinal column. This contact provided the perch from which Ron lifted Belman off the floor onto his back. Ron knew Belman would never again appear in any court of law.

Ron did not pause for a second as he lowered Belman and propped the body onto the high-backed chair. With great difficulty, he tried balancing the head to keep it from falling. Finally, out of frustration, he grabbed a ruler from Belman's desk drawer and inserted it into the neck and head to act as a binding rod. Ron essentially decapitated Belman if not for some fibrous spinal attachments.

Ron pushed the piano wire into his suit sleeve while maintaining a hold on one of the steel handles. He positioned his pepper spray into his belt loop back far enough to keep it concealed but ready for ease of draw.

Ron rushed into the reception room yelling, "He's gone berserk! He's crazy! He tried to kill me! Stop him! Please stop him!"

Covered in Belman's blood, Ron looked as if a madman attacked him.

The bigger guard rushed past Ron with his large caliber gun drawn. The smaller bull followed. As if rehearsed, Ron made a precise move to wrap the wire around Rick or Barney's neck; he knew not who. When the door closed, it turned out it was Barney who now rushed alone to Belman's aid in all the excitement. He never guessed his comrade laid on the reception room floor motionless and bleeding out.

***

Barney reached Belman's office and approached with caution. Seeing the motionless body covered in blood, he assumed Belman took his own life. He walked closer to check the carotid pulse for any sign of life. When his fingers fell into Belman's severed neck, it unnerved him. He jerked his hand from the grisly discovery, and Belman's head fell to the side, revealing the near decapitation.

Spooked by the gruesome encounter, Barney bolted from the room, never giving a thought about what happened to Rick. When he opened the massive door to the reception room, liquid fire pierced his eyes. He could neither draw breath nor could he exhale.

His gun fell to the floor, and he clutched at his burning face. Sounds of pain emerged as his vocal cords loosened, sounds that made no difference now that the others were dead.

With the skills of the surgeon he once was, Ron grabbed Barney's throat for the death grip. He never expected the resistance encountered. Strong hands reflexively grabbed Ron by his collar and whipped him around like a flimsy manikin. If Ron released his grip, Barney might recover from the pepper spray and defend himself unlike any other victim Ron encountered.

Holding on for his life, Ron tightened his clasp until he heard the cartilage snap, allowing him to finish off the writhing mass by folding the broken segment over the windpipe. Gasping for his breath and heart racing, Ron fell to the floor. He watched as Barney suffocated, and spasms of waning life ended.

After inspecting the scene for any chance of errors, Ron reeled with amazement, knowing he had taken out three formidable foes. His perverted sense of pride faded to shame. He fell to his knees and cried. He pondered how much longer he could perform in this manner? The grim possibility of capture or being killed set upon his rising thoughts. In a moment he regained his composure.

I can't wallow in self-pity and fear. How am I going to get out of here looking like a victim of Jack the Ripper?

Since Belman and Rick's clothes were no less blood-drenched than Ron's, the only option left was Barney's unscathed suit, at least five sizes too large. He struggled to remove it from the massive, lifeless form.

Ron stripped and washed with great care at the sink in the powder room. He donned the rubber gloves he kept with him to make sure he would leave no prints in the process of scouring the crime scene.

Ron located Belman's Mont Blanc fountain pen on his desk for show. He extruded ink onto his palms and smeared it over his face.

Upon his exit from the office, Ron glanced back into the reception area. He saw an Agam sculpture of Moses holding the sacred tablets.

What blasphemy! How could he own such a sacred symbol and have the gall to display it?

With pant legs and coat sleeves rolled up, Ron limped from the office looking the part of a downtrodden soul. His cover was so convincing a vagrant walked up to him and offered a sip from his bagged happiness. People walked by without glancing at Ron. How well he knew no one looks into the eyes of the homeless.

CHAPTER
THIRTY-EIGHT

PARANOIA PREYED upon Ron's psyche to a much greater extent than he expected. Around every corner he dreaded the peril of arrest. He understood the nature of the beast as a scientist, but it became a constant demon he had trouble suppressing. If he maintained control of his mind, he would be all right. However, letting delusion enter, a fall into the depths of despair would most certainly happen.

Ron fought with himself to castoff the obsessive and neurotic behaviors that become the seeds of tics and antics that draw attention, like Gary, who twitched incessantly. He tried to ignore the perceived sleuth lurking around every corner. He worked hard to stop thinking about the authorities who would assemble the parts to the puzzle that had Ron's itinerary branded upon its board of investigation.

Since the killings began, there was an abrupt silence in the lawyer advertisements aired on television and radio. They became a ghost of the once commercial successes feeding the profession.

During the last two weeks, a newcomer appeared on the airwaves, both brazen and bold in his promotions. He stated he would get his clients what they "deserve" from just about any injury imaginable. If you lived in New York City, you could not miss this offer to call for action.

The ads dressed billboards, buses, taxis, and all forms of media. They taunted Ron. Each time he heard this most irritating voice on the radio, it reminded him of the Mittenberg affair. All Ron's memories being at the mercy of Hill came back to haunt him. Ron wanted to end this campaign. In an odd manner of reasoning, he felt obligated to take action.

The eight hundred number broadcast in the advertisement seemed odd. Perhaps it belonged to a clearinghouse that funneled the callers to one of many personal injury attorneys who wanted to remain anonymous while open for business. This blatant display of advertising intrigued Ron.

Why would anyone wish to maintain such visibility considering the times? Perhaps they set a trap, the bait, to catch the American Strangler? I must find out.

"This is Mr. Dewey's office. How can I help you?"

"Yeah. Is this the lawyer's office I learned about on radio? If it is, I want to make an appointment to speak with Mr. Dewey."

"What is this matter regarding?"

"It's about a car accident."

"We can see you next Friday at four P.M."

"That's too soon. I'll be out of town until the fifteenth," said Ron, knowing he needed time to case the layout of the law office. He would take no chance of walking into a trap.

"How about the eighteenth at two P.M.?" the secretary offered.

"That sounds fine. I'll be meeting with Mr. Dewey. I don't want some underling to represent my interests here. The case isn't rock solid, so I need someone good."

"You don't have to worry. Mr. Dewey will be happy to meet with you."

"Great! I'll see you on the eighteenth."

Ron visited the address on the Upper East Side repeatedly over the following week. Clients entering the brownstone fortress never noticed the three plainclothes guards at the entrance, but to Ron, who surveilled the operation, it represented a well-protected environment. He understood why Dewey did not fear for his safety.

Concerned the stronghold could be a ruse, Ron wanted to use his appointment to inspect the inner sanctum of this mysterious law office rather than using the visit to kill Dewey. Once Ron learned the details of the operation, he would devise a plan to carry out the assassination.

On the eve of his appointment with Dewey, a bloated sky poured its fill, bringing a hazy dawn whose light never penetrated the clouded sky. The early morning darkness made Ron more melancholy than usual. He felt limited in his capacity to think and act in the way necessary for his mission.

Approaching the entrance, Ron saw the sophistication of the operation. Two of the plainclothes guards wore tiny surveillance earphones, mostly hidden by their hats. They appeared to announce arriving visitors to others within the compound.

Once inside the office, Ron realized it was a trap. About a dozen ordinary looking people sat in the crowded reception area. He assumed they were there to spell out their cases before the presumed personal injury attorney. Two men wearing hats sat in chairs strategically placed on each side of the entrance. They wore the same earphones as the men at the curbside.

Too late to leave without arousing suspicion, Ron reasoned he had nothing to fear. He had no weapon, and no one knew him. He would play along with the charade by telling his contrived story, then disappear.

The wait seemed endless for Ron, knowing he sat in the nest of captivity. His ever-growing guilt bred suspicion that the men seated at the door focused their interest on him alone. Surely the heavy pounding of his telltale heart would reveal his identity as a suspected killer if he did not regain control. Finally, it was his turn. A petite young lady called his alias.

"Mr. Royce, Mr. Dewey will see you now."

The young lady escorted Ron through the reception door, down a short hallway, and into an office with Dewey's brass nameplate fixed upon the door. Without saying a word, she motioned for him to take a seat.

Dewey sat with his back to Ron. After the attendant left the office and closed the door, an eerie silence ensued, lasting about twenty seconds. On safer grounds, Ron would have ordinarily broken the unexpected silence. Instead, he waited.

Without turning around, the voice from behind the chair spoke to him.

"I've been expecting you, Dr. Rellick."

As the chair rotated to face Ron, he saw Agent Grey dressed in an immaculately tailored suit. Every hair remained in place, heavily gelled, just as it had been on the first day they met back in Florida where the investigation of Mittenberg's murder began.

If standing, Ron would have collapsed upon the floor. Blood drained from his head, and he thought he would faint.

"Cat got your tongue, Doctor?"

"Hh ... how did you know?" Ron stammered with his lower lip quivering from shock.

"You may have fooled those city medical examiners, but forensics is a hobby to me. You made a little mistake. You almost got away with it too."

"What mistake?" asked Ron, now settling from the unexpected greeting.

"Whoever you placed at the bottom of the elevator shaft in Philadelphia had a shoddy, paste-filled root canal. You know, the kind they do in Europe. It just didn't figure a sophisticated surgeon would have anything like that in their mouth. Otherwise, you were damn meticulous. You had me fooled at first."

"So, it's all over unless I pull out a gun and shoot my way out," said Ron.

"Oh, it's over no matter how you look at it. You passed through our metal detector. You have no gun. There are five special agents out back and five more out front. You're at the end of the line, Dr. Rellick. But before I call them in . . ."

Grey held up his cell phone showing he could, at a moment's notice, call in the troops.

"I want to speak with you a bit. It's my hobby, you know."

"What can you possibly want from me they won't get at the interrogation to come?"

Unexpectedly, Grey slammed his hand upon the desk. Ron jumped.

"That's just it! The forensic guys will do the questioning, and I won't be any part of that story. You see, I'm great at catching scum like you, but they have other people for the interrogation they'll put you through. We all have our specialties, same as in medicine. So, I want the inside story. Who knows? Someday I'll write a book and retire on the royalties."

"Don't count on it. Got to be better stories out there," said Ron.

"What makes a good guy turn bad? Now that's a story," Grey stated.

"The system fucked me over," said Ron.

"Oh, please. Spare me. Lots of people get fucked by the system. That's no reason to go homicidal. Your crimes aren't like the lovelorn, estranged husbands who kill their wives and their lovers. Your story is about a professional man who has it all."

"Had it all."

"Come on, Dr. Rellick. You could have built it back. You had the means."

"Build it back so some other looter could take it again?"

Ron noticed a video camera mounted on the desk recording every word, presumably for Grey's personal file.

"I'm especially interested in the way you took out your victims. How you overpowered them so forcefully they couldn't fight back. We usually get some skin scrapings under their nails. Nothing, not a thing found. No physical evidence linking you to any of your victims. We found no signs of resistance, no blunt trauma injuries, just a simple wound to the throat. That surprised all of us."

"First it's the pepper spray. They needed their hands to clear their eyes. Then I had an open view of their throats. By grabbing the right spot, the victim wants to clutch at his throat to release the grip. Not being able to breathe produces a powerful survival instinct. By the time they tried to grab my hand, it was all over," explained Ron.

"So, they had no will to scratch, kick, or bite?"

"They had the will but not the time. It goes down fast. Once I cracked the throat cartilage, I could let go, and walk away. They suffocate. They had no chance to grab at my hand. Nothing would save them. At that point, it's an instant death sentence."

Grey stood and stepped behind Ron.

"I've studied many martial arts, and I've never heard of such a death grip. When I examined the victims, the bands of tissue in the larynx looked and felt the same. Tell me how you can find this cartilage so fast?"

Grey placed his hands around Ron's neck.

"Show me how to find the exact spot."

Ron reached up to engage Grey's hands. They seemed similar to those of a writer rather than a fighter.

"You count from the base of the neck, just above the collarbone," explained Ron as he lifted Agent Grey's hands to the exact spot.

In a sudden burst of speed, Ron leaped from his chair, spun around, and landed his hand upon Grey's neck. As expected, he tried to remove the grip.

"Listen close, Grey," Ron demanded. "Put your hands down, and I'll let you live."

Grey responded with immediate urgency knowing the deadly peril he faced.

"I will let you take in a small breath, so you won't have the urge to grab at my hand again. I know you can't resist if I deprive you for too long. Don't resist me, or I'll end your life as we stand here. Raise your left hand if you understand."

Fearful of an instant death, Grey complied most meekly.

"You will walk backward and step inside that closet. Remember, if you make the slightest move on me, I'll kill you."

They reached the closet, and Ron opened the door with his free hand. He removed one of the wire hangers and instructed Grey to place his hand inside the opening. With his grip at all times on the deadly target, Ron twisted the hanger around Grey's hand and over the closet rod, tying him in place and making his ability to defend futile.

"I'll deprive you of just enough oxygen to make you unconscious. When you wake up, in about ten minutes, I'll be out of your life, out of the country. Don't fight it."

Ron understood there was no way to abandon the instinct to survive. Standing to the side of a possible kick from Grey, Ron shut off his oxygen for three minutes and ten seconds. Death ensues in four minutes, even for the strongest. The strangle hold, as applied, would not kill Grey, but it would render him unconscious. Grey flailed around for the last minute before he fell limp, hanging from the closet rod by his bound hand.

Ron ran to Grey's desk and removed the memory disk from the recorder. He grabbed Grey's cell phone, pressed the intercom button, and muttered an unintelligible word. He got his answer from the other end of the line.

"What was that, Grey?" responded the agent receiving the call.

"It's him! He's gone out the back! Everyone, quick, out back!"

Ron jumped into the closet next to the unconscious Agent Grey and closed the door. He waited and listened. Two agents from the reception area charged through the door and continued to the back of the building.

Ron untwisted the hanger supporting Grey. He fell to the floor, improving blood flow to his brain. The reception area remained filled with clients waiting for their chance to reach the end of the rainbow. Ron walked by them and left the building the same way he entered.

THIRTY-NINE

OVER THE NEXT several months Ron expanded his master plan. He targeted for termination one high profile practitioner from each area of the law he thought destructive to American life. The press provided expanded coverage on each case against the wishes of the White House. Feuds between the media and the President became tactless. Outright hostilities erupted during Presidential press conferences. Copycat killers, again replicating the frenzied news reports, resulted in a total body count approaching two hundred.

The class action specialists lost Carl Bergman. His expertise and tactics weakened, and many times bankrupted highly capitalized companies. Carl's raids typically resulted in meager compensation for each of the thousands of members of the class looking for redress from the behemoth industrial giants while his firm raked in huge fees for their efforts. The many people who lost jobs when these industrial giants went out of business became the forgotten victims left in the wake of legal redress.

After each act of elimination, Ron returned to his home base in New York. Having no one to discuss his missions while away, Ron visited the local tavern knowing he'd find Gary, the ultimate fan of the American Strangler phenomenon.

Looking the part of a displaced loner, Gary stared into his morning drink. Upon seeing Ron, his signature twitch awakened, and he smiled.

"How about that last case?" Gary announced.

To dispel any suspicion, Ron played dumb.

"So many killings taking place, I can't keep track. What last case are you talking about?"

"The murder of the big-time sexual harassment lawyer. You know. It was in the news the other day."

"Oh, you're talking about the whore who ruined workplace courting. That jerk and all the rest of them, they're exploiters. Now everyone is ready to sue their bosses and coworkers for sexual harassment. And as usual, the laws were so poorly thought out they're filling the courts with bullshit cases."

Gary nodded in agreement. He always agreed with Ron.

Following Ron's foray into the sexual harassment arena, those suits all but disappeared. The litigation withered away in sharp contrast to the previous year.

At the bar, Ron basked in delight as Gary heralded the American Strangler update. To Gary, the killer was a hero. While everyone heard about the copycat killers, Gary preferred to think of the perpetrator as some omniscient being responsible for all the killings. He found joy in equating the perpetrator to a phantom that could be anywhere, anytime, all the time. Every related story on the news saw Gary transfixed, hostage to the message. His twitch sped up as any related story unfolded, reaching a crescendo by its completion.

"Ron, Ron, in war, people die. Innocent people die, Ron. The ends justify the means, Ron. Look around, for Christ's sake. There's a change in the air. It's here, Ron . . . the dawn of a new era."

Gary's passionate embrace of the homicides troubled Ron. He worried Gary would draw attention to both of them, or worse yet, Gary would act out his fantasy and somehow implicate him too.

"Calm down, for Christ's sake! Someone will hear you, and they'll think you're the killer."

"That's fine with me, Ron. I'd be damn proud to be that fuckin' guy . . . to walk in his shoes.

"Ron, look what happened. Around two hundred people died, and the country's a better place. We save billions of dollars for noble purposes. People's lives improved. The scales of justice evened out. We have fewer innocent victims of violent crime. The predator can no longer rely on a lawyer to keep him out of jail.

"Every night the news reports show how America has transformed. How many people died in past wars in the name of American interests? Soldiers died on many fields of honor to protect our interests. For democracy and freedom, we've lost countless heroes. So, what if we sacrifice two hundred people to make it better for all of us? Even if they were an innocent two hundred, same as the innocence of soldiers at battle, it'd still be worth it. But this is no innocent group. We're talking greed, pure unadulterated, self-serving greed, and they have to pay the ultimate price."

Ron understood Gary, and as his rant danced on, filled with the rapture of a madman, Ron lapsed into one of his periods of isolated thought.

Life is strange. How did I get here? How did I become what I've become? Whatever happened to the concept of community? It was an earlier age. I never lived it, but I read about it.

It was a time when villages and towns were small, a time when there was a sense of communal membership. People understood and lived personal_responsibility. It was a time when everyone in the towns and villages knew each other. That kind of living could never foster the savage hostilities that plague the world today.

Clergy, the elders, or the town sheriff resolved conflict, unlike today where the clergy and police are suspect; where the elders get cast as inept burdens instead of learned leaders filled with experience and wisdom.

The sense of community vanished long ago. Oh, maybe it still exists in small towns far outside the borders of the stinking, decayed cities. But for most of us, it's gone.

Ron's thoughts faded, and his mind returned to the smoky bar as the volume of Gary's words escalated and came back into focus. Ron's life seemed under the control of some master plan played out, complete with an alter ego, in Gary, whose words represented those sentiments Ron believed and acted upon but hid from public view.

"They mold society like clay with a force bent on destroying its structure and stability. The foundations of our society have been rotting much too long, attacked by the greed of lawyers.

"Do you understand me, Ron? It's time for change. You know our leaders can't do it. Most of them are lawyers.

"Too many vested interests perpetuate the decline. They let evil run us into the ground, consuming themselves in the process. Like the blind, they can't see what's happening. It takes a radical solution to solve a radical problem!"

"Gary, I know what you're feeling. Don't get upset. You'll get sick. I have to run. It's late."

Ron stood, and Gary rose in unison. He hugged Ron and patted him on the back. Ron glanced around to see if anyone saw them embrace. The members of the crowd remained too wrapped up in their personal moments to notice two odd mates blending into the smoke-filled chaos of life.

Ron patted Gary on the back again and repeated, "Don't work yourself up, man!"

"You're my only friend, Ron; you and the stranger changing the world."

"Right, Gary."

Suddenly the twitch stopped, and Gary's eyes began an ascent whereupon they hid under his upper lids.

"Are you okay, Gary?"

"I need some air. It's getting hot in this shit hole."

"Sure, come on. We'll get some air."

Ron struggled to hold Gary by his arm as he stumbled about while escorted to the street.

"Thanks, pal. I think I'll be getting home now."

Ron released his grip only to see Gary lose his balance and stagger forward.

"I think you'll need a little help to get home tonight."

"I'll be okay," insisted Gary.

"Like hell! Where are we headed?"

Gary handed Ron his key and told him the address. They walked toward the seedy side of the Village, past Avenue D. The stench of trash lining the streets, not yet collected, filled the air. Gary began stammering and spoke in a disjointed demonic voice.

"I was lured to the dark city, and I met the foul creature. But now . . . but now I swim the waters of Acheron to escape his hold on me."

"What on earth are you talking about?" asked Ron, worried about the immediate sanity of his friend.

"I tell you, I swim in the waters of Acheron. He can hold me no more. By tomorrow he releases me from his grip."

"Get a hold of yourself," Ron demanded with a sense of urgency.

Ron worried that Gary entered a psychotic episode with the potential of becoming lost forever. He walked him up the stairs to his tenement with great difficulty. Gary stumbled repeatedly and barely maintained his balance.

A display of utter disarray met them upon opening the door to Gary's apartment. Magazines, newspapers, tabloids, and paper plates with leftovers rotting in place scattered everywhere. A musty smell of the aged hung heavy in the air.

Ron helped Gary over to the bed where he let him collapse onto his back. He lay there motionless, each breath a strained labor.

Ron walked to the paper-strewn desk. In the middle of the clutter he saw a purple velvet box lined with satin. It housed the medal Gary often wore on the lapel of his overcoat. It was a Purple Heart awarded to those injured in battle.

Near the box sat a letter from the War Department, commending Gary for service to his country. Next to this letter he found a parchment document describing Gary's heroism for which he received a Silver Star.

It read, "In recognition of bravery, on June third, nineteen hundred and sixty-five, for having exposed himself to the line of enemy fire to rescue five members of "A" Company, Gary Saxon I hereby award the Silver Star . . ."

President Lyndon Baines Johnson signed the document.

Stacked alongside the medals sat every news clippings concerning the American Strangler killings. Each article had the name of the attorney-victim highlighted in yellow marker.

Under the news articles, Ron saw several military documents revealing that Gary trained as an expert in using explosives. On the wall above the desk hung a picture showing the front of the ACLU Manhattan headquarters. Next to the photograph, drawn in pen, sat a detailed schematic of a bomb. It described a rather simple plan to blow up the building dated for the next morning.

Ron never guessed his meek friend was a war hero. He picked up the Silver Star and admired what it represented, the highest form of self-sacrifice.

Unexpectedly, gasping for air, Gary struggled to sit.

"Ron! Ron!"

Startled by the call of his name and guilty for the indiscreet invasion into Gary's secret life, Ron dropped the medal and ran to Gary's side. Gary fell back and was silent. He stopped breathing. Ron searched for his pulse and knew Gary would breathe no more.

For an hour, Ron searched through the apartment gathering all evidence that Gary had sympathy for the American Strangler and engineered the bombing scheduled for the next day at the ACLU headquarters.

By hiding Gary's intentions and plan, it made him an unknown soldier in the army of the American Strangler. Ron lifted the Silver Star from the floor, placed it in Gary's clenched fist, and walked into the night.

The streets appeared darker than usual. A misty drizzle hugged Ron's face, making it impossible to feel the tears falling from his eyes. His teeth chattered. Ron experienced a profound, irreplaceable loss with the death of his friend. The darkness of his deeds stood before him.

CHAPTER
FORTY

"THIS BREAKING STORY . . . An explosion occurred at the New York headquarters of the American Civil Liberties Union in midtown Manhattan. After confirmation of eighteen deaths in the receiving area, they discovered many more fatalities inside the building. We await a final count. In a sad coincidence, last night many people populated the usually quiet headquarters hosting a strategy seminar concerning the American Strangler phenomenon gripping the country. Authorities want to determine if a connection exists between—"

The television screen blackened. The remote control landed hard on the desk.

"Just what we need now . . . utter chaos. Politically, the world is caving in on you, Jim. I wish I had the power to shore up the walls, but we can't seem to control the forces behind this plot."

Such was Maxwell Houston's assessment. He was President Jim Howard's most trusted advisor and confidant. They met at Stanford, where they spent their college days together, walked in each other's footsteps, and forged a bond of trust, mutual admiration, and a mirrored ideology. After Maxwell graduated number one and Jim number forty from Harvard Law School, they vowed to be a team. They hoped they could make a significant impact on the world by working together. Jim had the charisma, and Maxwell had the gray matter. He was brilliant.

"Max, I've always counted on you to pull me through. You pick me up when I fall. What can you do for me?" he pleaded with his dear friend.

"The situation deteriorated more than any of the pundits predicted," said Maxwell. "The copycat killings are spreading. A new wave of vigilantism has gripped the country. Jim, there are at least seven-hundred killings linked to these self-ordained protectors of the civilized world.

"It's not just the lawyers they're going after today. The latest report from the FBI tells us these misguided vigilantes now number over six hundred."

Staring out of the window with his back to Maxwell, Jim responded with a glaring tone of repulsion in his voice, "They're all going crazy. It has to be some mass psychosis taking place. Now I sound foolish for even mentioning such a thing."

Without commenting on the mental condition of the populous nor his friend, Maxwell continued, "These daily executions have exhausted our forces on the federal level. The FBI and Secret Service most often work in teams of agents on one case. They're now spread so thin, some sloppy killers evade capture by default.

"Come here, Jim," begged Maxwell. "I have to show you this video. Our people sent it down from Philadelphia. It's their uncut local news footage."

A whiny reporter performed the obligate setup for an event that already took place. She stood in front of her camera crew wearing an expensive, conservatively appointed suit. After clearing her throat, she began her story.

"It's not limited to lawyers anymore. The self-righteous are out to eliminate the cancers of a democracy run amok.

"Community members, fed up with not being able to walk in their streets, slaughtered several hundred gang members all around the nation. At first, authorities couldn't distinguish between the gang members killing one another and the new wave of vigilantes. It didn't take long to figure it out when police arrested a bold, defiant black man today in the Hunting Park section of Philadelphia's inner city. He claimed membership as a 'soldier in the People's Army,'"

The camera shifted to footage of the event played out just moments earlier. The police marched the elderly gentleman away in handcuffs, and the media pushed through the crowd to stage their traditional impromptu press conference.

"Why did you kill that young man in cold blood?" shouted the woman reporter whose local television news clip led the story.

The bent, frail man had leathery skin weathered by many years of a hard life. He sauntered slowly, sliding his feet over the ground, too weak to lift them. The question encouraged him to stop and turn to the young reporter.

"The constitution guarantees every American freedom, justice, and the pursuit of happiness. Don't it?" he snapped rhetorically.

"Why, I can't walk down my gosh darn street wit out da fear of being shot, or beat, or robbed. I be seein' da youngin gittin' kilt right outside my door. Damn gangs be killin' mo brothers than da Klan ever did.

"Life here ain't no freedom! We be better off when we be slaves. You go an ask da dead, if you can, and they tell ya. They be better off as slaves than as dead folk.

"Well, I done my part. I'm makin' a change here on my street. There won't be a child whoring for a master living in the blood of their veins. There won't be a slave master holding the white powdered whip on this here block.

"I won't accept a child's home in a cheap wooden box for all of time ever more. That nigger ain't gonna sell no smack to folks on my block no mo. He wit the devil now, where he belong. He ain't gonna shoot no one, no mo."

The camera panned the crowd of neighbors gathered to cheer as the detectives hauled Ben Johnson away in the waiting police wagon.

Maxwell stopped the video. They sat in silence. It was apparent this man belonged to a dying breed. A brighter, better time saw the rearing of Ben Johnson. Though his English was fraught with blunders, there was not a curse in his choice of words. His parents taught him better. They taught him respect. They taught him values. He was a God-fearing man who took the adage "an eye for an eye" as a means of survival. Ben Johnson taught his children the same.

"Jim, the drug gangs realize it's open season on them. They don't know who's coming for them next. It can be their enemies, the cops or the guerrilla-style vigilante eliminating anyone with an attitude.

"It's suddenly a liability to look tough. Drug dealers get killed at three times the usual rate. We no longer see kids standing on the corner for five hundred bucks a day selling dope. School has become a better, safer place for them. We're finally winning the war on drugs.

"Even the homeless have become targets. We see vagrancy and loitering starting to disappear. Beggars are no longer eyesores of the city streets. The storefronts and street vents have lost their allure as urban boudoirs. American cities stopped their descent into the ranks of the third world. The smell of urine no longer fills the subway concourses."

Jim looked into his friend's eyes and asked seriously, "You can't tell me you condone what's going on here, can you?"

"Of course, I don't condone what's going on. But it's interesting how it takes Draconian methods to change certain behaviors, yet a taboo-driven movement can change the landscape overnight. Behavior is suddenly modified for one reason."

"And what's that?" Jim said skeptically.

"The fear of retribution."

"We can't become Singapore, where they fine and flog their people for spitting in the street," Jim shouted. "This is America, and people have rights. I'll not take them away, and I won't let this

Strangler, this movement, take them away either. I have a plan to end this nightmare."

"You do?" asked Maxwell, revealing surprise in his voice and facial gesture.

"I do," Jim replied with a tone of authority. "I have a plan. I hoped you would come up with something better, but it looks like you're at your wits' end. My plan will break some rules. You are my dearest friend and chief counsel. I'll need your help to isolate me from any repercussions."

"What are you talking about, Jim?"

"I'm saying it's time to change the way we're handling the investigation. You must be the one who's officially in charge. If anything goes wrong, you'll take the fall."

"You know I'd do anything for you. I'm here to insulate your office."

"Are you sure, Max?"

"Cut the shit and fill me in!"

"In a few moments we'll meet with a fellow named Joe."

"Joe who?"

"It's just Joe. GI Joe, for all I know! That's all anyone knows of his identity. He's CIA. He's in charge of covert operations and will head up a unit operating outside of the realm of constitutional law. Once I give him the green light, he goes to work."

"What do you mean, outside the realm of constitutional law?" asked Maxwell with caution.

"Once I give you the details, we never spoke about this matter."

"Sure," Max said as he crossed his heart and put his finger to his lips

"This Joe, briefed me before, and he needs the green light to begin."

"Begin what?"

Jim's voice lowered, and he looked around the room while he spoke. Since no recordings took place in the Oval Office without the President's knowledge, his furtive behavior was guilt-driven.

"To proceed to a level one mission. The green light gives Joe the license to do whatever it takes to get rid of the perpetrators, the so-called American Stranglers. Many times his methods avoid due process. He's the mop-up man, the fixer. Without all the constraints, rules, regulations, laws, and loopholes a democracy affords the innocent who don't need them and the guilty who do, Joe will end our collective nightmare."

"You've got to be kidding me, or you've gone crazy," Maxwell said. "I can see it now. He'll fuck up, get caught, and I'll end up in Leavenworth."

"You don't understand. This guy is ready to die for his country. He's a real company man who'd never disgrace nor betray his superiors. Joe is the heart of the agency. We can trust him," explained Jim.

Maxwell stood in disbelief, waiting to hear the rest of the details.

The President summoned Joe into the Oval Office to spell out his plans. He entered with aggressive confidence in each step of his militaristic advance. Meeting the President did nothing to diminish his stature. He met with many Presidents.

Professional in every manner, from his obligation to salute the Commander-in-Chief to the friendly handshake he offered Maxwell, he waited for an invitation to take a seat.

Joe's smooth, unblemished skin pressed taut to the underlying bony structure of his face. Loose flesh beneath his neck revealed the only sign of a man older than realized on first impression. His comfort in the presence of powerful men signaled the sign of an experienced negotiator. He was rugged, handsome, and solidly built. Dark short-cropped hair contrasted with his light blue eyes. They were especially noticeable, making disengagement difficult and awkward upon first introduction.

"Joe, I told you I would proceed with your plan after consulting with my chief of staff, Mr. Houston. This meeting today never happened as far as anyone knows."

Joe smiled and asked, "What meeting? I'm in Algeria as we speak."

"If this mission ever fails, I never gave the order. If you need cover, Mr. Houston will take the heat along with you. That's what I understand you require based on our last meeting."

"That's correct," Joe responded.

The President smiled at Max and said, "I believe we can do business with this guy."

"I'd need some details first since I missed the meeting you two had without me," Max said with an uncommon suspicion in his voice.

Without hesitation and to avoid any waste of time on political discourse, Joe began his explanation.

"What we do in our sector is highly secretive. Only a select few of us share in the knowledge of our operations. You will get little or no briefing once I walk out of this door. The job *will* get done. You may, or may not, recognize what we do to accomplish our objective by the news reports you hear, but the job will get done. It *always* gets done."

Maxwell interrupted, "The President tells me you work outside the realm of the constitution. I don't mean to sound naive, but is there any way you can stick to the guidelines of the game? We want to preserve the rule of law."

"Sir, I *am* what preserves democracy. It's been men like me throughout the history of this country who tweak the laws, when needed, to maintain our freedoms. It may not sound kind. You may not appreciate what I'm saying, but people are animals. The way you maintain control in any society is through totalitarianism or through a controlled democracy. We, sir, are a controlled democracy."

Maxwell became visibly upset by this revelation espoused by a member of the most secretive unit of government.

"Controlled democracy. How can you say that?" said Maxwell tersely.

Joe did not wait for him to finish his thoughts. He attacked.

"It's inappropriate for me to reveal details of past operations. Just know, when someone or something gets too big and threatens our way of life, we have to neutralize their influences. It's ironic that this Strangler phenomenon works much as we do; only we're subtler . . . covert, if you will.

"It's come to our attention the American Strangler problem isn't being resolved through usual channels. The President called *me*, and here I am. If you're not ready for my services, I shall leave until I'm needed. We only act on orders from the top, never independently. Though, I can say there've been times we would love to have moved on our own. There are even times we would prefer to turn down a mission; however, it's not for us to decide."

The President, sensing the need to defuse an ideology conflict, intervened.

"Joe, please understand, in our administration, we haven't come upon this kind of national emergency. It is, in fact, unprecedented . . . hard to swallow. We need to take back our country. That's why I called for you. Now, please explain the plan to Mr. Houston so he may better appreciate what you do."

"It's rather simple. We've always had tremendous resources we could devote to the elimination of the perpetrators of the killings, but restraints kept us idle. Once we get the go ahead, due process no longer binds our hands. We have an extensive investigative network. We create our witnesses, search warrants, and juries when needed. We can work in one of two realms. We can capture the perpetrators and send them through the courts, *our* courts," he said with emphasis, "or we can take no prisoners unless the arrests have relevance as a deterrent."

"You mean you kill the killers?" asked Maxwell.

"That's just what I mean. We profile the assassins and wait for them to make the slightest mistake. The press will be oblivious to any new murders whenever we get to the scene before them. The country will stop reading and hearing about these phantom killers, and soon enough it goes away. Some innocent people may get killed in the actions we take. It's a cost often hard to bear, not unlike soldiers dying in battle to preserve our way of life."

"How do we call it off if needed," asked Maxwell.

"After the ball's rolling, it's hard to stop an operation like this. There are operatives who, once activated, become rather inaccessible. It can take days, even weeks, to halt activities. Please, gentlemen, if you're not ready to commit, let me leave now."

The President stood tall with a look of determination and declared, "I'm ready to commit. Let's do it, and put this bad dream behind us. Kill the sons of bitches."

Maxwell slapped his hand to the table and declared, "Jim, we can't become the vigilantes. You wanted a solution. Joe isn't the solution. I understand your frustrations, but it isn't proper this way. Maybe we could take the lesser of the evils. You know, take the captives through the courts."

The President turned to Joe and asked, "What's your take? You presented the two options, but you didn't mention which you preferred."

"You called me in to do your bidding. I'm the specialist. You want this matter closed," said Joe, staring deeply into the President's eyes. "If you let them drag their cases through the courts, you'll have a media circus. The next thing you'll see will be more psychos looking for their fifteen minutes of fame. If you need more time, I can come back when you're ready."

"No!" said the President. "We're ready. Well, there you have it, Maxwell, two votes to one. We've maintained our democracy after all. Joe will do it the right way."

"Jim, I'm your advisor and most trusted confidant. I would never expect you to take my advice unconditionally. Overriding the constitution is difficult, and I have to respect your view, though contrary to what I think. I'll always back you."

Joe rose from his chair and stretched his hand out to the President. They shook, and neither uttered another word. Joe nodded to Maxwell without offering his hand, walked to the door, and left.

"Men like him change history all around the world," the President stated boldly. "He was calm, confident, and convincing. I know things will turn around. It's just a matter of time. I feel good about this plan. We will get the upper hand now. I feel much better."

Maxwell looked to the floor, shook his head, and did not respond.

CHAPTER
FORTY-ONE

THE CAREFULLY PLANNED, sophisticated, implosive attack on the ACLU headquarters caused no injuries or damage to anyone outside the building or to any of the surrounding structures. Because the meeting dealing with the American Strangler took place inside the facility, over fifty people perished as collateral damage. The demolition process after the bombing involved long and tedious hours. A clear expert with explosives, Gary's post mortem deed proved his prowess and dedication to cause. News reports showed the FBI wanted to locate and interview past military demolition experts as probable suspects based on the forensic evidence.

A few nights after Gary's posthumous act, Ron walked by the cordoned-off site where police officers stood guard. He now understood Gary's reference to being released from the grip of the devil. Gary finally escaped from the torment plaguing his soul. He destroyed the symbol that, for him, represented the abuse of the freedoms for which he risked his life on the battlefield.

Ron walked on without motive, thinking more about Gary and his past, when two young gangster types approached. They stood tall at around six two, one thin and agile, the other stocky, bordering on fat. They wore low hanging pants, sported short dreads and walked with an arrogance announcing they owned the street.

The police had long ignored this thuggery, knowing they could do nothing. Authorities construed all edicts and efforts of aggressive policing to keep bad players in check as acts designed to deprive civil rights. This ploy helped make the streets ever more dangerous.

With intent, the two thugs moved to block Ron's passage. He moved left. They moved left. He stepped back. They moved forward.

I can't afford to have attention drawn to me. I can't end up in the hospital from the beating these creeps are about to give me, Ron pondered. *Perhaps I can talk my way out of this confrontation.*

"Look, fellas, I don't have no money, no jewelry. I don't want any trouble. Just let me pass."

"He don't want no trouble. Who wants trouble, man?" responded the thin guy.

"Yeah, man, he don't seem to know you and me *be* the trouble he don't want," said the thick one as he grabbed at his crotch twice to show dominance.

They snickered at the sense that they created some profound street poetry. It did not amuse Ron, but he dare not say another word, realizing any aggressive confrontation would put his anonymity at risk. He took a long stride to the right to maneuver about when the lanky one grabbed Ron's collar and pulled him to his knees.

Unexpectedly, Ron gripped the thug's throat in the same manner used for each strangulation. Immobilized and unable to speak, the goon fell beside Ron, arms flailing.

His friend reacted to offer aid, but too late to help. Ron knew the death grip completed the task, even once released. The victim clawed at his throat, though no effort would help by any means.

The unchecked gangster grabbed Ron by his shoulders and met the same rapid response. Both young men lay dying, and after a brief four minutes, they moved no more.

Shaken and feeling the effects of adrenalin released during the encounter left Ron trembling and light-headed. He wondered what essence made people so cruel. It seemed beyond adolescent behavior, more like some addiction to sadistic cravings living in the hearts of persons sporting bad will. It made no sense, but he recognized that joy in hurting and controlling others endured in many places and at many times throughout history.

Ron walked on, distressed, now pondering Gary's explanation of war as he headed back to his room. When stepping off the next curb, an impending sense of doom came upon him. He did not know if a peripheral vision or a prophetic vision caused him to turn and face the black demon bearing down upon him. A weathered old sedan moved fast, making no attempt to stop or avoid hitting him.

In the glaring headlights, he saw the angel of death about to choose its mark and strike. Losing his balance to avoid the fatal step into the street, Ron twisted his body and fell to the ground, grabbing at the coarse cement, attempting a crawl to safety. He could not move. The skin from his fingers shredded deep to the bone, though without pain, as he became numb from shock and in anticipation of crushing injury. Instead, a gush of air brushed his trouser cuffs, offering reprieve as the car raced by inches from his legs.

What saved me?

The horrid vision of flattening against the car grille, thrown into the air, landing hard and contorted presented Ron with an awareness of life's frailty. He questioned his very existence.

Was this a sign from God, my God, who watches over us all? Was this the omnipotent hand that can pluck us from life or spare us for some purpose obscure to mortals? Could there be a God who meddles in our affairs?

Though not religious, Ron always believed in a Supreme Being. This incident forced him to think about his relationship with God, now ever more alive in his mind.

How could You let me do what I've done? You give us free will. I did what I did through my free will. But couldn't You destroy me? Was that car meant for me?

Plenty of people throughout history were worse than me. What about the devil's children like Hitler, Stalin? Why were they spared long enough to wreak havoc upon the earth? Where was their step off a curb into oblivion? Were they and am I your agent doing some necessary deed?

Who am I to question Your ways? Am I not like the child who can't comprehend the punishment dealt out by a loving parent? Were the tormentors of humanity your angels, or were they the agents of Lucifer?

Terrible as Ron acted, committing wholesale murder, he could not fathom that he was a bad man. All the years he helped people seemed trivial and senseless considering the unprecedented grief brought to the lives of so many individuals by greedy, dangerous people. His barbaric acts seemed fair by comparison, or they could be an attempt at revenge.

Ron pulled himself together and walked onward with his knees stinging beneath the frayed holes in his pants. His raw knuckles throbbed to the rapid beat of his heart. The pain made him feel alive. Soon, an overwhelming release of endorphins flowed and blocked all painful sensations.

Ron felt closer to the divine. He always believed there was a God and now understood more clearly that man could not know Him. For Ron, this near-death occurrence became a sign that, though God could strike any time, the need did not yet arise. He smiled and walked on.

CHAPTER
FORTY-TWO

RON COULD NOT SLEEP, because he did not want to sleep. Since his dreams became filled with chaos, harboring demons—the creations of his past—he feared sleep. If exhausted, he might make it through the night without the ghastly awakenings. More often, he was not tired enough to avoid the startled arousal from his slumber that found him in a cold sweat with dark thoughts beyond reach once conscious. He dreaded these nocturnal panics.

To deplete himself, Ron found solace in television. It kept him awake to the point of collapse when his eyes forcefully shut. At that level of consumption, try as he may to stay awake, he could not resist. He knew the light of day would soon call and enable him to melt away the apparitions of damnation.

In the last hours before dawn he would finally sleep, but only if he experienced this forced bankruptcy of consciousness. The content of the television shows did not make any difference as long as it kept his mind away from the melancholy that overwhelmed him.

On this night, he happened upon a vintage war movie. How appropriate, he thought, having been unable to stop thinking about

Gary's explanation of war. The story line did not matter. It laid the trap of contemplation he so wished to avoid.

Ron watched as body after body fell on crimson-stained beaches. Warriors fired at faceless foes in defense of a belief, a value, an ideology.

How hard it is for the uninvolved, the uncommitted, to comprehend the need for war. If it's not your belief, ideology, or life threatened, it looks senseless. The Vietnam war had that feeling of meaningless. We had no threat to us on the college campus. The intellectuals embraced socialism. No wonder they protested. Why die in some God forsaken land in the name of a democracy the people didn't want? I didn't see it back then, but war is essential to human survival like the search for food and shelter.

Ron's head, drawn by the forces of exhaustion, fell to the side. He repositioned himself, refocused on the battle scene, and continued his thoughts.

The pacifists of my youth today live with unprecedented autonomy, and they hate the defense of the very freedoms they enjoy. They want to let the killers and rapists go free. Dump them onto the asphalt dung heap of violence and crime. They blame society for the behaviors of the criminals.

Let them experience a holdup by a sadistic maniac. Given the chance, they would hit, punch, bite, scratch, scream, and do whatever was necessary to save their asses. They would shoot to kill, yet if it's not an immediate threat to their cushy, protected lives, they tie the hands of society. They pervert every attempt to find justice for the soon forgotten victim.

My, how personal are the experiences of crime, punishment, and war. It's all right to go to war if the enemy is your enemy. As long as he's visible, a viable threat, it's all right to kill him. On the other side, we've become peacekeepers to the world, stifling the feuds of antiquity we can't comprehend. War is as natural as the breath of all creatures.

Greed, hate, jealousy, and lust have essential functions in maintaining lineage. One can't defend against an aggressor without the capacity to hate that aggressor. Lust and greed instill intensity to the defense of one's possessions. They cultivate a desire to live the good life, to get ahead, to invent, to procreate.

Am I insane? Could I be wrong in these matters? Isn't history on my side? Isn't war an integral part of, and as natural as, survival? It seems so twisted, but it's a logical contention with merit. Such a macabre philosophy isn't popular. Darwin wasn't very popular.

The scene of a soldier cleaning his weapon shifted Ron's thoughts to the gun.

It represents supreme power. It can end existence with relative ease. The control, the domination, the authority heralded by such a simple act of squeezing a cold metal trigger may be what engenders such a fascination with guns in our world.

Maybe society has become so complicated and controlling of our destiny that more people need to feel they haven't lost basic liberties. The gun lets them play God. It lets them eliminate their adversary with relative ease. It lets them end their own wretched existence when they reach bottom.

Ron's thoughts faded with the late hour. He understood Gary's passion. He understood the zeal and feel the eroticism evoked by such reasoning. The movie played on, begetting a particular blood-filled scene, and as Ron's mouth fell open, his eyes flickered like a fading candle until he was out. His infernal demons could not chase him now, for dawn was within reach.

CHAPTER
FORTY-THREE

THE WINTER-DWARFED days turned dark before the masses began migration back to their dwellings. This early dusk cast a sullen gloom over the minds of the city folk, much like the shadows of tall buildings throw murkiness onto the streets below. Stores closed early, leaving the eateries, taverns, and nightspots calling out for those inclined to interact after hours. On this cold night, a penetrating dank forced a brisk gait upon anyone not attired to escape the chill.

The walls of justice were closing in on Ron. It would not be long before authorities placed a net to affect his capture. Agent Grey could no longer continue his covert pursuit. In a matter of days, his superiors would have all the proof needed to mount the search for the man they once thought dead.

Ron planned to ask Jill to go with him to any town anywhere away from the usual retreats of those on the run. A rural setting seemed the place to hide now that the authorities discovered his identity.

Ron and Jill finished a late dinner in their favorite haunt, a small Italian restaurant where the waiters, chef, and maître d' spoke to one another in their native tongue. To the patrons, they spoke broken English as they served the flavors of Italy through the savory foods.

Every week they escaped to this place where a bottle of cheap wine helped cast their worries aside. After an hour of caring about nothing in particular, they passed the threshold of the storefront and returned to the City.

With hands clasped, they strolled the streets and joined the other travelers of the night. The mosaic of life's passions called out. Conversation, laughter, song, and sounds of the city heightened the visual experiences. The live entertainment from the local clubs spoke to the pedestrians, inviting them to spend time as young artists sang songs to the audiences of preoccupied socialites.

The contentment and inexorable inner peace Ron experienced became a concern. Tranquility was the anesthetic putting caution to sleep and weakening his guard. He could not maintain the status quo much longer for someone in Ron's precarious position. He would savor every moment but knew his days of calm would soon end.

A local band performing enchanting songs lured Ron and Jill into an intimate bar. They took seats near the stage to get closer to the stranger pouring out the universal travails of life most hypnotically.

After a few drinks and more song, their troubles moved further away from the moment. With senses heightened, their appreciation for life together became the foundation for an enduring bond.

The aroma of Jill's perfume drifted toward Ron, and it excited him. It was pure and clean and reminded him of his past. Like many triggers of nostalgia, it brought him to a better time and place clouded by the fog that forgets tribulations and glorifies good memories.

I never noticed the simple things in life. I guess preoccupation ruled over me. How did I become so sentimental?

Ron stared into Jill's face, oblivious to those around him. She stared back and, without words, they connected with a profound sense of devotion.

Things are too good. I don't deserve a respectable life for all my deeds. Whenever life is going along without issue, beware. It has always been that way. You work hard, you achieve-then boom! Something, someone, some occurrence comes along and takes it away. Is this God's manner of preparing us to deal with the inevitable? Does it help us embrace the end? Is this somehow connected to preparation for our passage from this world?

A flush swept over Ron's face. Delving into the forbidden over-thinking about mortality awakened his fears of lost vitality. He had to suppress his thoughts before becoming overwhelmed by panic.

"Let's get out of here. Come on, let's go," he snapped.

Jill looked at Ron with hesitation.

He took her hand into his and whispered, "I want you so much."

She squeezed in affirmation. They arose and headed toward the exit. Knowing a carnal union was moments away, Ron felt troubled having thoughts of remorse and loss. Happy as Jill made him, he could not escape the guilt-ridden death gnawing at his conscience.

On the trek back to their hotel, the empty streets appeared to shrink, becoming narrow pathways lined by buildings towering above them. The intimidating solemnity of an abandoned city combined with cold night air forced a fast-paced march.

Ron and Jill turned the corner, and the silhouette of a huge unidentifiable man appeared from the distant shadows. A hanging belt from an oversized trench coat bounced from side to side, and the outline of open-topped boots provided the confirming signature. Jill stopped in her tracks as memories of terror flashed into her head.

"What's the matter?" Ron asked, responding to the panic in her face and the rigidity of her stilled body.

She froze in place and started trembling. The ominous figure now moved fast, as though sensing fright in his prey.

"It's him," she muttered in a barely audible utterance.

"What?"

"It's him! The . . . the . . . the . . ." she stammered, "the street guy who beat me!"

"Lots of street people look—"

Ron never noticed the rapid approach of the hulking assailant as he tried tending to Jill's panic. A solidly placed punch to the side of his head cut his sentence short. While falling to the ground, it all clicked. The shadowy figure, so distinct, so recognizable; he should have trusted her fearfulness in knowing her attacker.

The daunting blow sent Ron reeling into a stupor. He tried to rise, but his animation froze in place. The blurred figure grabbed Jill's purse and neck.

Ron heard the garbled voice commanding, "Give it up, cunt!"

Half-helpless, Ron seized the assailant's arm, using it to balance himself more than as an offensive retaliation. The effort was futile and met with a misplaced kick to the groin.

The heavy boot landed on Ron's outer left thigh, cracking the canister of pepper spray he always carried with him. The intense burn of the blistering fluid reached the tender tissues of his groin. The pain overwhelmed Ron so much that he never felt the final blow to his face rendering him unconscious.

Jill ran into the middle of the street screaming. A burly motorist stopped to assist her. Cell phone in hand, he dialed 911 and stepped toward the assailant. It appeared the thug never expected such resistance. He dropped the pocketbook and disappeared into the night.

It took about twenty minutes until the ambulance came, a good response time for big city, crime-laden nights. Jill sat next to Ron, holding his hand, rubbing it as if stained with some indelible substance.

A police detective questioned Jill while the EMS personnel placed an intravenous line. Probes attached to Ron's body fed vital signs to the sophisticated array of hi-tech monitors, part of the crowded mobile medical theater.

The wail of the siren became the distant backdrop to a vision filling Ron's semiconscious mind. Caught between reality and dream, there remained enough faculties to realize the difference. Soon, the jarring ride in the ambulance lulled Ron closer to the dream state where he found himself at his Temple during the highest of the holy days. The Kol Nidre service, the ceremony that starts the Yom Kippur day of atonement, where the Jewish people ask the Lord for forgiveness and to include them in the Book of Life for another year, just began.

A dozen congregants stood on the pulpit, all proud to hold Torahs, the ancient book of laws, the Holy Scriptures, the ultimate honor reserved for the most respected members of the community. They often defined the measure of "most respected" on the amount of money given to help support the Temple. Age and reverence did not determine the recipient of this accolade as in past generations. They gave the honor based on charity anyone could buy.

Of all the men standing in their glory, there were ten well-known attorneys or businessmen, and two doctors. Ron knew all twelve men personally or by reputation. Of the six attorneys, four were notorious for their lack of conscience, two having served time in prison for fraud. The four businessmen included one known by all, except his wife, to be a philanderer. Another gained a reputation for ruthlessness, and no one trusted him.

The doctor representatives were a split group. One was the most upstanding member of his community and well respected by his peers. The other was an accident doctor who served time in prison for fraud, bilking insurance companies out of millions of dollars.

Instead of being based on traditional melodic tunes, they recited the prayers much like a Gregorian chant. Ron sat transfixed in his usual Temple seat. A distorted voice spoke to him with the deliberate slowness of a recording played on the wrong speed.

"I am your Lord! Go upon the pulpit and take the Law into your own hands. Seek thy honor. Be cherished by your congregation. Let the people praise you."

Ron struggled to speak, and finally managed to call out, "These are not all good men, Lord!"

The voice responded with a booming resonance, "I know of these men, though they do not know of me. I cannot reveal my presence or my power to the people, for if I did, there would be no faith in My Being. It would show fear in the reality of My Being. It would be a relationship of servitude. The only way I can bestow free will upon My Creation is to let My Flock seek Me out. They must show faith by their actions, not by fear of My retribution."

The words made for pure clarity in Ron's mind. He found no other explanation in a world where the bad go unpunished and the good have bad things happen to them.

Ron found comfort in believing the certainty of a divine plan. Along with the comfort, he felt insignificant. He always believed mortals had to rely on faith, but he never understood why divine knowledge had to live in secrecy.

The voice continued, "Go, Ron, take your place amongst your people."

In the next moment, Ron stood on the pulpit, scriptures in hand. The chanting continued.

Ron cried out, "These are not my people!"

When the words rolled off his tongue, all the chanting halted, producing a grim silence.

The stark realization entered Ron's mind that he desecrated the Law worse than anyone on the altar. He killed, not once, but many times. He trembled.

The ominous voice broke the cold silence. "How insolent are My creations to think their transgressions have no consequences? How impudent are the unfaithful coming before Me begging forgiveness to elude My wrath? Your every act in life harvests outcomes for which you are responsible."

The Temple rumbled from the ire of an angry God. The ceiling opened, revealing a turbulent firmament to those congregants now cowering below and fearing for their lives. From the seething heavens, bolts of lightning fired one by one, vaporizing the seven wicked men. Ron shivered as he waited for his judgment, but it never came in the form of retribution.

The heavens cleared, and the voice returned.

"The Lord, the Lord God, merciful and gracious, keeping mercy unto the thousandth generation, forgiving iniquity and transgression and sin will not clear the guilty forever. Never forget the Lord knows what is in the hearts of all, and goodness shall prevail!"

After the edict, heavy rain poured down upon the remaining bearers of the Law. The cold drops saturated Ron's face, body, and inner soul.

CHAPTER
FORTY-FOUR

IT WAS NOT uncommon for the President to get late night calls from Maxwell, the only advisor permitted this intrusion upon the President's private time. If the world ended, the message still had to go through Maxwell.

"I want to talk," Maxwell said with urgency in his voice.

The President had no hesitation about any request made by his friend and trusted advisor. They met in the Oval Office where many times the light burned throughout the night.

When Maxwell arrived, he looked pale and breathed with a discernable wheeze. A Secret Service agent assigned to the night detail ushered him to the waiting President and left them alone behind closed doors.

"What's wrong, Max? You sound terrible, and you look worse. What's happening?"

"I have worries about the effect of what we're doing. Christ, I know we agreed to green light the Agency, but now I'm having serious second thoughts."

"What are you talking about?"

"Look at the papers," he said as he tossed the latest daily print-outs from several major cities onto the finely carved, ornate, mahogany desk. "Almost no crime reported. The courts . . . empty. The headlines . . . all human-interest stories if you exclude the articles associated with the American Strangler. Instead of chronicles of aberrant human behavior, the newspapers started reporting mundane bullshit. If we eliminate the Strangler, will we go back to the same old thing?"

"Do I hear you right, Maxwell? Whose side are you on here?"

"Jim, you're missing my point. You don't see the real picture. For years we've lost deterrents to crime, greed, lust, and most evil acts. People like us don't see it. All the things we think of as deterrents aren't affecting the new breed of criminal.

"God used to be the deterrent to crime and inappropriate behaviors for the masses. Now marriages don't last. Kids are fucking their cousins and stepsisters not knowing who their fathers are. Theft and cheating are all around us. The deterrents from faith in a God are fading.

"Do you remember Nietzsche, Jim? God is dead! So where do we turn for law and order? We look to society. We make laws to deter crime. These laws work just fine if there's some punishment to go along with them. The system fails us, because there's no punishment, no deterrent."

"Come on, Maxwell, you're talking like some conservative nut."

"No, Jim! Look around, for Christ's sake. Open your eyes. Do you remember when you were a kid? The world changed, and we lost sight of what happened because it occurred so gradually. It's taking place right before our eyes.

"Look at the statistics. How can you deny there isn't a tragic problem? More young men are dying from gunshot wounds than any other cause. Do you realize the magnitude of that happening?

"Did you forget, just a few years ago, someone murdered the director of the CIA while on a canoe trip? We'll never solve that case. People are shooting each other for honking a horn, for Christ's sake. And what happens to these reprobates? They run free, or they serve some time in our hotel prisons. We've become numb to the violence.

"You can't go to huge sections of every major city without risking your life. It just wasn't this way when we were kids, Jim. Our children are growing up in a hostile world! Society gave us the charge to fix the problems, and we failed them."

"So, what do you propose? We get behind the vigilantes?" asked Jim, eyes glaring in disgust.

"We *are* the vigilantes, Jim. That's what's preying on me. I can't sleep. I can't live with myself. I don't know what's proper anymore. Now I'm trying to determine what's less wrong. I want to cancel the operation with Joe."

"We don't want to do that, Maxwell," demanded the President. "What's less wrong is doing away with these thugs. Please, don't get any ideas about calling him."

"You don't have to worry. I can't reach him. Not that I didn't try. He's listed as on a mission in Algeria, just as he said. The agency is the strangest outfit, the way they operate. His superior doesn't know what Joe does or how to reach him."

"That's why they're so effective. There's no one to second guess once the operation begins. Just let it be, Maxwell. We decided, and we did the right thing."

"You think so?"

The President did not have a response. He put his head into his hands for a moment, looked to the rain-stained ceiling above, and whispered, "God help us. I don't know the answer."

CHAPTER
FORTY-FIVE

VOICES OF URGENCY RESONATED EVERYWHERE. Rain-soaked EMS technicians removed Ron from the ambulance. The torrential shower hampered emergency operations and disrupted Ron's delirium. He understood how reality forms in the mind and can become a scaffold for a dream, but he had trouble discerning his true state. Thunder and lightning happening in his hallucination, and in this real-life moment added another level to the drama and confusion in his thinking.

Jill stayed by Ron's side as they rushed him into the emergency room. When they approached the inner sanctum, a nurse pulled her away.

"You can't help him in there. We'll bring you back as soon as he's stable."

Ron's pulse slowed to a dangerous level. A code blue team worked furiously to keep him from drifting toward his final breath. While cutting off his clothing, one of the apprentice nurses felt the wet pants saturated with pepper spray liquid. She forgot to don her gloves in all the excitement.

"Oh, my God! I touched his urine, and I'm not gloved!"

"Urine never hurt anyone!" shouted the lead doctor. "Just wash up and get gloved. STAT!"

The frightened young nurse ran to the sink, but before she washed, her tender skin started to burn. Experiencing such intense pain, she could not turn the spigot to relieve the mysterious contamination. She stood motionless screaming, "It's burning me! Help me! It's burning me!"

"What the hell? Go see what she's yelling about," the doctor snapped, having now lost his composure.

The head nurse, suspecting a caustic solution, located the crushed pepper spray dispenser in Ron's pants pocket and held it up for the doctor to see.

"Make the call," he commanded.

In less than ten minutes the first agent arrived at the emergency room. There weren't many injuries involving pepper spray, but a team of FBI special agents showed up for every recorded case during the past three months. All hospital emergency rooms in the nation received a notice they posted that read: "All personnel must report any injury caused by or involving Mace or pepper spray!" An eight hundred number for the FBI national task force listed in bold, red font conferred a level of importance rarely seen.

No one at the hospital understood what the directive meant, though many suspected some connection to the American Strangler.

Instead of the usual cursory investigation, the first FBI agent on the scene seemed more interested in this case. Ron had no identification. His girlfriend, Jill, knew nothing about him. He fit the loner profile of the killer and had the caustic spray in his possession.

Jill watched with suspicion as an agent who introduced himself to others as Agent Colby made a cell call from an ultra-small phone. She heard him connect to the what seemed to be his superiors.

Within fifteen minutes an ominous character arrived and introduced himself to Agent Colby as Joe, just Joe. He looked the part of some law enforcement agency being well-built, ruggedly masculine, exuding confidence, and demonstrating leadership.

Jill had an intuitive feeling of imminent catastrophe. Too much activity all around, and too much interest in her furtive lover, led Jill to believe the man of whom she knew little was the target of something ominous. The clamor among the hospital staff showed Jill that Ron represented an element of threat. She went undercover and made her way to a nurses' lounge where she changed to dress the role. With her hair pulled back and topped with a white scrub cap, she blended in well.

From this new vantage point, Jill walked around unimpeded and saw Joe ordering what seemed to be many X-rays and tests. She listened intently, but didn't understand what was happening. "Get me a ceph, a pan, and intraorals. I want the prints sent out now, and get me a match STAT!"

In a fortuitous action, Joe ducked into the nurses' lounge for privacy only seconds after Jill. She retreated there to evade the suspicions of a doctor who might have realized she did not belong with the team of medical personnel. Based on the timing, she feared Joe was coming after her. He never saw her enter and remained unaware she watched his every move as she stood behind a dressing screen.

Joe removed a thin aluminum case from the interior breast pocket of his suit. It contained a pair tuberculin syringes, the small injectors used by people with diabetes for administering insulin. He filled the syringes with separate solutions from two different vials also contained in the aluminum case. After tapping out the air bubbles, he carefully recapped the needles.

While Jill understood little about medicine, she realized Joe was not a doctor. She suspected if the tests came back with an affirmative confirmation, her lover would be on the sharp end of these two needles, and they weren't for his health.

CHAPTER
FORTY-SIX

"MR. HOUSTON, there's a man on the phone who says he must speak with you. He said it's urgent. He wouldn't give me his full name. He said to tell you it's Joe, and you'd understand."

Maxwell's housekeeper, the proper type, would be quick to hang up on a crank phone call. The man at the other end of the line intimidated and convinced her she best put him through to her employer.

Maxwell expected Joe's call a week earlier and now dreaded the decision he had to make. He could act as if he was requesting an update on the mission or try to call it off against the wishes of his President.

"Joe, I was hoping to hear from you," he said.

"Usually when I get a call from the boss, it's regarding a change of heart," responded Joe with empathy. He knew how to make his superiors feel comfortable with the psychology of their often-gut-wrenching decisions.

Maxwell, distraught and wavering over this critical mission, took the bait and proceeded as if he now spoke for the President.

"You understand, this plan we have has made me very uncomfortable," he stammered, "I mean us, the President and me. We've decided maybe it's best to let the sticks fall as they may."

"You want to call it off. And understandable," said Joe. "I told you there're times we at the agency would prefer to do our own thing. If I had my choice, if I were commander-in-chief, I'd let this American Strangler guy play out too. The pendulum has been way out of balance for decades, and these things take on a life of their own."

"So, you can do it? You can call it off?" exclaimed Maxwell.

A hollow pause foreshadowed the negative response.

"It's not that easy any longer," Joe stated in a gutsy manner. "I had a call from the President earlier today. He asked me to step up the operation. He wants to put this whole thing behind him as soon as possible."

"He, what?" shouted Maxwell, unable to conceal his surprise, embarrassment, and displeasure.

Joe caught his fish and reeled him in with more explanation but devoid of any question about Maxwell's veracity or motive.

"He allocated extra emergency funding so we can step up the operation. Since *he* is the commander-in-chief, I can't change this order unless it comes from him.

"The mission might be finished already for all we know. We have over a hundred independent operatives working on this matter as we speak. A report just came into headquarters regarding one of my men in New York with a mugging victim matching the profile. They're waiting for confirmation and are ready to act."

"I can't believe he would do that without consulting me. He does nothing without my input and my guidance," Maxwell lamented.

"Mr. Houston, this conversation is off the record now. Your boss is the one who helped perpetuate the problems we have by his policies. Now he wants to trash the rules to keep his way of life intact.

I'd just as soon let the sticks fall as they may on this American Strangler, like you said.

"This call . . ." Joe hesitated in a way begging a response, but Maxwell remained speechless. "I know you made it without his approval, but don't worry. I said, it's off the record. If it's any consolation, I'm glad *you* have a conscience."

THE "OTHER JOE," in New York City, held a conference at the cordoned off nurses' station. He and three well dressed FBI agents spoke quietly, covering their mouths to maintain secrecy.

Having left the nurses' lounge without notice, from which Jill discovered what appeared to represent an ominous outcome for Ron, she worked her way back to the emergency room. Rather than being treated in the usual curtain-lined cubical, they held him in the private surgical suite. The interest in his identity and the nature of his suspected involvement in the American Strangler matter made secure confinement a priority.

The federal authorities posted a local police guard at the entrance to the room. This assignment did not seem to have the same importance for the young officer as it did for his elite superiors who made him keeper of the gate. He barely looked up from reading his *Daily News* when Jill rolled a cart past him on her way into the room.

Ron, now conscious, with vital signs stable, looked bewildered when he saw Jill.

"What happened?" he asked.

"Someone attacked you and knocked you unconscious. You're in the hospital."

"I remember nothing. Why are you wearing a nurse's uniform?"

"Something's terribly wrong. The hospital staff called in the FBI. When they admitted you, they found a pepper spray in your pocket, and when I couldn't give them any information about you . . . what's this about?" she asked with trepidation and longing.

Ron did not answer. He thought for a moment and made the connection.

That's it. The pepper spray, no identity . . . that's the key. Agent Grey must have put out a description to find me. Maybe they're just looking for the copycats—pursuing every lead. I can't take any chances.

Ron responded with urgency and without explanation, "I have to leave!"

"You really do have to get out of here, love! They called in some special higher-up, and he wants to kill you!" Jill whispered with tears pooling at the base of her eyes.

"What are you thinking? These people don't belong to the Mafia, Jill."

"Trust me, Ron. I may not see many secret agent movies, but this guy is here to kill you! What's going on? Please, explain."

Without responding, Ron pulled the IV from his arm.

"Is there a guard at the door?"

Jill nodded to confirm without speaking a word. She became stiff as fear took control of her body.

Ron's faculties returned, and his mind raced for a plan.

"I see one way out," he said.

"Oh, and you think the nice officer on the other side of this door will let you walk out of here?" said Jill with tears escaping and now rolling down her cheeks.

Ron looked at the door, then turned his attention to the cart Jill used as an excuse to enter the room. His former role as a surgeon would provide the gateway for his escape.

Even while Ron's mind cleared, he found his body not as resilient as he hopped off the bed and met with near collapse. Although nothing appeared broken, the pain of movement against his injuries caused severe throbbing from the chemical burns sustained in his contact with the assailant. Ron suffered some serious contusions and blisters, but most critically, he'd been in shock. In the cold night air it would not take long for Ron to relapse with the chance for coma and death to ensue.

Scrubs, masks, caps, and booties filled the supply cart Jill wheeled into the room. Ron dressed in a half dozen pairs of scrubs so the extra layers would provide some insulation from the cold. He had to bear the pain of nerve endings firing wildly from the weight of the bulky clothing pressing upon the denuded skin of his groin. A surgical mask hid his bruised cheek and jaw.

Ron now looked the as the rest of the anonymous health care providers who wander the halls of all medical centers.

"Take this clipboard. When we walk out that door, you pretend you're writing everything I'm dictating," he ordered in quiet but authoritative commands.

Ron looked around as if something was missing.

"Where are your clothes? Your pocketbook; what happened to your pocketbook? We need money for a cab," he added anxiously.

"We'll get money back at the hotel," said Jill.

"No! We can't let anyone know where we're going! They can't find your wallet, your identification."

"Okay! Okay! I'll take care of it. After we get you out of here, I'll get my things from the nurses' lounge and meet you, but where?"

"Meet me across from the entrance to the ER and have a cab waiting. I'll find you."

Jill led the way. When she opened the door to the emergency operating suite, the officer, engrossed in his newspaper, nodded in a friendly manner. Ron spoke in medical terms and acted as if the officer was not there. Jill made notes on her clipboard just as Ron instructed.

The plan worked well until five steps out of the room when a voice called out, "You! Stop! Who let them in that room?"

Following the command, thundering footsteps came from no more than thirty paces away. The officer guarding the entrance became startled by the commotion and ran into the room to check on his prisoner.

Ron grabbed Jill by the neck and called out to the approaching agents, "Stop or I'll kill her!" He held his hand to her back as if armed. The agents came to a reluctant halt and pulled out their weapons.

A standoff would not work out well for Ron. He knew they never do. Reacting with precision and speed, he pushed Jill onto a gurney sitting idle along the corridor wall. He whispered, "Hold tight, love," and sent it toward the agents. This diversion gave him the seconds needed to turn the corner of the hallway where a host of staff busily walked the halls. Ron yelled, "He's got a gun! Every-body down!"

With his words just spoken, Ron jumped to the floor and cradled his head lying close to the wall. He knew, in a world on edge, and in the presence of an active shooter, everyone would comply by falling to the ground. He now lay huddled with some thirty fearful strangers. When the law enforcement officers rounded the corner, a hallway lined with doctors and nurses taking refuge in the fetal position greeted them. The agents ran onward, past Ron and the others, in pursuit of the escapee. Ron picked himself up, and with calm, walked in the opposite direction to exit the hospital.

With little difficulty now that the agents redirected their operation, Jill made her way back to the nurses' lounge to retrieve her pocket-book. Another challenge appeared as two police officers guarded the door. They noticed Jill draw near, and she could not turn back without arousing too much suspicion. She approached while trying to control the trembling she felt weakening her limbs.

"I'm sorry, ma'am, no one can go in there," said the more alert looking of the two guards.

Shaken but with confidence, Jill countered with a valid plea.

"My coat and purse are in there. I can't get home without my license. It's cold outside, and I'm coming off a long shift. Please."

Sympathetic for her predicament, one officer opened the lounge door to reveal several Special Agents and the devil himself, Joe, viewing many X-rays. Jill's heart dropped as he turned around to face her. She realized if she did not get out of the building before they reported Ron's escape to this command center, she would never get out. Surely, they would close all exits at any moment.

"Excuse me, sir. She's going off duty and needs her coat and pocketbook."

The officer motioned toward the corner of the room where the staff left their outerwear and personal effects. He spoke to Joe, who appeared perturbed by the interruption.

Joe motioned Jill into the room and demanded, "Make it fast!"

He turned back to his labor. While Jill rushed to gather her belongings, she heard him say, "One more film and we have a match."

She wondered what mystery tagged the man who became her hope of escape from a life without meaning. Why was Ron's identity given such urgency? Should she meet him, or should she walk away from this perceived danger? The moment defined something menacing. But no matter, she wanted to stay with Ron, even if it meant her death. Ron had become her reason to live. She had to follow the plan, or she would never see him again.

CHAPTER
FORTY-EIGHT

THE COLD NIGHT air greeted Jill with the fear Ron might have collapsed and lay dying in some hiding place used to elude his pursuers. The blocks surrounding the hospital were long and dark. When she turned the next corner, all brightened as the emergency room entrance lit up the sky. After hailing a cab as instructed, she waited across from the hospital.

Out of a dark service entrance, Ron appeared, stepped into the cab as planned, and they slipped away from the fury of the late-night accident ward to the lifeless streets of an approaching dawn. Their flight, a mission of stealth, provided more fear and danger than Jill ever experienced, in spite of her sordid past life.

They did not speak a word during the cab ride. Quiet travelers were typical for the cabby, who chauffeured many an exhausted late-night traveler. For Ron and Jill, who embarked on a new realm of their relationship, the silence was haunting.

Ron had the cabby drop them four blocks before their hotel. He knew it would not be long before the nation's crime busters would follow every lead to track him.

Intentionally, Ron asked, "Is this the L line?" pointing to the subway entrance.

"Sure, but I can take you a hell of a lot safer this time of night!" the cabby urged.

"Thanks. It's a long ride, but we'll take our chances. Thanks again."

Ron used this charade to divert the feds should they interview this cabby.

By the time they entered Jill's room, Ron near collapsed. She helped him onto her bed and stroked his hair.

"What have you done? You must be an important guy from the attention you got back there."

"Jill!" Ron grabbed her shoulders. "You can walk away and remember the good times. If you don't leave now, I'll have to explain everything, and I'm afraid my life, my past, will repulse you."

Jill's eyes filled with tears, and she fell cheek to cheek with Ron. She spoke softly into his ear, "I can't leave you, not now, not ever."

With reluctance and gravity, Ron realized he had to come clean about his past and present, even though his future looked rather bleak at the moment.

"I was a respected man, a professional man. My downfall came at the hands of my unrealistic principles. How can I describe it best? I've become all I detest. I've sinned worse than the people I wanted to destroy. I don't know how to say it. Here I am at confession, and I can't say it," he stammered and shook his head left to right.

"Ron, you can tell me anything. It's about the murders of all those lawyers, isn't it?" she said as she lifted his hands to her lips.

Ron pulled away from her clasp and stood abruptly.

"Yes, yes, I started it all. I'm the embodiment of all the copycats out there. I've sinned, and I'm worse than the problem I tried to bury."

Jill stood, embraced Ron, and placed her head on his chest.

"You're a hero to more people than you can imagine," she said as she stroked his arms and lovingly kissed his chest.

"They're all sick. The entire world wallows in depravity. You could never live with me knowing what I've done."

"No, Ron, you're wrong. I'll always love you."

To Ron's joyful disbelief, Jill embraced his deeds the same as torrents of people all around America. The sentiment for the American Strangler had taken the high road.

"You have to get away! Please, Ron, take me with you."

Realizing his identity climbed out of the grave he so carefully created, Ron understood he had to leave New York. He could not hide from his past misdeeds. Only a future somewhere far away offered any chance of hope. In a matter of days, law enforcement would plaster his picture on every television screen and post his image on every website and social media contrivance across the land.

"We have to leave the country, but I have no identification. I can't get a passport. I'll never get away," said Ron in despair.

"We'll get you a forged passport."

"Jill, how many forgers do you know? Let's face it; we're not career criminals. I can't risk it, even if we found someone to help us. They have a reward on my head."

"I have a plan, Ron. I'll need a few days to take care of a final matter, then we can leave the country. You must grow a short beard."

"A beard?"

"Please, trust me on this. Grow the beard."

"There's one last thing I must do before we leave," said Ron.

"Please, don't press your luck. You don't want to ruin everything now. We're so close to finding a future," pleaded Jill.

"I swear to you, this venture will in no way jeopardize our plans, but it's something I must do."

CHAPTER
FORTY-NINE

THE REFLECTION of the full moon floated rhythmically upon the gentle waves of the mighty ocean. Only twelve days all year did the glorious sight manifest its most extreme size and brightness. Ron knew tonight Susan would be on the beach as sure as the moon waxed bright.

Ron and Susan took their customary stroll on these precious moonlit nights. She taught him to appreciate all God's gifts. Susan used this pleading many times to get this most exhausted doctor up and about for a stroll, no matter how near to collapse a hard day took him. He wanted her to be there. He prayed she would be there.

Ron wanted Susan to go on with her life, but tonight he hoped she would be alone. He waited on the beach remembering the words in his note to Susan before he fled from her life, "until we meet again when the world turns around." The words echoed through Ron's mind in a mantra-like chant, inducing a warmth that sustained him as he stood alone on the cold, dark beach.

When the door of the massive shore house opened, Ron's heart swelled with happiness. Watching Susan walk down the staircase, he experienced a rush of nostalgia fostering memories of better times.

Susan approached the boardwalk leading to the beach where he waited. A sense of regret and gloom erased his exhilaration. He now had second thoughts about this meeting. However, he realized he could no longer remain silent, not since the FBI dug him up in their quest to bury him for eternity.

Ron suspected the authorities had already been in contact with Susan. They would have told her how he remained alive and committed the dreaded killings. They would have explained how the suicide note, the body in the elevator shaft, and the original dental films were a well-planned hoax that eluded the best of their sleuths.

In conclusion, they would have described their further suspicion, based on investigation and research, that Ron continued his killing spree and escaped their dragnet. The question remained, would Susan now fear the man she once loved and turn on him?

Surely, Susan would expect Ron to resurface. The authorities likely would watch her for a reunion. If they wanted to use Susan to get Ron, it had to be by wiretap. Ron searched for and saw no surveillance outside of the house.

Susan approached at a brisk pace. While landing on the last step leading to the sand, she noticed the frozen figure of a stranger in the shadows. She repelled to find a safe footing for retreat, forcing Ron to call out gently, "Susan, it's . . ."

His voice indelibly imprinted upon her mind needed no introduction.

"Ron!" she cried out, gasping as she repeated, "Ron! Ron! My God, it's you!"

Susan ran to him and leaped into his arms. Between hysterically crying, incoherent words flowed spontaneously. Suddenly she found her recurring dream come true. He came back after heartbreak and longing. The love she thought dead the past two years returned.

Susan experienced laughter and joy between thoughts of abandonment and pain. The bittersweet state of mind produced an explosive charge of vitality she thought could never be hers again.

Ron tried to calm Susan, but to no avail. They walked toward the glistening surf with both his arms wrapped around her trembling figure. She held his arms and kept touching, squeezing, and massaging them to make sure this embodiment was not a dream. They strolled along the shoreline, allowing time for her uncontrolled emotion to settle. While cherishing the affection of peaceful presence, not a word left their lips. The sound of the tide became the music for their symphony of devotion.

The quiet stroll lasted five minutes, but it was pure bliss. Ron stopped. He turned Susan to face him, and he spoke.

"There's no way you can forgive me for what I've done to you and the children. Not only did I ruin my life; I ruined yours too. I've wrecked our family because of impulse, passion, and principle. For what? So they can hunt me like a dog?"

"Don't punish yourself, Ron! We all understood. Me, the kids, we suspected it was you out there, or at least your spirit that ignited this movement. You're a folk hero to so many people."

Again, Ron was shocked that people accepted his deeds and what they represented. He never realized the magnitude of popular reception for his vendetta. He found himself torn between the epithet of a murderer and martyr; vindictive slayer as opposed to emancipator of a failing system.

"Come back to the house, Ron. You're home now."

She kissed him, but something felt wrong. His cold lips told a story Susan feared asking.

"Ron, what's the matter?" she inquired, her voice filled with alarm.

"You must accept it. I'm your past life. You know it, and you have to live with it. You're being watched. The kids are being watched. They tapped the phones. I'm already a dead man, Susan! They can't afford any martyrs."

"I'll go with you! I can't lose you again!"

"You'll never lose me." He shook her gently and said, "Never! Do you understand?"

Susan nodded, and tears rolled down her saddened cheeks as the reality of their fate became apparent.

"Do you remember the words you pledged on our wedding day? I am my beloved's," as Ron continued, Susan repeated the second part with him, "and my beloved is mine."

Susan dropped her head into her hands and sobbed gently. Ron took her hands into his.

"We'll always be together even in death. Even though this death is not of the body, it must separate us physically, but I'll always be with you. You must stay. Go on with your life."

"Where will you go? What will you do?"

Ron had no answer. He just stared at her, overcome by sorrow. He felt a pain deep in his chest and knew his heart broke into a thousand pieces at that moment.

"I can't stay any longer. It's not safe."

Ron pulled Susan close, kissed her with a renewed passion, but just for a precious moment, and he walked away.

Sobbing, she called out, "Don't go. Damn you. Please! Don't leave me."

He turned back to face her, and in a gentle voice pleaded, "Please, please, please, go on with your life!"

She called back to him in a barely audible whisper, knowing her last words, if heard, would only make the pain of his departure worse.

"You are my life!"

CHAPTER
FIFTY

"WELL, Jill, I thought I'd never see you again."

Brad Allen poured drinks as he stood behind the lavish mirrored bar decorated in the splendor of a bygone era. The Dakota housed some of the biggest moneymakers in all of Manhattan, and Brad Allen, Esquire, lived with the best of them.

Brad was a pathetic Gatsby type. Never popular with the ladies throughout his many years of schooling, he did, however, learn fast, once the accolades of success came to pass, "Lots of foxy women will fuck money." This vulgar adage became his oft-repeated mantra. Not being born very attractive, did not stop him from bedding down some of the most desirable women in town. In his wildest dreams, as an adolescent, he never imagined he would partake in so much prime sex.

At fifty-five years of age, living the good life to excess, he looked worse than most. His gut hung over a belt drawn too tight. He was five-seven in his stocking feet but gained two-and-a-half inches from shoes fitted with custom lifts.

When on the town, Brad always sported taller women. He liked to flaunt his towering, model-type escorts to the bystanders who could never understand the match. His short brown beard looked too dark and strikingly colored to be natural. It did not match his graying brows or the wrinkles of his face that spoke of a life filled with sun and stress. His shaved head made him look odd as it revealed several lumps and irregularities.

The scene repulsed Jill. In the past, she ignored the creepy mannerisms, potbellies, and salivating lust of her clients. Suddenly thrust into a last encounter that epitomized her former life, she felt uneasy, and it showed.

"Relax, baby. You look like an uptight junkie or something," Brad said in a manner he perceived as being cool.

He walked around the bar to where Jill sat and handed her a Black Russian, heavy on the vodka. He fancied his women intoxicated. It offered him the control required to help him overcome sporadic episodes of impotence.

Like a predator eyeing prey, Brad slinked behind Jill. Her bare shoulders excited him. Her skin, so pure, so flawless, begged him to touch as he did many times in past encounters. Brad could not resist. He ran his fingers along her neck and let them roam over her shoulders and back. His hands, cold and wet from the glass he held, added to Jill's discomfort, but he remained oblivious.

"You like that, don't you, baby? I can feel you quivering."

She did not respond to his query and concentrated on her mission.

"I missed you, Jill. You walked away, not a call, nothing. You shouldn't have done that to me, baby. You know I'd always take care of you."

"I know, Brad," she said, "but I met a guy. I just couldn't—"

"Fuck him. I always told you I'd take care of you," he said heatedly.

Brad had no scruples, and he expected that was the norm for one and all.

"So, what happened with this guy?"

"He split."

Brad moved his hands down along Jill's chest. His fingers traveled slowly, as if on a mission of stealth, approaching the rim of her low-cut dress. As he explored lower on her chest, he grabbed her nipples between his fingertips and twisted them side to side in a rough manner. Despite his loathsomeness, they were firm and erect from the coldness of his hands. Brad was anything but gentle. His folly hurt her just like so many other times.

Jill learned that a good whore masks discomfort as pleasure, and pain as climax to please the fantasies of the john. This credo served her well with Brad since he believed good sex involved hard sex.

Brad led Jill to the bedroom. He pushed open the double doors to reveal a spectacular floor to ceiling, dramatic panorama of the city skyline. This glorious view saw many women pay the price of admission to a lifestyle of glitz and glamour with a guy like Brad Allen.

To disengage Brad's escorting embrace, Jill did a little twist and push, tossing him onto the bed. He was like many powerful men she knew. Sometimes they wanted control, and sometimes they relinquish it to the object of their desire. Jill had to make sure Brad would be servant to the ultimate dominatrix.

"Do you still have your toys, Brad?"

"Sure, baby! Sure, I still got them," he stated with a look of curiosity.

"Then I have a surprise for you. Lie here and give me the key," Jill demanded.

He reached into his pocket fishing for the key to the lockbox that served as home to his sex toys. He paused, and a sly look swept over his sweaty face.

"You want the key? You'll have to come and get it."

How clever, she thought.

Jill played along, slipping her hand into his pocket.

"I don't think there's any room in this pocket for a key," she said as she stroked his erection along with his ego.

Jill had to be careful because Brad often hair-triggered upon direct stimulation. If she played too much, he would climax, and hours would pass until he'd be ready again.

Once she had the key in hand, she knew where to get the play things.

"You wait here, Brad, baby."

Jill exited, leaving Brad to his fantasies. She walked to the den and opened the false top to the intricately inlaid end table hiding the lockbox. Inside, she found the Holy Grail. Buried under the sex toys, she retrieved a pistol and Brad's passport.

Carrying two hands full of the most bizarre vibrators and assorted sex paraphernalia, she returned to Brad, the lecher in waiting. By now he lay naked, fondling himself to keep his wood from fading.

"Let's try something new tonight, honey. Lie on your stomach," Jill coaxed.

Brad tossed himself over with no hesitation. Jill started rubbing his back and massaging his neck. Without speaking a word, Jill reached into the night table to locate tethers Brad used to bind his women. She wrapped them around each arm and foot, securing Brad to the bed on posts designed and intended for this purpose.

Jill's offering of unique intimacy, a new game of lust, thrilled Brad, and he cooed approval.

"Oh yeah. Oh, yeah, baby!"

The fruit was ripe, and Jill began the harvest. She picked up a dildo at least fourteen inches long, including the leather handle decorated with rhinestones. The actual probe was narrow at the tip, then it became bulbous, making initial penetration easy followed by an explosive expansion. The firm but flexible shaft then narrowed for a brief reprieve and widened as it penetrated.

Jill began gliding the device over Brad's back and shoulders. She moved it up to his neck and face to make sure he would cast view upon the monster phallus.

"You know how much I love this one, Brad! How hot it makes me when you work it deep inside? Remember, baby?"

A demonic tone to her voice, and a devilish look possessed her, all of which Brad never noticed as he remained cradled in ecstasy.

"Relax those cheeks, honey," she coaxed.

Brad lifted his body to spread his legs further, readying himself for the delivery.

"Jill, I've never done this before," he explained.

"Don't worry, baby. You'll do great! It doesn't take a whole lot to learn this trick!"

Brad was incredibly tight-assed, but after a short struggle, the plunge met with a roar.

"Whoa!"

"Great, isn't it, Brad?"

"Easy, baby," he responded.

His reply encouraged her to push even harder. She watched with glee as the thickest part of the shaft buried deep. Brad twisted wildly to grab the wand only to find the restraints all too effective.

"What the fuck are you trying—"

His outburst stopped mid-sentence as she withdrew the spear, then forcefully reinserted it.

"Stop! God damn it, Jill! That fucking hurts like a motherfucker!"

"What are you talking about, Brad baby? You know how much I love when you stick it in real deep."

Brad's face turned red with rage.

"You sadistic mother fucking whore. I'll have you put away. You'll never see daylight!"

Jill kept the device in place and left the room. Brad struggled desperately though futilely to free himself.

In a matter of seconds, an innocent-looking Jill returned. Brad twisted his torso to face her. He decided upon a different approach in his appeal for freedom.

"Come on, baby. I never knew it felt this horrible. Untie me, and I'll make it up to you."

Jill appeared distant, in another place, in a trance. She did not respond to Brad's plea, and from behind her back she drew his pistol. The angelic visage turned cold. Her stare became fixed and maniacal.

Brad called out repeatedly, louder and louder, "Stop! No! Don't! Wait!"

Finally, the harsh sound of his voice freed Jill from the grip of her trance.

"What are you doing?" he demanded, his declaration now filled with panic.

Jill responded in a voice of calm, "How many lives have you ruined? How many people live in despair while you bask in splendor?"

Brad's expression changed, and he became bold. "You can't shoot me, bitch!" he shouted. "Where you gonna go? You'll never get away with this!"

The reprimand did not work. It only triggered a foreign rage in Jill. A shot rang out. Brad screamed in pain as a bullet pierced his rear thigh.

Brad had a terrifying realization. Jill was not a scornful lover. He faced a psychopath who would not respond to reason or emotion, the two worlds Brad could manipulate. He feared final judgment stood before him and began crying like a child. He pleaded with Jill to spare his life. Jill laughed at the sight of Brad reduced to a whimpering, pathetic soul.

"Brad, you are pitiful. I will let you go."

His bawling stopped, and he looked up to her.

"Oh, thank you! Thank you! I knew you couldn't do this! You wouldn't—"

She interrupted his words of gratitude. "I will let you go . . . straight to hell!"

Calmly and with methodical intent, she emptied the gun into the doleful form. Brad twisted wildly and screamed from the next two blasts, then spasm dictated his movement.

When Jill saw his body no longer contained a breath of life, a profound weakness overcame her every muscle. The gun fell from her hand, and she dropped to her knees. Her eyes became heavy and dry, causing her to blink repeatedly. She knew she had to leave but had no reserve to carry her away. Unable to resist, she curled up on the floor next to the bed and closed her eyes. She entered a slumber deeper than any she had experienced since she was a child.

CHAPTER
FIFTY-ONE

HARRIED souls came and went in droves, unrecognized and numb to their surroundings. Their faces blurred as they sped by in the airport's concourse. People raced everywhere, going nowhere, as they swept past Jill and Ron, who walked arm in arm toward Gate Ten. They blended into the crowd like any other couple but out of necessity wished to remain hidden.

Remaining anonymous became more difficult as the FBI plastered pictures of Ron on walls and counters everywhere. They alerted all airports, train terminals, and seaports to watch for him. Walking past one gate after another, it horrified Ron to see the airline personnel boarding passengers holding his picture.

Embarkation already began for Fight 613 to Ecuador. The staff scrutinized each person as they made way to board.

"What are we going to do?" said Jill in a voice filled with nervous apprehension.

"How do I look?" he asked while stroking the short, but distinctive beard he grew to go with his shaved head. Ron made these changes to match the picture on his new passport, but they did little to hide the characteristic features of a unique face.

"I don't think it will work. I can see you under it all. Maybe we can stay and find a safe place to live."

"It's too dangerous. My face is everywhere, not just in the airports."

"If you're recognized, what should we do?" asked Jill.

"We won't even know the boarding crew recognizes me. They'll let us board, then in about fifteen minutes several gorillas will drag me away in cuffs. We have no choice. Are you ready?"

Jill acknowledged the need to move forward with the plan by shaking her head in affirmation.

"This is it then," she said, resigned to the fate that lay ahead.

The line they picked was twelve passengers deep when they got the courage to board. Orders followed to the tee required the attendant to scrutinize each passenger as they handed in their boarding passes. This gate keeper appeared methodical and efficient. He closed each encounter with a friendly, "Enjoy your flight."

Jill went first and had to pretend she did not know Ron. To avoid any connection that could implicate Jill as an accomplice, they planned on remaining strangers until meeting in room 232 of their chosen hotel in San Clemente. Only then would they embrace and resume their lives together.

Jill had no problem boarding, as expected. Ron stepped forward. He felt embarrassment and distress causing his pores to drain. It started on his brow, and he hoped the sweat would not progress further. How futile, he thought, knowing the impossibility of controlling a nervous system under duress. Soon he felt as though his entire body perfused the cumulative guilt of his turbulent past for all to see. His underarms produced an awkward drip. He tried to stand still as if to crush his confession.

How could I kill so many, yet fall apart when the Promised Land is steps away?

Presenting his boarding pass became a test of nerves. The attendant studied Ron's face. He compared it with the FBI placard at his station. He nodded conspicuously, handed the document back to Ron, and said, "Have a great trip, sir," followed by an unobtrusive salute.

Not knowing how to read the encounter or what to expect, Ron responded with caution.

"Thank you."

An awkward hesitation froze time for a moment before Ron repeated himself, "Thank you very much."

Ron could not tell if he just received an enormous gift or the salute of condemnation. He knew the lad recognized him and decided to either let him go or set him up for capture. Ron boarded.

Moments after all passengers took their seats, the pilot announced an unexpected delay in departure and offered no details. Jill feared the worst. She envisioned stormtroopers bursting through the door at any second. Visibly upset, her appearance concerned for Ron. He feared she might fall apart from the intensity of the ordeal.

A sudden thud next to Jill caused her to jump and turn around in her seat. She reacted to an umbrella dropped by an elderly woman reaching for the storage compartment. Jill looked pale, and her eyes fluttered.

Ron recognized the signs of syncope that could lead to unconsciousness. To avoid a scene that would bring unwanted attention and more delay, he had to intervene.

"Ma'am, you look upset. I bet it's flying. Right?" Ron said, while patting Jill's cheek to arouse her.

He winked at Jill, comforting her as he spoke.

She welcomed the intervention, and the simple conversation let her escape morbid thoughts. It gave her strength and the connection she needed at that moment. She played along well, protecting their cover.

Finally, the plane taxied toward the runway. If lightning did not strike them out of the sky now, they would make it to Ecuador, Ron reasoned.

The flight was long. For Ron, it offered a period of solitude during which he reflected upon his life. Never in the depths of his wildest imagination could he fathom this predicament and destination. It was all too strange, too outlandish.

He knew from where he came and used to think he knew his course, if not the expected outcome of his choices. He once thought he had some control over his future. No longer could he predict the day's end much like a vagabond under the influence of happenstance.

The jostling of the plane and the screech of tires clawing at the runway announced the long-awaited landing. Ron now envisioned a special operations unit whisking him away upon deplaning and taking him to a CIA dark house to finish the task the agents missed back in the Manhattan hospital.

The tedious and slow process as each disembarking passenger had to empty the overhead compartments allowed Ron's imagination to race onward. Jill seemed comforted in assuming the escape succeeded. They strode along the aisle, Ron right behind Jill. When they passed the waiting pilot, he appeared to nod in a peculiar manner. The smile that followed assured Ron he was free to move on without trouble.

When Ron stepped into the cab behind the one Jill entered, he noticed the deep frown in his brow release as worry melted away. The ride to the hotel was a welcome experience of aesthetic beauty.

The roads of the coastal lowlands traveled flat and narrow. The glorious vegetation stared at voyagers from the vibrant green jungles following the road's every curve.

The other side of the highway fed the senses with passion of the sea. The green and blue shades and hues appeared unlike most coastal waters anywhere else on earth. The vista gave mortals a glimpse of the heavens above to make them long for a place of eternal peace.

A land of much poverty and primitive culture, it was nothing like Ron expected. He did not choose Ecuador as a new home for its sophistication. He made this choice based on the extradition laws and undeveloped lands he thought would allow him to hide from the world of his past vigilante undertakings.

Guayaquil, the central city, did not turn out to be the antediluvian haunt Ron envisioned. The crowding became clear as they traveled through on their way to San Clemente.

The city looked the same as big cities everywhere. Soon the congestion cleared, and they came upon Hotel Palmazul, a first-class beachfront Mecca. In recent years, the promise of peaceful resorts lured tourists into developing the economy further.

The cabby offered comfort by explaining the country, the people, and the customs in a most promising manner. It sounded like a better haven than Ron planned. The diversity of the land included mountains, plateaus, rain forests, beaches, farms, and cities. A paradise, albeit a hot one, waited for Ron and Jill to explore and settle.

At the hotel, they embraced. In celebration of their escape, they made love with the same passion experienced their first time together. Afterward, wrapped in plush robes, they looked out on the Pacific Ocean from the terrace. They talked about new dreams and plans. They wanted to live a life of freedom, devoid of a past they wanted to leave behind.

CHAPTER
FIFTY-TWO

THE AGNEWS BUILT a wonderful life for themselves out of tropical splendor. Integrating themselves into an isolated cacao plantation along the coast, they assumed the identity of early retirees from the States. This picture played out more and more in recent years. Escape from the madness of modern life became a premium destination. No one asked questions in this impoverished land where money did all the pertinent talking.

The hoard of diamonds Ron brought to this new land protected him against the ever-increasing rate of inflation and elevated him to the status of land baron. In less than six months, he took title to the farm and let the mestizos work it for him.

Ron and Jill had little to do. They found pleasure in reading the classics that modern life made obsolete for all but the academics. Philosophizing replaced consumption of the media they fed upon back in the States. They had no exposure to television, movies, or theater unless they ventured into the city.

In short order, they realized and appreciated the cause of vast overpopulation in third world tropical nations. The hot and humid days sapped the energy and left a lazy mood that welcomed the act of mating as a staple. The lack of stress and things needing to get done provided the time to make love daily. A life so free and easy was foreign to Ron, who only knew the way of the workhorse.

The plantation rested on a fifty-acre parcel of land. Ron and Jill lived in the main house, about a hundred yards from where the laborers' quarters stood next to storage bins.

The main house sat in a clearing surrounded by cacao plants on the north and east side, with the lush jungle hiding a host of natural treasures to the south and west.

Ron and Jill walked through the fields and into the jungle as part of their daily routine. The rainforest haven offered refuge from the heat.

Tall trees standing as an endless array of giant umbrellas cast shadows stunting the tropical sunlight. What little glare filtered through the leaves of the jungle's canopy produced a kaleidoscope of emerald shapes that burst forth the sun's golden flashes with every turn of the head from the ground below.

Sounds of the rainforest filled the air. On occasion, Ron and Jill reached the source of the sounds, at which point they saw some of the most curious life forms found anywhere on earth. Colorful birds sporting crowns of fascinating shapes, insects whose strange features echoed a lost world, and flora of such diversity that yet undiscovered species remained shrouded by the dense cover lived everywhere.

After many months, Jill needed to bring closure to their past by confronting it. Repression left a void in their relationship keeping her from feeling whole.

"Ron, we haven't talked about the past since we came here. We've been acting as if it never happened. Maybe it's not healthy to block it out."

"I know you're right, but it's a bad dream I don't want to relive. I'm in a good dream now, and I don't want it to end."

"I'm sorry. I won't speak of it again," Jill responded.

"No, you're right. I'm just afraid to go there. We can't act like we had nothing in our lives before we came to this paradise."

"What happened? What made you do it? Sometimes understanding our motives helps us accept their consequences," offered Jill.

"It's too simple," said Ron. "I couldn't take the injustice anymore. It became an obsession. Seeing what our country became repulsed me. It was everywhere. We come to this pristine land, and it's another world. It's a world without chaos. Why?"

"What do you mean?" said Jill.

"Look all around this country. Ten million people and most are living in poverty. Compared to the poorest people back home, this is *real* poverty. One percent, the ruling class, control the wealth, the commerce, everything here. They live the good life like us. What keeps the masses so content? Why aren't they killing and robbing like back home? What allows them to accept their poverty-stricken conditions?"

"Maybe because there's no one to rob," Jill said, smiling.

"No! No! That's not it. If these peasants turned on the 'one percent,' what would they have?"

Though not a rhetorical question, and since Jill expected he had his answer, she kept quiet.

"They'd have nothing, absolutely nothing! It's so clear when you live in this kind of world. It's the 'one percent' that builds community, institutions and the very pillars on which a society sits. What is there without the 'one percent'?"

"Ninety-nine percent," she added for humor's sake. Ron offered a smile but remained earnest and on point.

"That's true, ninety-nine percent, all the rest—lots and lots of people whose biggest aspiration is to exist. Most are content to work hard for their food and survive. They want to eat, drink, party and make love. They're the most satisfied sons of bitches anywhere.

"If you take away the 'one percent,' the forces of nature will destroy these easygoing souls. It could be by war, famine, disease, storm, or earthquake. The 'one percent,' the ruling class, is the guardian of the masses, like the parent is guardian of the child.

"It seems to be a kind of natural respect and understanding for the guardian when they look out for the masses. And the masses behave out of the fear of a dictatorship or hostile guardians.

"Other times, the masses revolt, bring them down, and take control. The results can vary with some good revolutions and others that bring the chaos of self-governing fools. The vital element that makes one nation a powerhouse and another succumb to the forces of nature and the evil of humankind is how the leadership behaves."

"How do you explain the violence and greed in the states where they have the best and the brightest of leadership?" asked Jill.

"It all has to do with the institutionalized acceptance of moral decay. We've brought it on ourselves. Too few taboos remain in American society, so anything goes. Greed, anger, and envy have become the norm. The very freedoms we cherish, without moral conduct, bred perversion and violence.

"Our murder rate exceeds all other civilized nations in the world. A real holocaust is taking place back home, because priorities are all screwed up!

"People in high places condone envy. They encourage it. It's from their hostile rhetoric that crime breeds in a fertile cesspool of contempt. The politicians have such concern about taking power from their opponents, they try to align the masses against the 'one percent.' They make them think they don't need those individuals who produce the wealth of the nation.

"Instead, they convince them they should have a bigger share of the pie. Not because they contribute anything to society, but because successful people are greedy and don't need what they have. It's about class envy. The thing they don't tell them is that without the 'one percent,' they'd be no different than any other third world shit hole.

"Our politicians, they've become despicable. Once they were the leaders, real protectors in their own right. Now they've become the enemy of the people. They're just concerned about their power and don't care what they have to promise or say to get it.

"I couldn't take it anymore. I cracked. I thought I could change it . . . the system. It's too ingrained in the souls of the people. I guess there's no hope. I tried and look where it got me."

Jill never saw Ron get so worked up since they started their new life, but she thought it best that he got it off his mind. She took his hand, and they continued their walk; nothing more said.

CHAPTER
FIFTY-THREE

THEY PLANNED a city trip for the next morning. For the excursion they expected more excitement than usual. Ron ordered medical provisions he wanted to keep around to help the farmhands. He saw them suffer from various maladies he could remedy if he only had a few instruments, some local anesthetic, and antibiotics.

Jill waited for her copy of Boccaccio's *Decameron*. While bookstores abounded in every mall and business district in the States, books remained a precious commodity in this land of illiteracy. Orders once placed took months for delivery. They learned that many things used every day cost more than imaginable in this world of cheap and abundant sunshine.

Ron had trouble falling asleep this evening. He attributed the restlessness to anticipation of the upcoming visit into town, and after a while fell into a restless sleep. Jill experienced an eerie uneasiness each time Ron's abrupt tossing awakened her. He moved erratically and mumbled words of despair that pulled her from slumber to startled dismay.

She shook Ron ever so gently and asked, "What is it, hon?"

Ron jumped to a sitting position, almost terrified, breath labored and heavy.

"God, since we've been here, I haven't had this dream. It's like I can't breathe. Like I'm suffocating. I used to get this recurring nightmare, and it makes no sense. It's hard to explain, but somehow I find myself at the bedside of Uncle Eli."

"Who's he?" she asked, because every detail of Ron's life, of his being, interested her. She wanted to understand him, to hold him when he faltered.

"He was an uncle, maybe a close friend of the family. I don't remember."

Ron thought for a moment and continued.

"Yeah, he was an uncle, definitely. Probably my father's distant uncle. He never had children, and he outlived all of his brothers and sisters. At ninety-two, I guess he outlasted almost everybody he knew.

"Well, in this dream, I'm at his bedside, and he's lying there near death. He can't see me. He always had thick glasses, and by this time he turned blind.

"He's just lying there alone and lonely. He can't tell I'm there by his side. He can't see or hear. I'm afraid to touch him, yet I know I should reach out, to give him the support of a compassionate embrace. He's lying there dying, and I can't give him a final scrap of comfort. I can't. Something holds me back.

"I see he's having trouble breathing the same way I feel right before I wake from this recurring nightmare. While this desperate old man is gasping for his last breath, I finally try to reach out. Then I wake up in a cold sweat. It's like I'm that guy lying there, Jill, all alone."

Ron stared wide-eyed toward the candle they let burn each night on the dresser. The flickering light held him in a fixed gaze.

"Don't worry, darling. You'll never be alone. Never. I'll always be there for you," said Jill, not sure Ron heard her pledge of loyalty and devotion.

She embraced him, and he responded by pulling her close. They spoke no more. Ron's slow rhythmic breathing showed Jill the crisis passed. Knowing Ron remained comfortable allowed Jill to drift into a deep sleep.

———

Ron remained silent, but far from the grip of slumber. His mind raced back in time, offering a moment with his children he missed so much. Though a faint memory from days long ago, he remembered they laughed and acted silly. They played a game with Ron, a special game, the details lost to him now, but he knew it was their favorite game.

The faded image offered great comfort. Hard as he tried to see what they were doing, the image remained distorted. The years separating his mind from the details of the past proved too frustrating. Soon the happiness garnered from this incomplete recollection faded, replaced by the stark recognition of days forever lost.

FIFTY-FOUR

"GOOD MORNING, Dr. Agnew! I see you and the Señora rise early. It's that time of the month for your city trip. You picked a hot one, Doctor. The sun shines bright today."

"It's a great day, Jesús," said Ron while packing the back of the Land Rover with provisions to take to the workers' quarters. Air conditioning burned too much precious fuel, so the car ride offered the only semblance of a cooling breeze available on the entire plantation. It afforded a welcome relief on the hottest days.

Though the early morning sun had not yet awakened to its potential, Ron bathed in his sweat. He blotted his face and made mention, "Make sure the hands get plenty to drink, and don't forget the salt tablets."

"Doctor, Doctor, we appreciate your kindness, always worried about our well-being. Don't you know? We live and work in the fields. We know no other way. It is our life. We understand the heat and know how to manage."

Jesús, the caretaker of the plantation, looked after the estate as if it was his property. Tall for an Ecuadorian, he stood at almost six feet. Through an open linen shirt stained by sweat, his muscular brown body peeked out, molded by hard labor in the fields.

Of Spanish descent, Jesús spoke English well but with a pronounced accent. Jesús was a good man, a devout Catholic, faithful to the church, his job, and his family. Most of the farm hands worked hard and led pious lives. The missionaries did a stellar job in teaching the Gospel.

The spread of American pop culture had not yet invaded the lives of the people who worked the land. It was the youth who migrated to the city looking for American styled dreams of wealth and wild times who posed the greatest threat to the safety in these otherwise pristine lands.

The young radicals who desired to live movie violence and machismo lifestyles wanted more than poverty, toil, and the dull lives their parents endured. They rejected the values and morality of their elders for the promise of street-level wealth and power.

Anticipating the arrival of their new goods made the ride into town a special event for Ron and Jill. Whenever they ventured into the city, excitement prevailed. Once finished their chores, they felt relief upon leaving. The city in their souls let them savor the experience, but spending their days in the timeless paradise of the plantation became the place their hearts called home.

Ron and Jill picked up the medical provisions at the FedEx office, then strolled on to the bookstore, more of a one-stop shop for written materials. Devoid of anything literary, they only stocked some of last year's American bestsellers, a newspaper and political manifestos of the various parties in contention for the minds and the support of the masses. In this shop they could order anything in print, wait a month to get it, then pay four times the cover price for such luxuries.

Jill glowed like a child exploring a novel toy as she flipped over her newly gained treasure to read the reviews on the back cover.

"I can't wait to get home! We'll read this book together each night after dinner."

"Sure thing," said Ron. He paid the clerk, and they exited the store.

Jill ran ahead to drop off a letter, her request to order books through a publishing house to expedite her desire for reading material. Her run turned into a skip as she approached the postbox.

The vibration of booming base approached as an unrecognized intrusion at first, then vibrated so deeply that it resonated in the chest of everyone nearby. Throbbing pulsations set the cadence for a primitive driving beat, like a heart ready to burst. It reminded Ron of evil. The sound was foreign, and at first he could not place it. As the pounding got closer, it was clearly American, the sound of hip-hop music broadcast for all to hear and feel.

Two young men wearing oversized jeans of the past years' style strutted toward Ron and Jill, who now advanced fifty paces ahead of him. The taller boy carried a boombox on his shoulder and walked with the exaggerated swagger of a bully seeking ownership of the street. The shorter youth wore at least twenty gold chains around his neck, the sign of involvement with illegal activity in a land where only the elite or the criminal afforded such an excess of glitter.

Ron picked up his stride in anticipation of trouble, but no time remained to react from the twenty paces now separating him from Jill. Ron froze. He watched as one youth grabbed Jill's package; her cherished *Decameron*. She struggled.

"Let it go," Ron shouted, but the gangster tune, originating from the loudspeakers, and the harsh sounds of the city muffled his outcry.

A slow-motion nightmare materialized as Ron watched the youth pull a gun from his waistband. He lifted the weapon, aimed it at Jill. Ron saw the brightly colored tattoo of a bold eagle, wings spread on the arm of the assailant. It reminded him of the faded emblem worn by the movers who came to empty his home of worldly possessions in what seemed so long ago.

A shot rang out. One shot and Jill's hand fell limp, releasing the package. For an instant, she stood in an upright position, and for that moment in time Ron paled. He only hoped the bullet missed. As he ran forward, Jill fell to the ground, limp from the point-blank gunshot. The thugs darted in the opposite direction, tossing the novel into the street, realizing it had no value to them.

Jill collapsed hard with neither animation nor grace. When she hit the ground, Ron heard bones shattering. He grabbed her lifeless form and held her in his trembling arms.

It did not take much for this trained trauma surgeon to recognize a shredded, ascending aorta. The rhythmic, pulsating flow of Jill's blood poured onto Ron's chest and groin. He felt the hot nectar of life chill as it dampened his clothing.

"Jill! No, you can't leave me alone!" His words poured out in uncontrolled, rabid bursts.

"You said you'd never leave me! Jill! Oh my God!"

Ron realized Jill did not hear him in this world. He prayed her spirit remained near and would know of his total devotion to her in death as in life.

"I love you, my darling! I'll always love you! *Always!*"

In absolute shock, Ron sat rocking her lifeless form. He cried and made incoherent utterances. Suddenly, a feeling of serenity muted his grief. He smiled with an empty face that turned into a trance-like countenance. His mind wandered to happier days and drifted to that place where forgotten memories live. The vision from his past came into view.

Ron sat on the living room floor with his children, Lawrence and Faith. They played a silly game he invented. The recurring, previously forgotten notion revolved around this, their favorite game. While his remembrance was lost in the shade of his faded past, the image cleared as bright as the sun now shining upon him.

"Here he comes!" Ron threatened as he walked his two fingers across the carpet toward Lawrence.

"Here he comes!" Ron repeated.

The approach of the fingers excited the children. Their eyes widened, smiles lengthened, and giggles flowed freely. They gasped trying to avoid breathlessness.

"Look out! The Gotcha's coming!" Ron warned.

The two fingers stopped. He blended them into the other fingers of his hand. The fantasy creature disappeared from view.

Faith called out most anxiously, "Where's the Gotcha, Daddy? When's he gonna get us? When will he get us?"

"Come on, you know!" Ron replied with jubilation.

"No, we don't, Daddy. Where'd the Gotcha go? When's he gonna get us?"

"Come on, guys. When does the Gotcha get you?"

In unison, they all responded, "When you least expect it!"

With those words, the Gotcha reappeared and jumped up to tickle Lawrence, then Faith. They shrieked hysterically. They laughed. The Gotcha disappeared, having gotten them when they least expected.

ABOUT THE AUTHOR

Dr. Robert M. Fleisher holds a BA in psychology and DMD with a specialty in endodontics. Engaged in writing for the past thirty-five years, he has written for professional journals as well as having produced several non-fiction books. *The American Strangler* is his second novel and eighth published book. Dr. Fleisher looks forward to telling his stories to an audience interested in difficult subjects. He is an active member of *International Thriller Writers*.

facebook.com/robert.fleisher.908
x.com/DoctorRobert5
instagram.com/robertmfleisher

ALSO BY ROBERT M. FLEISHER

The Divine Affliction

From Waiting Room to Courtroom

Bedside Manner

The Sexless Marriage Fix

Dating Again

Forty Something

Fifty Something